WINTERVEIL

JENNA BURTENSHAW

WINTERVEIL

⤙ THE SECRETS OF WINTERCRAFT ⤚

GREENWILLOW BOOKS
An Imprint of HarperCollinsPublishers

Winterveil
Copyright © 2012 by Jenna Burtenshaw
First published in 2012 in Great Britain by Headline Publishing,
an imprint of Hachette Livre UK. First published in 2013 in the United States
by Greenwillow Books.
The right of Jenna Burtenshaw to be identified as the author of this work has been
asserted by her.

The text of this book is set in Horley Old Style MT.
Book design by Sylvie Le Floc'h

Library of Congress Cataloging-in-Publication Data

Burtenshaw, Jenna.
[Legacy]
Winterveil / Jenna Burtenshaw.
pages cm.—(The secrets of Wintercraft ; [3])
"Greenwillow Books."
First published in 2012 in Great Britain by Headline Publishing under the title
Legacy.
Summary: Silas and Edgar try to rescue Kate after she is abducted
by vicious Dalliah Grey, who wants to use Kate's power to bring
down the veil between the living and the dead.
ISBN 978-0-06-202646-0 (trade ed.) [1. Fantasy. 2. Dead—Fiction.] I. Title.
PZ7.B94569Wi 2013 [Fic]—dc23 2012041112

13 14 15 16 17 LP/RRDH 10 9 8 7 6 5 4 3 2 1
First Edition

Greenwillow Books

For beautiful Belle—
my canine writing companion, who
explored Albion at my side from the very beginning.
Champion tail wagger & mistress of the howl.
2001–2011.

CONTENTS

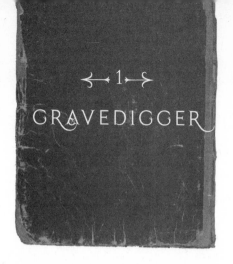

1

GRAVEDIGGER

High above the chilled waters of a sunlit sea, a dark tower rose like a wizened thumb from the crags of a blackened cliff. It cast a broken shadow across the rubble-flecked land behind it, standing crooked but strong in the rising daylight as it kept its ancient watch over the waves below.

The waves crashed against the foot of the cliff, their rhythmic surge echoing along the eastern coast of Albion, but few human ears were there to hear it. There, in that isolated place, a man climbed out of a hatch in the tower's roof and carried a small wooden crate draped with cloth up into the open air. He left the crate near the hatch and walked to the edge, where a spyglass stood upon its stand, pointing out across the sea. His stubbled face was half hidden beneath a wide hat, and his hair hung tattered across his shoulders as he cleared the lens and pressed his eye to the eyepiece.

Tarak had spent months freezing in that tower, watching

ice drifting sluggishly across the horizon. That bleak seascape
had become his world, but not—he hoped—for much longer.
He knocked his hat back, exposing deep green eyes. The sword
he kept propped beside the spyglass had claimed the life of the
man who once guarded that place, and a mound of earth near the
tower's foundations marked the spot where the body now lay.

This was the day he had been waiting for. Everything was
going according to plan.

As the sun rose higher, a distant shape on the water drew
his eye. He adjusted the lens until he could make out every
wave on the surface of the sea, raised the spyglass's eye to the
horizon, and settled at last upon a dark, welcome sight. A ship,
heading toward the coast, with a mass of black sails raised high
and full.

"The *Gravedigger*," Tarak whispered, his face softening
into a satisfied smile. At last, his time in that vermin-ridden
place was coming to an end. He buttoned up his coat and set
to work.

He crossed the tower roof and dragged the cloth from
the crate. Powerful wings beat hard against the latticed sides
and four beady eyes blinked up at him as he carried it to the
wall. He cooed gently to keep the birds calm and carefully
unlatched the lock before reaching in and lifting out a pigeon.
He tucked the bird under his arm and slid a prepared note into
a ring attached to its bright pink leg. "It's time to do what we
came here for," he said.

The bird wriggled excitedly, sensing the freedom of the open sky. Tarak held it out and sent it fluttering into the freezing air, where it settled into a smooth glide and flew across the water heading toward the Continental lands that lay beyond the icy sea.

Tarak watched it swoop past the dark sails of the oncoming ship. He had spent many months of his life stationed on that weather-beaten deck. The black hull bore the scars and burns of countless battles, and just seeing it again brought back memories of combat, war, and death. Enemies often underestimated the deadly power carried beneath those sails, but the *Gravedigger* was the strongest vessel in the Continental fleet. It had earned its name many times over.

He prepared a second note and attached it to the leg of the remaining bird, which sat peacefully in his hands as he held it out over the side. The pigeon flapped into the air the moment he let it go, circled once, and settled in the opposite direction to the first bird, heading deep into Albion territory, straight toward the distant graveyard city of Fume.

Tarak closed the crate. With the ship in sight and his messages sent, his work in that tower was done. He waited until both birds were no more than dark specks against the sky, then grabbed his sword, headed for the roof hatch, and descended the tower steps two at a time. He spiraled his way down past the living quarters and out onto an overgrown patch of land that was half buried in snow.

His horse was where he had left it, inside the tower's single tumbledown stable. He slid the blanket from its back, saddled it quickly, and led it outside. Salty wind whistled past the tower's stones as he mounted the beast, flicked the reins once, and rode along a gravel path, following a narrow trail that ran along the cliff top, traveling south.

Winter still held Albion firmly in its grip, and the clear morning sky was already under threat as heavy clouds massed on the horizon. Tarak glanced out to sea and spotted the winking light of a lantern signaling from the ship to the shore. He worked the horse harder, forcing its hooves to slam into the crumbling cliff, traveling past long-abandoned buildings that stood perilously close to the edge. The watchtower had not always been alone. It had once stood guard over a coastal town that had almost finished crumbling into the sea. Now only a few forgotten houses were left to mark the inland edges of the vanished settlement. The ground here was riddled with old tunnels, weakening the cliff and making it a dangerous place.

Tarak led his horse into a sheltered spot between two buildings, tied the reins to a bare tree, and picked his way on foot through what was left of the town. He headed for an exposed patch of land, perilously close to the cliff edge, and walked slowly until the ground sounded hollow beneath his boots. There he bent down, scrubbed away a thin layer of earth, and heaved open a hidden door, revealing a steep flight of steps cutting down into the cliff.

Two threads pinned across the entrance were undisturbed. No one had passed through that door in days.

Tarak followed the steps down into a twist of old cellar tunnels, and the glare of the low sun dazzled him at the point where the base of the cliff met the shore.

The tunnel's mouth opened out into a small cove, with the watchtower's crags on one side and a curving face of jagged rock on the other. A small, battered fishing boat lay abandoned within a low cave close by. Smugglers sometimes used that place, and it was not unusual for them to leave things behind.

Tarak crossed the cove quickly, tugging at a leather cord hung around his neck. A circular disk of polished crystal slid from his collar and sparkled in the sunlight as he pressed it into his palm. The ship's lantern flickered again. He held the lens up to catch the sun and flashed a signal across the water, letting the crew know that their landing place was secure.

The *Gravedigger*'s crew pulled in the sails. Ropes snaked out over the ship's starboard side, and a boat with a curved roof was lowered slowly down onto the water. It was hard for Tarak to see anyone in it clearly, but he knew whom to expect. A woman and a girl were due ashore that day, accompanied by armed officers wearing their distinctive uniforms of red and black. Tarak straightened his shabby coat. He would be glad to clean himself up, cut his hair, and wear the colors of his true station again. Those men were his comrades, his brothers, every one of them honored to be part of the

Continental army's elite force known as the Blackwatch.

He was standing proudly at the water's edge, waiting to welcome the boat ashore, when the sound of a whistle carried down from the top of the cliff. He looked up to where a man was leaning fearlessly out from the cliff edge, flickering a signal. Tarak raised a hand in reply. The horses had arrived.

He turned back to the sea and watched the boat advance slowly toward the shore, until thickening clouds swept over the sun and sharp spits of hail began to fall. The wind churned, and the air filled quickly with swarms of stinging ice, while storm clouds swelled like a bruise, filling the northern sky. Tarak stood braving it out, until the hail became too heavy to bear. He had hoped to provide a dignified welcome, but if he stood there much longer, he would look like a fool.

Cursing the weather under his breath, he headed to the cave for shelter. He pulled up his collar and made for the hollow where the fishing boat's prow jutted out over the sand. His hand had just touched the cave's clammy wall when he hesitated. Something about the boat looked different. There was a red net draped over the side that he was sure had not been there before. He edged closer, until his boot pressed down on something firm just beneath the sand.

A strained cry rose up from the ground, like the whimper of a wounded animal. He raised his foot and saw what looked like four long fingers curling upward, but the moment he saw them they were gone.

Tarak drew his blade, not sure what he had just seen. He tested the ground again, pinpointing the muffled sound, then bent down and sank his fist firmly into the sand. His fingers met something that felt like cloth. He grabbed hold of it and dragged it out. The cloth was a dirty sweater, and wearing it was a young man who spluttered loudly as his sand-covered face and mop of black hair were revealed.

"Who are you?" demanded Tarak.

The boy was too busy coughing to answer. Tarak was about to question him again when he sensed something cool and sharp press against his throat, and a dark voice spoke into his ear.

"Release the boy."

A trickle of cold fear ran through Tarak's blood. He had been threatened before; he had been close to death more times than he could remember. His fear had nothing to do with the blade at his throat but everything to do with the person who was wielding it. He hesitated for a few seconds before releasing his grip. The boy scrambled away from him.

"Drop your weapon," said the voice. "And turn. Slowly."

Tarak did as he was told, letting his sword fall flat upon the sand. The blade of a dagger played gently around his neck as he turned to face a pair of dead gray eyes.

He was standing in the presence of a man whose height towered far above his own. Those lifeless eyes stared down at him with no hint of emotion. The rugged face gave away nothing but indifference as his ambusher held a rough dagger in one hand and a sword made of blue-black steel in the other.

"Silas Dane."

Fear pulled the name unwittingly from Tarak's lungs and out into the air. This man's reputation had spread farther than he could imagine. People on the Continent called him a man without a soul, a perfect warrior. The soldier who could not die. Tarak was trapped in the shadow of a predator that could not be outfought, outwitted, or outrun, but he would not flee and die with a blade in his back. Pride kept him standing tall, knowing that all he could hope for was the mercy of a swift death.

"The ship," said Silas. "How many of the crew are coming ashore?"

Tarak remained silent. He would not betray his men to the enemy.

"How many are above us with the horses?"

Silas's blade bit a bloody mark into Tarak's flesh, but still he said nothing. How had he not noticed that the fishing boat's hull was damp from recent use? Why had he not stayed by the water, braving the weather, rather than venture close to the cliff?

No matter what happened to him, his birds were already on their way. Not even Silas Dane could stop what was to come. He rolled his shoulders back, forcing himself to look his enemy in the eye. If he was to die, he had done his duty. There was no dishonor in that.

Silas gave him time to answer, letting the silence stretch on. "If you will not talk," he said at last, "I have no time for you."

In one quick move the blade cut deeper, slicing swiftly through the pulse beating in Tarak's neck. Warm blood spilled across cold skin. Tarak felt the weight of his body slump heavily to the ground; his life stolen away in a single cut. Darkness and pain closed in. The warm current of death swept through him, and then his spirit was gone.

Silas looked down at the body in the bloodied sand, then stepped over it and watched the sea through the swirling hail. The young man with him was a shabby seventeen-year-old named Edgar Rill, who stared at the dead man, not sure what Silas expected them to do next.

"Bury him," ordered Silas, cleaning his dagger on a patch of sand grass. "And stay out of sight."

"More Blackwatch are heading in on that boat," said Edgar. "We don't have time. Have you seen how close they are?"

"I have eyes. Dig."

Edgar grabbed an oar from the fishing boat. His stomach, which had been growling with hunger just a short while earlier, squirmed with discomfort at being so close to the dead man. He used the oar to scrape away a hollow in the sand beside the body, working as quickly as he could. "Are you going to help?"

Silas had tucked the dagger back into his belt and was listening silently to the ice-filled wind.

"I'll take that as a no." Edgar's hands were shaking. Through fear or cold, it was impossible to tell. In the past day alone he had been stabbed, dragged back from the waiting hands of death, and ferried across a frozen sea. His only company had been a man whose conversation stopped at giving orders. Silas's presence still made the hairs bristle on the back of Edgar's neck, despite his having been the one who had saved Edgar's life.

"Next time you can be the bait," said Edgar, digging quickly. "What if he had decided to kill me as soon as he grabbed me? What then?"

"I would have stopped him."

"Why couldn't I have hidden in the boat?"

"Dragging someone out of a boat makes them an enemy," said Silas. "Dragging them out of the sand makes them a curiosity."

"Well, I'm glad that logic works for you. Feel free to step forward a bit quicker next time."

Edgar knew the makeshift grave was not yet deep enough to fully hide a man, but the Blackwatch were getting too close. He had to finish the gruesome job quickly. He jabbed the oar into the sand and decided to improvise. Two drags—one on the man's shoulder and one on the knees—sent him rolling into the shallow trench, where Edgar spotted the bright glint of a crystal lens light hanging around his neck. Something like that was too useful to leave behind, so he tugged it loose and pocketed it.

"And the coat," Silas said, without turning around. "He has no use for it anymore."

Edgar's own coat was torn, filthy, and drenched through. He was surprised he had survived so long in that state. He may not have liked stealing clothes from the dead, but Silas was right. He dragged the patched garment off the man and claimed it for himself. Sliding his arms into the wide sleeves, he realized with a grim shudder that they were still warm. He whispered an apology, covered the man's face with his hat, and kept working.

It took less than a minute for Edgar to pile a mound of sand on top of the grave, while Silas kept his eyes upon the ocean, completely ignoring his efforts.

"I'm assuming you have some sort of plan?" asked Edgar.

Silas said nothing, and Edgar knew better than to ask again.

As soon as Edgar finished, he joined Silas within the shadow of the cave wall, watching the boat moving closer to the shore. Whatever plan Silas had in mind, Edgar would be ready when the time came. Until then all either of them could do was wait.

← 2 →
THE
ONCOMING
STORM

Kate Winters was standing on the forward deck of the Blackwatch ship when the eastern coast of Albion crept into sight. She had hardly slept during the voyage. Her only view of the outside world had been through a tiny window facing back toward the Continent, and she had spent hours looking out of it, staring into darkness, watching the stars glinting against a black velvet sky. It felt good to be out in the open again.

The sea breeze stung life into her cheeks as the ship's crew toiled on the deck below and a woman in a long gray coat strode between them, watching them work with a critical eye. Kate could not recall much beyond her short time upon the ship, and whenever she tried to remember, she found it hard to concentrate for very long. She had a memory of traveling in a carriage and arriving at a port, but anything more detailed than that refused to make any sense. It was like trying to remember a dream when most of it had already faded away.

The wind tugged at Kate's long black hair as she leaned against the guardrail separating her from the sea. The coast of Albion emerged slowly as an inky sprawl of cliffs in the distance, and as the ship drew closer to the shore, the gentle energies of the veil began to settle around her. The powerful influence of the woman on deck prevented her thoughts from venturing too far into the realm that lingered between the living and the dead, but that, she had been told, was for her own protection.

Dalliah Grey claimed that Kate was her student and she was her teacher and had promised that Kate's memory would gradually return over time. When Kate looked at the woman, she expected to feel some flicker of recognition, or at least a slight hint of trust, yet all she felt was a dull creeping sense of unease.

Dalliah left the captain's side and climbed the steps to join Kate where she stood looking toward the coast. "The veil is at its most powerful in these lands," said Dalliah. "You will experience changes as we approach the shore. That is natural. Make sure you are prepared."

Frost played across Dalliah's fingertips and gathered on her eyelashes as the veil's influence swept in across the water. Kate remembered what she had been told. She breathed in deeply and gripped the guardrail as tightly as she could. The chill of air in her lungs and the ache in her fingers grounded her physical senses more strongly to the living world, but even that could not prevent her own skin from frosting briefly as the veil whispered around her.

Kate wanted to let her soul reach out and reconnect with her country, her home, but she could feel Dalliah watching her, quietly studying her reaction to the land's unique atmosphere. Just being close to Albion again made Kate's blood pulse with steady energy. If she pushed herself, she was sure she could break the restriction Dalliah had placed upon her, but she had the unsettling feeling that she was being tested. If what she had been told about her life was true, nothing would be lost by being cautious. If something else was happening and she pushed too far, Dalliah would simply strengthen her hold. It was better to appear weak than to risk showing too much resistance, at least until she could discover the truth about their journey.

Kate tried to close her mind against the veil, but she did not let go of it completely. She let its presence linger as a gentle whisper at the back of her thoughts and watched the souls within it drifting as a hint of gray haze seen at the very edges of her vision. She tucked her hands into her sleeves, concealing the frost that was spreading across her fingers, then closed her eyes against the cold wind and listened secretly to a sound that few people could hear. It was a hollow sound, empty and dull, like an echo of a voice fading in an empty room. It was the kind of noise most people would forget about as soon as they heard it, but for those who recognized what they were listening to, it was the most amazing sound in the world.

Kate was one of the Skilled, one of the rare few who could hear the voices of souls that had not yet made the full journey into death. She could hear thousands of whispers, thoughts, and cries bleeding from the shores of Albion, becoming louder as the ship traveled in toward a small cove. She could not make out any distinct words, but the more she listened, the clearer her own clutch of scattered memories became. She remembered fire and smoke and a circle made of carved symbols drawn upon an old stone floor. She tried to hold the memory and let it grow, until Dalliah's cold hand touched hers, forcing her to open her eyes.

Dalliah's face was inches away from her own, her eyes sharp with curiosity. When Kate tried to step back, the woman held her still.

"What can you see out there?" she asked.

Kate did not want to admit how strongly the veil was calling to her, so she focused upon something solid and physical instead. "The cliffs," she said. "They look beautiful from here."

The older woman gave a slight smile of satisfaction, making Kate believe that her secret was safe. She may not have known why it was important for her to keep it, but as long as she had even the slightest doubt about her situation, she would trust her own instincts far more than any living soul upon that ship.

She returned as warm a smile as she could manage toward

the woman who claimed to be her protector. Dalliah was a tall woman who looked no older than sixty, with short hair flecked with gray and a strong body. Her clothes were old and well worn, and she wore twists of dried flowers and leaves around her wrists, marking her as someone who often worked with the dead. When her eyes met Kate's, they were critical and cold; they belonged to someone who had lived too long, had seen too much, and had many secrets to hide.

Dalliah was no ordinary woman. She had lived far longer than anyone alive. Her extraordinary connection to the veil allowed her body to heal itself almost instantly, stretching her unnatural existence until she was now almost five hundred years old. She had spent most of those years in exile on the Continent. Now she was traveling back to Albion for the first time in two centuries, taking Kate back to the ancient city of Fume.

"Is your memory returning?" Dalliah's question was simple enough, but the look she sent with it was heavy with threat.

"No," Kate answered quickly.

"Da'ru tried to lie to me, too," said Dalliah, "when she was a girl, not very much older than you. You would be foolish to follow her path."

The name was familiar, but Kate did not know from where.

"Da'ru was your predecessor," said Dalliah. "She might

not have possessed your level of natural ability, but I would have preferred you both worked together toward what we must do. Sadly, that is not possible."

"Why not?" asked Kate.

"Because she is dead." Dalliah said the words as coolly as if she were commenting on the weather. It was a statement, given without a hint of real interest or emotion.

"What happened to her?"

"A student who cannot defend her own life is of no use to me," said Dalliah. "The details are not important. Da'ru had her chance. It took fifteen years to teach her what she knew. You have only a few days. Do not waste time by lying to me again."

She turned away from the sea and spoke to an officer who was standing at the top of the staircase leading down to the main deck. The officer glanced at Kate and nodded firmly before heading that way to gather a group of his men. Kate looked down across the deck and watched the Blackwatch work. Some were lowering a small boat over the side of the ship, while others pulled in the sails, bringing the huge vessel to a steady stop.

Ahead of them, a tower reached up from the rocks like a ghost swathed in icy air. The small cove nearest the ship appeared deserted, yet Kate's eyes were drawn immediately to a shallow cave worn into the side of the cliff. Something about the darkness drew her in. There was a presence inside, something neither fully dead nor fully alive, waiting in the dark.

"We will go to the shore together," said Dalliah. "Do you have the book?"

Kate rested her hand on a small lump underneath her coat pocket. Even without her memories, she felt protective toward the book that was concealed inside. Dalliah had warned her not to open it until they reached Albion's capital city, but Kate had defied her and secretly flicked through its pages during her time alone in the cabin. The words inside looked familiar, and she found that she did not have to read everything to know what was written there; the slightest reminder was all it took for her mind to fill in the gaps. She had read that book before. It felt like a vital part of her that she had to guard at all costs.

"Do not allow anyone to take that from you," Dalliah said. "Keep it safe."

Kate nodded her agreement. She would keep it safe . . . even from Dalliah. She followed Dalliah down the short staircase to the main deck, where the Blackwatch were already lowering the boat.

"Your assistance has been appreciated," Dalliah said to the man in charge as she unhooked a small traveling bag from the side of the deck. "I have no doubt your military plans will run just as smoothly, when the time comes."

"We are prepared," said the officer. "Three of my men will row you to shore, and I have already sent word for horses to be readied for your arrival. You and the girl will be escorted to Fume, as we agreed."

"And the city gates?"

"Entry has been arranged," said the officer. "My men will get you inside. They have procured the item you asked for. Beyond those gates, the city is yours."

Dalliah nodded her head in thanks, and the officer backed away. "Climb down quickly," she said to Kate. "Fume is two days away, on horseback. We will need time to work before the Continental army begins rattling its swords outside the capital."

Kate descended a long rope ladder leading down into the waiting boat. The tiny vessel was barely big enough for a handful of people, and its rear half was covered by a wooden roof raised on posts, allowing passengers to see out and the wind to surge in. Two officers were already seated near the middle, each manning an oar. Kate took her seat on a small bench under the roof, and Dalliah sat beside her, followed by another man, who knelt at the front of the boat, sweeping a spyglass across the cove, searching for any signs of life. Once he gave the all clear, the boat's tether was released, and the officers worked the oars steadily toward the shore.

The rhythmic sound of wood upon water accompanied them across the choppy sea. The small group traveled in silence, leaving the great black ship behind them, but before they had rowed very far, Kate heard a fluttering sound nearby.

She looked back at the ship and spotted a shadow moving among its sails, something too small to be one of the crew and too large to be one of its resident rats.

A bedraggled crow had settled in the rigging with its wings hunched up, glaring directly down at her. Its inky feathers completely absorbed the light from the rising sun, making it look like a shadow except for a bright streak of white feathers that slashed across its chest.

"Kate."

Dalliah's voice made her look away, not wanting to draw attention to the bird.

"You will carry this." Dalliah slid her traveling bag from her shoulder and dropped it at Kate's feet. Its upper flap had folded open, revealing a collection of old books and loosely rolled scrolls packed neatly together. Most of them were written in a language Kate did not know, but a few of the symbols she spotted were familiar: an open eye, a wolf, a sword. . . . As she agreed to take care of the bag, the crow skittered out of sight behind the ship's sails. When she looked up again, it was gone.

The officers rowed together, steering the boat into the cove. The watchtower's point of land blocked the coast farther north from view, while the cliffs turned inward to the south, leaving nothing but a vast expanse of sea. Crags of dark rock, their upper edges glistening with frost, loomed high above the travelers.

Dalliah's hand rested upon Kate's, and Kate felt a wash of calm creep over her. Her thoughts threatened to retreat again into a distant part of her memory, ready to be locked away, barely remembered, as Dalliah continued to keep her mind under control, but Kate had no intention of allowing herself to be subdued like a child. Tiny flickers of memory had begun to return. She did not want to forget them again. This time she resisted.

A flurry of hailstones rattled hard upon the boat's roof and stabbed into the waters around them. Kate barely felt the chill of the ice as it swirled in around her. Instead of deadening her senses, Dalliah's interference had only made her more determined to hold on to everything she did not want the older woman to know. She focused upon the soft gray light gathered at the edges of her vision and was certain she saw movement there, close to the boat, drifting upon the water. Shades of the dead were not restricted to moving upon land. They could drift freely within the confines of the veil, separate from the living world but still reflected within it as shimmering mists and points of soft white light, to those whose eyes could see them there.

Dalliah moved her hand from Kate as the veil drew more powerfully toward them. She had been away for a long time. The veil's influence did not spread very far beyond Albion's soil, and Dalliah had been forced to struggle and experiment to connect with it while living so far away. Now that she was heading into the very heart of its energy, her face filled with relief.

Enthralled as she was by the veil, it soon looked as if she were no longer aware of anyone else in the boat with her. Kate was glad of it. The last thing she wanted was to hold Dalliah's attention for too long. The clearer her thoughts became, the more her instincts screamed at her to get away from the woman as soon as possible.

The rowers landed the boat on the sand with a smooth grating bump. The scrape of the hull distracted Dalliah. The two rowers climbed out and dragged the boat farther up onto the sandy shore, where Dalliah stepped onto dry land, letting her long dress trail through the wet sand.

"The first step toward a new world," she said. "The veil is falling, Kate. You can feel it here. The land feels it. We will show our people the truth they refuse to see. We will educate them, and they will have no choice but to listen to us."

One of the Blackwatch officers held his hand over the side of the boat, but Kate ignored it, preferring to climb out herself.

"Where are the horses?" Dalliah's voice was sharp and impatient as she strode through the hail.

A tiny light flickered from the cliff top.

"They are here. Waiting above us," said one of the officers.

A small shadow swept over the boat as the crow from the ship flew directly over them, heading for the cliff. It perched upon a rocky crag, looking down at the people below.

"Kate," said Dalliah, "come with me."

Kate grabbed the bag and glanced once toward the darkened cave. Blackwatch officers flanked her on both sides, and the third stayed next to the boat as she followed Dalliah toward a tunnel mouth and into the very heart of the cliff.

"Let's go," said Edgar, peering out of the cave once the group was out of sight. "You can take on three Blackwatch. Let's get Kate and get out of here."

Silas ignored him.

"She's right there!" said Edgar.

"There are Blackwatch officers above us, two at Kate's side and one posted as a lookout," said Silas. "The moment we attack, that lookout will send a signal to the crew. You would be dead within moments, and I could not guarantee Kate's safety. We would be squandering our only advantage."

Silas kept a close eye upon the lookout, while flurries of ice blew around the boat. It was not long before the two officers who had accompanied Kate and Dalliah returned to the shore without them. The three men pushed the vessel back into the water and boarded it quickly, then rowed back toward the ship that sat like a scar upon the gray waters.

Silas moved out into the open with Edgar following closely behind. The hail provided some cover against anyone watching from the ship, making it hard to distinguish two moving figures from the dark backdrop of the rocks. There was no way of knowing how many of the Blackwatch were above them, but with the ship on the move at least they would not have any reinforcements. Silas could dispatch them at will.

He headed for the hidden staircase and listened for signs of any movement above. He climbed the steps up to a hatch, but there was no sound of any horses. No one talking. No one moving. He clicked the latch and pushed the trapdoor open. The crumbling buildings on the cliff top looked completely deserted. Dalliah Grey had had no reason to remain there any longer than was necessary. Getting Kate to the capital city was all that mattered to her.

Edgar reached the top of the staircase and hugged his stolen coat around himself against the bitter wind. "Where did they go?"

Silas climbed out and assessed his surroundings. The wild weather made it hard to tell how many animals had been brought there recently. He doubted Dalliah would risk transporting Kate alone, but the Blackwatch would not have dedicated too many men to honor an arrangement with the woman when it had greater plans at work in Albion. Two, perhaps three officers would be enough. They would travel swiftly, taking minimal rest and avoiding any settlements along the way, preferring the wilds over any place where they could be identified as the enemy. The weather would be against them. That would force them to stay on open paths and prevent them from taking risks. Silas, however, had no such constraints.

"We must reach the city before them," he said as Edgar stood beside him.

"You can't just walk back into Fume. The wardens are still looking for you. They think you are a traitor."

"They are wrong."

"I know that. But if they catch you, they'll bury you."

Silas glared down at him.

Nuggets of hail peppered Edgar's hair. "I still say we should have taken our chances at the cove," he said quietly.

Silas saw movement along the cliff to the north and spotted a crow gliding toward them, carried upon the sea breeze. The bird circled over a clutch of abandoned houses and fluttered down onto Silas's raised wrist. Its feathers were damp, and it shook itself dry before climbing up onto Silas's shoulder, where it stood pecking at its claws.

Silas allowed his senses to shift briefly into the veil, searching for the crow's memories that would be waiting for him there. The half-life fell over his consciousness like smoke as he closed his mind to everything except what he was there to find. He could not risk alerting Dalliah to his presence by reaching out to Kate directly; but the crow's spirit shone brightly, and his thoughts connected with it, allowing him to see what it had seen.

"Kate is starting to remember," he said, witnessing the memories as a single thought.

"The crow told you that?" asked Edgar.

"It earns its place beside me. Unlike some."

During his time on the Continent, Silas had learned that Dalliah Grey's only goal was to bring down the veil across Albion, allowing the souls of the half-life to roam freely across the living world. Kate was the key that would help her complete centuries of work, so long as she could keep the girl under control. No matter what it took, Silas could not let her succeed.

"They won't want to be seen," said Edgar, ignoring his comment. "They will avoid settlements, maybe even ride around them. That will slow them down. Not much help since we're on foot and they're on—" Determined to prove himself more useful than a bird, he stared at Silas. "That man you killed. He didn't walk here, did he? What if he had a horse? The Blackwatch wouldn't have taken it. They brought plenty of their own. There has to be a horse here somewhere!"

Edgar's freezing body warmed with a sudden rush of hope. He set off between the abandoned buildings and soon spotted something moving among the driving hail. "There!" He headed toward it, glad to do anything that did not involve standing still and freezing to death, and found a gray horse sheltering beneath a half-fallen roof, tethered to a tree. "I was right!" he shouted back at Silas. "Look!" He reached out a hand to pat the horse's muzzle, but it shied away from him, whinnying and pinning its ears against its skull.

"Stay back," said Silas, walking toward the beast. "This is an old battle horse. It can smell the blood on you."

Edgar spotted the dark, curling brand on the animal's flank that marked it as a soldier's battle horse and immediately backed away. Battle horses were strong and well trained but dangerous in the wrong hands.

The horse stamped as Silas approached.

"Few of these are found outside active service," said Silas. He whispered something to the horse, and slowly it began to settle. "It may not be the fastest beast, but it is sturdy enough."

Silas climbed up into the saddle and Edgar kept his distance, trying not to think about the dead man's blood still staining his coat. The last time he had been on a horse he had been close to death, and he was not eager to relive the experience.

"Climb up," said Silas. Edgar took a deep breath and accepted Silas's hand; he hooked his foot into the stirrup and climbed onto the horse behind Silas's saddle. The horse's coat was sleek and well groomed; it would not take much for Edgar to fall. He clung on to Silas's coat for his life as the horse turned away from the cliffs.

Silas knew that coast well: every watchtower, every trail. He directed the horse across a wild expanse of tangled land, far from any path the Blackwatch might have taken. Dalliah believed she had stepped onto Albion soil unseen, but Silas would not let the rest of her plan unfold so easily. He already knew his targets' destination. He intended to reach the graveyard city first.

On that freezing morning, two very different journeys began to cross Albion's wild counties. Silas and Edgar rode their horse across barren fields heading directly west, while Kate's group behaved exactly as Silas had predicted, following the trail a short distance north before curling in toward the dense forests that were scattered across Albion's eastern lands.

Kate was riding a brown horse led by a Blackwatch officer riding in front. Another officer rode to her right, with a third behind her and Dalliah completing the formation to her left. The Blackwatch men had arrived disguised in black robes like those worn by Albion's wardens, ensuring that no one would dare challenge them on the road. Kate had been given a robe of her own, and she pulled it tightly around her as the hail shifted into relentless rain that stung her cheeks and blew into her eyes. No one saw the shadow of a crow flying steadily above the treetops directly overhead.

They rode on through the afternoon and early evening, until darkness pulled in like a heavy cloth, blanketing the Wild Counties in a coverlet of moonlight and stars. Trees glimmered in the cold. The horses' breath steamed in pale gusts of white, and the rain that had fallen turned slowly into ice, leaving fingers of glassy icicles clinging to the trees. Kate shivered beneath her robes. Her lips were pale, and her fingers gripped the reins without even trying, as if the cold had frozen them into place.

Dalliah did not feel the cold. Her body did not need the ordinary comforts that burdened other human lives. She could have ridden easily for days without rest, but the girl, Dalliah remembered, was not as resilient as she. The horses tired, lowering their heavy heads as they walked, and in the distance faint lights sparked as a settlement came into sight.

"We should set up camp for the night," said one of the officers. "The horses need to rest."

"You and your men can sleep in whatever muddy ditch you wish," said Dalliah. "The girl and I will spend the night in the closest approximation we have to civilization." She pointed to the lights. "There. I have no intention of scrabbling about in the dirt."

The Blackwatch officers might not have agreed with Dalliah's decision, but they had orders to act upon it.

"One of us will camp with the horses," said the lead officer. "The others will accompany you."

"Discreetly," said Dalliah.

"Of course."

Dalliah and Kate dismounted and walked toward a rough fence encircling what looked like a small trading village. A few silver coins bought them entry past the guard on the gate, and the eyes of the few people still out in the cold fell on them immediately. Dalliah was not the kind of woman to pass unnoticed. Her presence alone made people uncomfortable. No one stayed near her for long.

The only stone building in the settlement was an inn with a red rose painted on a swinging sign. When Dalliah stepped inside, everyone huddled around the fire fell quiet. She paid for a room and took her bag of papers from Kate.

"Servants belong downstairs," she said. "We will leave at sunrise."

"I'm not your servant." Kate's voice was loud enough to be heard by most of the people in the room.

Dalliah took hold of Kate's arm in a way that could have looked gentle to the onlookers, but her fingers wrapped around Kate's wrist and twisted hard, just enough to crick the bone and hold her attention. "You will do as I say, or you will spend the night in the gutter." She spoke through a well-practiced smile, but her eyes were filled with a venom that Kate had not noticed before. "Sit down and do not talk to anyone." She continued. "You will stay silent. Do you understand?"

When Dalliah took her hand away, a bruise blossomed around Kate's wrist. "Yes," she said.

"Remain here. If you wander, you will regret letting me down." Dalliah turned to the innkeeper, who was staring at her warily, in case she turned her anger upon him next. "This girl is to be left alone," she said. "When I return, she will be waiting for me, unharmed and untouched. You will watch her." She scattered a handful of silver on the counter, and the innkeeper's eyes widened when he spotted three glimmers of gold among them.

"Y-yes, ma'am."

"Good."

Dalliah climbed the steps to the upper floor without looking back, and the man scooped up the coins at once, hiding the gold pieces in his palm before the people around the fire could spot them. He smiled at Kate, recognizing her as a route to quick money. She turned away from him, looking for a seat well away from everyone else, and found one with its back to a corner of the room.

The inn was drafty, but infinitely more comfortable than hours spent sitting on a horse's back. A small fire was burning steadily in the grate, and when the flames threatened to burn too low, an old woman knelt down to tend it. The flames dulled a little as they caught on the leathery edges of what had once been books, now torn apart and good only for kindling. The old woman pushed the books in one by one, and the sight of the flames chewing around the edges of the papers stirred an uncomfortable feeling within Kate. Something twitched in her memory. The smell of burning paper . . . kneeling in a small space . . . someone beside her, whispering in the dark.

"Been traveling far?" Kate had not noticed the innkeeper walking up beside her, carrying a tray with a mug and slices of buttered bread. "You look as if you could do with this." He put the tray down in front of her and refused to be discouraged when she did not speak. "We've had a few like you in here. Traveled in from Fume, I suppose. It's not a place many people want to be right now."

Kate looked up. She wanted to ask questions, but knew that for the right coin this man would tell Dalliah everything about their conversation, so she stayed quiet instead.

"Eat up, then," he said. "I won't tell her upstairs."

Kate was too far from the fire to feel much more than gentle warmth, but it was enough. The herbal drink warmed her from the inside, and the food settled her stomach while the people around her talked among themselves, chattering about their lives and speculating about the "servant girl" and her mistress. They were so engrossed in this new subject that no one looked twice when one of the Blackwatch officers entered the inn. He had removed his warden's robe and now looked just like any other traveler. He mingled perfectly with the villagers, laughing with them and even accepting an offer of a drink before he took a seat in the corner farthest from Kate. She tried to ignore him and turned instead to the company of the book hidden secretly beneath her coat. People glanced over at her whenever they thought she wasn't looking, but the innkeeper made sure that she was left alone.

Kate opened the book to a page near the back, and a black feather slid out from its place tucked against the spine. The feather was old and tattered. The place it had marked held details of a Skilled technique that could bind a dying soul to that of a living person in order to prolong its life, but what had begun as an attempt to save the life of a dying subject had become something far more sinister. Different writers had added to the book over the years, and those who had worked on that technique reported that it did not just prolong a life but also prevented the one woman who had been experimented upon from ever knowing the peace of true death.

Dalliah was that woman, still living, centuries on, but her story was not what had drawn Kate to that particular part of the book. She had the feeling that there was something more there, something important that she had not seen, but no matter how many times she read that section, her broken memories would not tell her what it was.

Kate remained alone at her table, sometimes reading, sometimes sleeping in her chair, until a loud thud woke her. Something had hit the window next to the inn's main door.

"Was that a bird?" A woman's voice rose from a chair

next to the fire, where she had been sleeping with a baby in her arms. "Are there more out there?"

Two men scratched their chairs back and looked out the windows.

"Can't see nothin'," said one of them.

"Where there's birds, there's wardens," said the other. "I'm not lettin' them take me!" He pulled the bolts across the inn door and backed away from it as if death itself were waiting for him on the other side.

The innkeeper threw a spoon at the man's back, making him jump wildly. "Stop scaremongerin'! No warden has ever put a booted toe across that threshold, so don't you be frightenin' people off with your talk. Hear me?"

The woman rested her baby in a cloth sling across her chest and went to look for herself. "I was in Harrop when they harvested it last," she said. "Some of us got out over the walls; lots of us didn't. The wardens took half the town away that day. None came back."

"We all have stories," said the innkeeper. "There's a right time to tell 'em, and this isn't it."

Kate and the Blackwatch officer kept quiet as everyone gradually agreed that the noise was nothing to worry about and they all settled cautiously back to their business. The innkeeper walked around to unbolt the door and, despite his assurances, opened it just wide enough to take a wary look outside. His hand was shaking, and his fingers rested on the bolt as he hesitated, in two minds over whether to lock it or not. The view of the street reassured him, but just before the door swung shut Kate was sure she saw something he had missed: someone standing out there in the dark.

"Nothing to worry about, miss," said the innkeeper, returning to his counter. "You're safe as houses here."

Kate was not ready to take his word on that. She carried her book to the window and slid a lit candle to one side so she could look out. The moment she was close enough to see through the dimpled glass, something moved behind it. A crow was sitting on the windowsill. It perched there for a few seconds, its black eyes turned her way, and then took flight, swooping over to land on the shoulder of someone waiting in the rain.

A man was out there, standing on the other side of the muddy road. His eyes shone white in the moonlight as he stepped out of the shadows. The black feather was still in Kate's hand, and she turned it between her fingers, remembering something small, yet significant. "Silas," she whispered.

Silas watched Kate carefully. Everything depended upon keeping her attention. He knew how strong her link with the veil had become. If he could use that link and remind her, just for a moment, of the memories she had lost, he could see how deeply Dalliah's influence had spread.

The crow settled on a wall behind him, its work done, while Edgar kept watch over one of Dalliah's guards a short distance away. Silas did not know if what he was attempting would work, but he had to find out what he was dealing with. If her mind could be saved, that was reason enough to spare her life. If not, he could end Dalliah's plan there and then with the edge of his blade.

The world around Silas slipped into shades of gray. The candle on the inn's windowsill dulled to a faint blue flame, and Kate's eyes shimmered as she let the veil take hold. Silas had looked into Kate's memories before, but this was very different. This time she was the one who had to see the truth. He did not have to share her thoughts; he had to let her see into his.

The inn's sign creaked gently in the wind, each swing becoming slower and slower until all movement stopped. The inn walls dissolved into gray, and he could see the souls of the people within it as soft blurs of light filtering through the shadowy barrier of stone. Kate's soul shone the brightest of them all. Silas's blood chilled until it flowed like icy water through his veins. Then he sensed her. Kate's spirit was so tightly attuned to the veil that its brightness intensified when viewed through it, like sunlight through a magnifying glass. Dalliah had recognized that strength within her. All Silas had to do was remind Kate of what she already possessed.

Kate's consciousness blossomed in his mind like a glowing ember rising into a gentle flame. Instinct carried her through his memories. Half-remembered pieces of his past crystallized into sharp focus for brief moments before dissipating again as she searched for any sign of her old life, anything that would tell her who she was and why Silas was there.

Kate saw everything that Silas knew: every terrifying event he had caused in the past and every moment of the time they had spent together in Fume, she as his prisoner, he as her captor. She sensed the strength of purpose that had carried him into her life and relived the moment when he had turned against the High Council to save her from the enticing pull of death. She witnessed his vicious treatment at the hands of the Blackwatch as seen through his own eyes, as well as the offer Dalliah had made to him before they had left the Continent. Dalliah's voice spoke clearly within the memory. *We can regain our souls and be whole again. Surely that is worth the life of one young girl, Silas. Don't you agree?*

Kate broke away at once. Their connection lasted only a few moments, but her absence left a feeling of emptiness within Silas as he let her go. Kate stared through the window, her face gently blurred by the glass, and there was recognition there. After everything Silas had shown her and everything he had done, she remembered.

The inn's sign squeaked back into motion as the living world dominated Silas's senses once again. Kate looked back into the inn's main room and stepped away from the glass, while Edgar made his way toward Silas, crossing the street and sticking closely to the shadows.

"That Blackwatch officer looks like he'll be sitting there for a while," he said, completely oblivious to what had just happened. "Have you seen any sign of Kate?"

"She is inside," said Silas. "Under guard."

"So, why aren't you going in?"

"Dalliah has not remained free all these years without being cunning," said Silas. "If we take Kate now, she may still find a way to go ahead with her plan. She would hunt Kate down. Kate would never be safe."

"But she would be back to normal. With us."

"Dalliah has affected her mind once," said Silas. "It would not be difficult to do so again."

He studied the scene that Dalliah had created by choosing to stop in that place. The well-populated village, the positioning of the guards, even her apparent separation from Kate all had the markings of a subtle plan being put into action. Experience had taught him that Dalliah did not do anything without thinking many steps ahead. She was a strategist who served her own very personal agenda, with five hundred years of persecution and pain to help shape her decisions. There was no way to predict her methods or how she would react when under attack. With this enemy, ordinary rules of engagement did not apply.

"We have done all we can here," said Silas. "Get the horse."

Edgar glanced over at the empty window. "We can't leave her there."

"Kate can look after herself," said Silas. "She is more use to us where she is."

"You said we can't let her and Dalliah reach the city."

"I said we had to reach it first."

Edgar would have argued further, but Silas's demeanor warned him that his orders were not to be questioned.

The two of them left the village the same way they had entered it, climbing over a cracked section of fencing that leaned against a storehouse. No one saw them arrive, but everyone in the village felt them leave. Silas's frustration leached from him like a poison, infecting the village with a sense of dread that made sleepers stir in their beds. The air grew still. Whispering sounds not caused by the wind spread between the buildings, and shades moved across the ground like creeping smoke. The guards were suddenly more alert, raising their lanterns to inspect the surrounding trees, and the few people out on the streets stood still with fear, feeling the creeping sensation of eyes watching them from the dark.

When Silas and Edgar turned their backs upon the inn, they did not see Kate standing in the doorway with her hood laid back across her shoulders. Her link with Silas had stirred old shades up from the land, but it had also cleared her mind like a breeze blowing down a leaf-filled lane.

The battle horse carried its two riders away at a racing pace, while Kate's silver-tinged eyes saw the shades that drifted through the village, each one caught in a cycle of repetition, their essences pressing through the surrounding buildings, reliving aspects of their lives that had been passed in that place. She no longer recognized Dalliah's influence over her and knew her "mistress" for exactly what she was, an enemy, and easily the most dangerous creature to set foot upon Albion soil since Silas himself.

Kate let the cool bite of the air clear her lungs of the inn's once-welcome heat. She wanted to be out in the open, to claim her freedom and leave Dalliah far behind. The memories she had regained bled into one another, and together they unlocked thousands more, letting her see the entire balance of her life with complete clarity. Her hand went immediately to her necklace. She had not even noticed it on her journey there, yet now she could not imagine herself without it. Her fingers grasped the familiar shape of the oval gemstone that had once belonged to her mother, and she remembered. Everything.

She would not let Dalliah take that away from her again.

Kate stepped back into the inn to a spate of grumbles from a man disturbed by the cold from the door. He was about to complain to her directly, but one look at the figure in black was enough to make him think again. The girl standing by the door was not the same as the one who had stepped out of it. She held her head a little higher, her eyes were a little sharper, and one look at them made people feel exposed, as if she could peer into the well of their deepest secrets.

The man lowered his head and pulled his collar up around

his neck, while Kate sensed Dalliah's presence descending the staircase before the woman stepped into view, no doubt to check upon the girl whose life she was so willing to trade in order to reclaim her own. The remnants of Silas's influence still clung to the air, and he had left Kate with far more than just his memories. He had stoked the fire of rebellion within her, but she knew enough to take care around the woman. Silas had left her with a warning.

"What are you doing, Kate?"

Looking at Dalliah with veil-touched eyes was like looking at a phantom. Her living body was strong, but inside, the little that was left of her spirit was withered and worn, like a tree too often bent and twisted by the wind. Her soul was broken, but that alone should not have been enough to distort her essence in such a violent way. She had caused that damage to herself, during decades of experimentation and desperation. Dalliah's will to survive had carried her for far longer than her physical body should have been able to endure, even with her connection to the restorative energies of the veil. Kate was surprised by the twisted sight before her, but she did not flinch, focusing instead upon Dalliah's living form.

"Someone thought they saw a warden outside," said Kate. Since Silas had been in the village, there was just enough truth in her words to be convincing.

"The wardens have no reason to waste their time on a place like this," said Dalliah. "Do not get dragged into these people's superstitions. Leave them to their useless lives and sit down."

Kate twisted her fingers into fists, but she did as she was told.

"Something has changed," said Dalliah, looking out of the window where the crow had been. "The dead are restless."

Some of the inn patrons looked at her, and the woman with the baby dared to speak up.

"What's that you're sayin' about the dead?"

"Wait a few days," Dalliah said, glancing coldly at the child. "You will see."

She sat down beside Kate, and the people in the room gradually sought comfort in their drinks, their dreams, and the quiet crackling of the fire.

Kate did not have the luxury of ignorance any longer. Silas and Edgar were gone, and Dalliah Grey was a force beyond anything she had encountered before. Silas's unspoken warning hung heavily within her thoughts.

Face Dalliah with care. Overt disobedience will end in death.

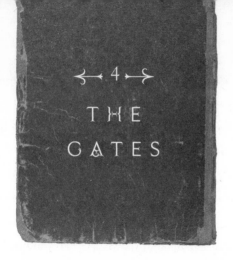

4

THE
GATES

Silas's battle horse pounded through the forest, thundering along a maze of overgrown smugglers' trails and snapping through a wall of never-ending trees. The wilds raced by in a crackle of twigs. A waxing moon illuminated the stony sky, eventually giving way to the rising sun of a new day, and still the horse kept running. Silas rode with one hand on the reins and the other resting against his mount's powerful neck, channeling the veil's energy into the running beast. If its muscles tired, Silas's influence kept them pumping, lending the horse a burst of new life, replenishing its aging bones and returning its old heart to the pounding strength of forgotten youth.

Edgar gradually became used to the rhythm of the hooves striking the earth and the movement of the horse's body as it broke out of the forest and into an open patchwork of what had once been ancient fields and hedgerows. Nature was already reclaiming what people had left behind. Neat boundary hedges had long since outgrown their straight lines and now spread outward into webs of evergreen touched with tips of white.

Whenever they stopped during that second day, it was for only a few minutes at a time, allowing the horse to drink and giving Edgar time to forage for food while walking off the pain in his legs that came from riding for so long. Sluggish clouds blotted out what little sun the winter had to offer during the short day, and rain fell like a constant mist, clinging to their skin.

Silas did not speak. Any questions Edgar asked were left unanswered, and they rode on, until the sun slipped once again toward the horizon and the high walls of Fume spread like a chain of black pearls in the distance.

With the fiery sun behind it, the city looked like a dark crown upon the landscape. Its curved walls reached farther than the eye could see. Black towers bristled against the sky, silhouetted by burning clouds as their spires blotted out the light of the setting sun, and a wide river encircled it all like a fiery slick reflecting the orange clouds above.

The road was exposed enough to be dangerous to anyone daring to ride so close to the ancient city. Watch posts bulged from Fume's walls at equal intervals, and any gate guards on duty had orders not to let anyone inside without direct permission from the High Council itself. Travelers were almost always turned away, and those who challenged that decision often met their end at the point of a warden's arrow.

Once people made their homes in the capital, few ever had

reason to leave the safety of its boundary again, yet it appeared that people had done so recently. Silas slowed the horse to a steady walk. He would have expected to see one or two trails, but the road was churned into a mess of hoofprints, wheel tracks, and bootprints, every one of them heading away from Fume. Many of the tracks were fresh. People had been leaving, this time by the hundreds.

Edgar was dozing lightly behind Silas, staying just alert enough to keep himself from sliding off the horse. The crow had spent the entire journey shadowing them from high overhead, and when Silas stopped, it fluttered down and strutted across the ground, hunting for food in the dirt.

Silas turned. "Wake up."

Edgar sat up, half asleep. "Why have we stopped?"

"Something has happened in Fume."

Silas edged the horse forward a few steps and inspected the walls far ahead. He could not see anyone standing upon the watch posts. It was sundown. The guard should have been changing and the sentry lights should already have been lit. Silas knew every inch of that city: every alleyway, every patrol route, every rhythm. Just weeks ago he had been responsible for the movements of each warden within those walls. To him, any change in routine, no matter how small, was significant.

"We will walk the rest of the way," he said. "A horse like this will be noticed out here."

Edgar clambered down, remembering the last time he had

seen the city from a distance, when he and Kate were being carried away from it against their will. He had seen too much during the past few days. All he wanted was for it to be over.

"What's the plan?" he asked as Silas unbuckled the saddle and pulled it loose.

"We are going to find a way in."

Silas slid the bridle from the horse's head and patted its flank. Remembering its training, the old battle horse took that as a signal to rest and wandered a little way off, into the night.

The gates of Fume stood as imposing webs of ancient iron that reached even higher than their towering walls. Beyond those gates, the city was a haunting place. The windows of the memorial towers stared down like sunken eyes watching over a maze of stone streets. Gas lamps flickered and flared, illuminating roads that wound in upon one another, twisting between buildings that had been there since the city's first days and past the newer houses of Albion's richest families and their servants. The new veined deeply into what was left of the old, but the essence of the city remained just as it had been for centuries. Immovable. Eternal. A city of secrets.

Fume was a place built for the dead, not for the living. It was the country's capital, and Silas should have been there, protecting it. The day he turned away from the High Council, he had been forced to abandon the place he had sworn to protect. Enemies had already spread into the arteries of the city. Dalliah Grey was not far away, and the wardens were making mistakes. It was time to put things right.

One by one, the watch posts came to life. Guardrooms swelled with light, and silhouettes of wardens moved along pathways on the wall tops. Silas passed Edgar his dagger. "We will infiltrate one of the watch posts," he said. "Make our way in over the walls."

"*Over* them? It would be easier to go under them."

"We do not have time for foolish ideas," said Silas.

"Maybe you don't know as much about Fume as you think you do."

Silas regarded Edgar carefully.

"Trust me. I have a better way in," said Edgar.

"Show me."

Edgar set off to walk the short distance to the city's encircling river. As rain clouds lingered overhead, it was dark enough for them to go unnoticed so long as they did not move too quickly.

Silas might have known how the wardens worked, but Edgar had a few tricks of his own. Every warden posted on the walls carried a light with him at all times. If you could see a lantern, a warden could see you. Edgar kept a close eye upon two fiery lights, waited for one to disappear into the shelter of a watch post, and tracked the second as it moved out of sight behind a raised section of the wall's battlements. "Follow me."

He crouched at the edge of the riverbank and slithered down its steep side. A thin trail of bricks had been sunk into the mud beside the water, and he walked along them with Silas close behind. From what Edgar had heard, there were at least twenty secret tunnels beneath those walls; all he had to do was find one.

The river was clean and webbed with ice along its shallower edges. The water rushed over layers of submerged rocks and splashed over Edgar's boots as he picked his way along its slippery course. He was not sure what he was looking for, but as long as the bricks remained underfoot, he was sure he was heading the right way. He held on to the muddy banks for balance, and soon his fingers touched something that was not meant to be there. Pressed flat into the steep bank was a slab of stone caked in a layer of mud, and beside it was a slice of rusted metal.

"This is it." Edgar felt a sudden pang of guilt about showing Silas a pathway people had used to hide from him and his wardens. "Er . . . don't tell anyone I told you about this," he said.

Silas's wide shoulders blotted out the moonlight, and his eyes shone with a faint gray glow. "Your secret is safe," he said, with the slightest hint of a smile.

Edgar pulled at the metal door, and a glut of stale air gusted from a passageway on the other side. "The land out here is covered in graves," he said. "People emptied a few of the larger crypts ages ago, hollowed them out, and cut tunnels into them."

"While no doubt casting any bones they found into the

river," Silas said with a hint of disgust. "I thought I had brought down the last of these passageways."

"You knew about them?"

"Not all of them, clearly. I would have found this one, given time."

Silas bent down and entered a space that was too low for him to stand in, but high enough for someone to scramble along at speed if he needed to. The passageway was neatly made. The walls were perfectly straight, running directly toward the city, making it easy to navigate without a light. Edgar followed Silas inside, his boots squelching through a layer of mud where moisture had leached in from the land above.

They kept walking until the soft glow of a street lantern silhouetted Silas's body up ahead. A small door led out into a narrow alleyway, barely wide enough for two people to stand side by side. The tunnel had cut straight through the foundations of the outer and inner walls and into the very edges of the city.

Silas had spent most of his adult life within Fume. He had patrolled it as a warden, returned to it as a soldier, and fled through it as a traitor. Despite everything that had happened to him there, he felt as if he were returning home.

"This entrance is badly hidden," he said as Edgar joined him in the open air. "The wardens should have found this tunnel."

"It's a good job they didn't."

"My men do not make mistakes."

"They're not your men," Edgar told him. "This isn't your problem anymore."

Silas walked down the alleyway, whispered something to his crow, and sent it fluttering up above the rooftops before he headed straight out into a lantern-lit street.

"Wait!" said Edgar. "You can't go out there."

Silas walked into the center of the road and stood there within full sight of anyone who might be looking out of the houses nearby. He was standing in one of the older districts of the city. Memorial towers rose from the ground all around him like fingers clawing their way out of the earth. Their old stones leaned in toward each other, while their upper levels gradually crumbled beneath the weight of time. High up in their farthest reaches, statues and cracked gargoyles looked down over the streets. Silas could tell exactly where he was from the skyline alone. It all appeared exactly as it should have been, except for one detail.

"Where is everyone?" asked Edgar.

"There are people here," said Silas, looking at the buildings around the square. To his right, a curtain moved. A shadow passed across a pale window directly ahead. "They are hiding from something."

"Maybe they saw you coming."

"Not this time."

With the city so quiet, the sound of carriage wheels carried freely through the air. Silas moved instantly and was already at the edge of the square before Edgar even realized he had gone. A warden patrol was due to march through that section of the city, but instead of hiding away from the oncoming vehicle, Silas sought it out. There were no wardens in sight, only a lone taxi carriage searching futilely for a fare.

Fast footsteps sprinted along an alley to Silas's left, and Edgar ran out into the light, his face relaxing with relief when he spotted Silas again.

"Warn me before you do that next time," he said. "I almost lost you."

Silas looked past him, his eyes settling upon the frontage of a theater that should have been filled with people at that time of night. Its doors were closed, its tall windows black, except for a small face peering out from behind the glass.

"Remain . . . still."

"Why?" Edgar froze at once as Silas walked past him.

The girl's breath did not steam the pane as her nose pressed against it. She blinked as Silas watched her and her eyes were touched with spirit light. She was, there, as clear as any living creature, but her life had ended long ago.

Unable to resist any longer, Edgar turned to see what was happening. "There's someone in there!" he said. "Don't let her see you."

"You can see that girl?"

"Of course I can." Edgar noticed the chains locking the doors together. There was no one with the girl as far as he could see. "Do you think she's all right?"

"As well as she can be," said Silas. "She is dead."

The girl drifted back into the walls as Silas's dark presence approached her, until the theater's glass door was empty once again. Edgar stared, unable to believe what he had just seen.

"She was . . ."

"You should not have been able to see her," said Silas. "This could be why people are fleeing the city and hiding in fear. They are not running from the wardens. They are running from the dead."

Edgar glanced back at the theater and saw the little girl's face, just for a moment, before it dissipated again.

Silas soon caught up to the idling taxi carriage, which was standing at an empty crossroads. He grabbed the side of the driver's chair and pulled himself up beside him. The man's face crumpled with fear.

"Do you know who I am?"

The man nodded silently. His hands, wrapped within the reins, were quivering.

Silas signaled for Edgar to climb into the back. "You will take us where I tell you. You will not stop unless I instruct you to do so."

"Yes, sir."

Silas patted the man hard on the shoulder, making him wince with fright, then stepped down and entered the carriage, sitting with his back to the driver's seat. He slid open the small hatch between him and driver and gave his orders. "The Museum of History," he said.

The driver kept his head down and stirred his horse into action.

"Why are we going there?" asked Edgar.

"Preparation, Mr. Rill, is everything."

As they rode, the streets they moved through gradually became more populated. Not everyone was ready to give up everything he had earned because stories were being told of the restless dead. Edgar tugged the short curtains closed on his side of the carriage, not wanting to be seen by anyone outside, but Silas kept his open. The people of Fume did not need to see him to know that he was there. His presence oozed from that carriage like oil across water. He had not been inside the city for some time. Now that he was back, it would not take long for word to spread.

"The wardens are going to find us," said Edgar, unable to hold his nerve with so many eyes upon the carriage. A cluster of paper notices was pinned to a panel behind his seat. He pulled one down and held up a small wanted poster with drawings of Silas's and Kate's faces printed upon it. "People don't ride straight through Fume when there is a price on their heads."

Silas did not look at the poster. "I do," he said.

When they arrived at the museum, Edgar stood looking up at the huge old building with its long windows of green glass while Silas spoke to their driver. Edgar was surprised that he and his horse did not just trundle away into the night the moment they stepped out. Whatever Silas had said to him, he waited there quietly while the two of them slipped inside.

The museum's main hall was a cracked, dirty shell of what it had once been. Floorboards were torn up and cast against the walls. Bones from old exhibits, tangled in wires that had once suspended them from the ceiling, were strewn across the floor, and in the very center of it all was a listening circle, a carved ring of stone symbols left by the Skilled long before that abandoned place had ever been used as a museum.

Edgar had bad memories of that hall. Silas marched straight across it, heading for the winding corridors and the staircase leading to the floors below, while Edgar stayed close to the walls, still wary of the circle that he had once seen open up and reveal its true purpose. It was a dormant gateway into the half-life that, when activated, had allowed him, Kate, and Silas to see deep into the realm of the restless dead.

Silas's voice, calling him, echoed around the vast empty building, and Edgar could not shake the feeling that there were eyes watching him from the high galleries above. He hurried after Silas, lit a candle from the wall, and followed the voice down through numerous cellar floors, along into the deep part of the museum that Silas called his home.

"Get yourself cleaned up." Silas stepped out of a room up ahead and threw a towel into Edgar's hand. "There is running water in there. Clean clothes through the door opposite. You have ten minutes."

Edgar's clothes were filthy. The coat was not too bad, but the rest almost had to be peeled off his body, they were so engrained with mud, blood, and sand. He washed quickly and was soon clean and dry. He scuffed his hair dry with the towel and sneaked into the second room.

The candle wavered in the doorway, and Edgar wasted time just staring at a maze of garments hanging from slim wooden rails. He had the pick of anything from leather-strapped soldiers' uniforms to robes belonging to past councilmen. Tempting as it was to choose one of the uniforms, Edgar settled on a black vest with deep blue edges that hung down long at the back. The trousers he chose fitted well enough, but he bulked out the vest with two shirts layered on top of one another. It took a while to find boots that fitted, and he topped it all with a dark blue jacket that reached to his knees. When he was ready, he stepped back into the corridor, where Silas was already waiting.

Gone were Silas's bloodstained and travel-worn clothes. His dark hair was washed and loose. He wore a bloodred shirt, black trousers, and polished boots and had a short black jacket with silver buttons sweeping from his right shoulder to the scabbard holding his black-bladed sword against his left hip. Edgar might have taken the opportunity to wear clothes fit for Fume's upper classes, but Silas looked as though he were truly one of them.

"The driver is waiting," said Silas, walking straight past him.

"Where are we going?"

"To help this city."

True enough, the carriage driver was still waiting outside. When Silas appeared at the top of the museum steps, the thin man dropped from his seat and held the door open for them both to climb in. "Sirs," he said with a nervous nod.

Edgar smiled awkwardly, but the driver dropped his eyes at once.

Silas did not have to give an order. The driver already knew where they were going, and the moment they were seated the carriage was on the move again. Edgar began to feel trussed up and uncomfortable in his unfamiliar clothes. The route the carriage followed, however, was all too familiar. As the gargoyle-guarded streets passed swiftly by, a knotted feeling of dread twisted in his stomach. He knew this route. He had traveled this way before.

"I know where we're going!" he said suddenly. "We can't go there. You have to stop the carriage." He leaned forward and shouted at the driver, "Stop the carriage!"

"He will not listen to you."

"Then *you* should listen. This isn't a plan. This is insane!"

"Sit."

At last the carriage stopped at the end of a long, straight street leading to a place that Edgar knew well. The driver knocked open the little hatch behind Silas. "Are you sure about this, sir?"

"Perfectly."

The hatch clicked shut, and the carriage continued on, climbing up a slight hill toward a collection of grand ancient buildings circled by an old iron fence. Edgar sank back in his seat as they stopped in front of a heavily guarded gate. Wardens converged upon the vehicle, and Silas opened the window as a hooded man's face filled the glass. The warden looked in at the two passengers, and his eyes widened in surprise. For a second Edgar thought he was going to order his men to attack, but instead he bowed slightly in Silas's direction.

"Officer. Open the gate," said Silas.

The warden stepped back and immediately raised a hand to his men. Two of them pushed the gates aside, opening up a clear path into the most protected part of Fume, the chambers of Albion's High Council.

"This has to be a trap," said Edgar. "They wouldn't just let us in."

The carriage horse walked slowly forward, and Edgar spotted three more wardens standing close by. The carriage rolled past their post, through an archway and across a courtyard, heading directly toward the chambers' main door.

"There's still time to turn back," said Edgar. "The council will set every warden they have on us the moment they see you."

"True loyalty does not die when it becomes inconvenient," said Silas. "Fume is under threat. This is where we must be."

5

SILVER &
DUST

When Kate and Dalliah arrived at the city on horseback, the disguised Blackwatch officers approached the gates first and spoke with two wardens standing on the other side. Dalliah had ordered Kate to keep her hood up once they were close to Fume, and Kate peered out from behind it as the wardens signaled for the two of them to move forward. One of the men unlocked the great iron gates and pushed them open while the other bowed his head in greeting.

"Lady Grey," he said, "welcome to Fume."

Kate thought there was something unusual about the man. His accent was softer than the sharp voices that were common across Albion.

"The city is not as secure as its High Council believes," said Dalliah.

The warden smiled. "It never was." He handed Dalliah a cloth-wrapped package that was small and thin. They talked quietly for a short time, and Dalliah hooked the package onto her saddle.

The disguised officers stood alongside the wardens, and Kate overheard them giving the gate guards orders. She knew then that the latter were not wardens but Blackwatch agents. Albion's enemies had infiltrated beyond Fume's gates.

"We ride on," said Dalliah, taking the reins of Kate's horse and leading it alongside her own.

The air trembled as the two women crossed the threshold of the city. Shades shifted in the shadows, filtered through the stones, and mingled in the air, making the flames in the wardens' lanterns shrink and fade back to the tiniest spark. A shiver of fear and expectation ran through every soul and every memory still locked within that place. Kate felt it as a chill colder than any winter wind, as if a door had opened to the coldest part of the world, letting freezing air blast against her skin. Fume's streets were bare and ghostly. The gray and black buildings stood out sharply against a white sky, and it felt as if the towers themselves were listening.

The Blackwatch remained with their associates at the gate. The city's silence was disturbed by the screeching of metal hinges, and Kate looked back to see the huge gates pulled shut. None of the wardens posted nearby had noticed the presence of intruders in their midst.

Since she had seen Silas, Kate's memories had burned into clarity like flames spreading through a forest. She could remember everything that had happened in her life: the loss of her home to the wardens' flames, the experiments conducted upon her by the High Council, and her trial at the hands of the Skilled, who had rejected her even though she had gone to them for help. But worse than all the others, the one that made her wish she could forget everything all over again, was the memory of events that happened just before her journey across the sea.

She remembered Dalliah's influence spreading around her, stifling her: Silas Dane, weakened and injured but never broken, and her best friend, Edgar, stabbed by a Blackwatch officer and left to die. Under Dalliah's influence, Kate had walked away from both of them, leaving them there. She had seen the building they were trapped in burn and blaze, sending thick black smoke into the sky. Silas had survived, but she had seen no sign of Edgar in the village. She could not escape the guilt of leaving him behind. No matter what had happened, she would never forgive herself for that.

Kate's hatred toward Dalliah seared inside her. She wanted to shout and rage at the woman who had torn Edgar away from her. She wanted to scream at her . . . make her pay for what she had done. But instead she stayed quiet. She had seen Dalliah's cruelty at work and had already been overwhelmed by her once before. She needed to keep her mind clear. She needed to wait. If her time with Silas had taught her anything, it was patience.

Dalliah slowed the horses at the base of a memorial tower that looked very different from the dozens of others they had already passed. Its basic structure was much the same—rounded walls of black stone punctuated with small windows—but this tower's stones looked as if they were veined with silver. Fragments of what could have been metal reflected the moonlight in thin trails across them, but as Kate looked closer, she saw the truth. Ordinary people would never see anything unusual there. Those veins were threads of energy, invisible to all but the most Skilled of eyes. A dull ache of sadness permeated the air, and Kate could feel the watching presence of at least two souls that were bound to that place, unable to leave.

Dalliah ordered Kate to dismount and stood with her hand against the tower's solid door. "It has been a long time since I was last here." The tower reacted immediately to her touch. The silvery glow faded back until it was barely visible at all, retreating from her hand like ripples on a lake.

She pulled a key from a pouch on her belt and slid it into the lock. The door was stiff, and the air that belched from inside smelled dead and dry. Kate choked in the swirling dust, but Dalliah was unaffected. The two of them stepped into the forgotten building, and then Kate heard the voice.

"Do not go."

Dalliah showed no sign of having heard it, but to Kate the voice was soft and clear.

"Please."

Inside, the tower was unexpectedly bright. Light poured in through slitlike windows pierced into the walls alongside a curling staircase that rose from the vault below and led up to the levels above. Kate covered her nose with her sleeve to allow herself to breathe and spotted something slumped against the wall. It was a broken skeleton, its skull set crooked and empty eyed, its bony fingers hooked around the handle of a rusted blade.

"Hello, Ravik," said Dalliah. She kicked the skeleton's foot as she passed it, sending bones rattling across the floor. "You'll be wanting this back, no doubt." She dropped the key between the skeleton's ribs, and something moved in the air above the steps. Kate looked just in time to see a pale apparition of a young man sinking into the wall.

"Ignore him," said Dalliah. "He was useless in life, worthless in death."

"Who is he?"

"A previous student of mine," said Dalliah. "He did not believe in what we are about to do. He made things difficult. He might have lived a little longer if he had put his intelligence to better use."

Dalliah crunched a loose bone beneath her boot as she followed the steps upward. Kate hesitated, concerned that Dalliah had locked the door behind them, and the moment the woman was out of sight she crouched down, slid her fingers between the dead man's ribs, and hooked out the little key.

"Do not go."

The air chilled beside her, and she spotted something next to the old blade. Something had been scratched within the stone. She moved the dagger to one side and discovered a thread of spiked, thinly cut letters, etched to form a shaky word.

MIRROR

Kate's fingers brushed gently against one of Ravik's thighbones as she stood up, and she saw the final moments of his life through his own eyes. *Standing at a desk. An intruder behind him: heard but not seen. A knife—like fire—plunging into his side. The attacker making his escape. Ravik's bloodied hands staining the walls as he stumbled down the tower steps. The door . . . locked.* Kate heard his weak cries for help as if she were making the sound herself, sharing his pain and desperation as he spent his last scrap of life scratching the message into the floor.

"Kate." Dalliah's voice carried around the curved staircase, and she quickly moved her hand away from the bone. Ravik had not been surprised by the locked door in the memory. He had expected it, only half hoped that his attacker had forgotten to seal it again on the way out. Kate had noticed deep scratches around the lock where someone had tried to prize the door open from the inside. Whatever Ravik was doing in there, he had not been doing it by choice. He had been locked in that tower many years ago. He had been murdered there, and now his spirit could not leave it. Ravik moved through the walls, circling her, but staying out of sight.

"Don't let her find it. The message must be passed on."

Kate stood up, pocketed the key, and read the scratched word once more. "I'll try," she said, still not sure what it meant, and Ravik's spirit passed invisibly beside her, leading her up the tower steps.

At the very top stood the room where Ravik had spent his final days. Dalliah was standing to one side, next to an old bed frame, and there were low cupboards running around the rest of the curved wall, each one ravaged by damp that seeped in through narrow windows that looked out to the east and west. Every flat surface was covered with old bowls made of tarnished silver. A box filled with a variety of unusual tools stood propped against the wall, and a collection of knives had been stabbed into the cupboard tops, each one surrounded by deep welts where it had been forced into the wood over and over again.

"Ravik was a troubled young man," said Dalliah.

"People don't like being locked away," said Kate.

"Do not believe everything the dead tell you," said Dalliah. "Isolation was essential for his work."

Kate touched the handle of one of the knives and saw an

image of Ravik stabbing it into the cupboard, just for a second. "What was he doing here?" she asked.

"My ability to supervise work here in Fume was limited while I was on the Continent," said Dalliah. "In my absence, Ravik's task was to test a theory of mine. The theory was correct, of course, but Ravik refused to see the procedure through to its natural end. We must complete what he began, and we must do it right the first time, with no hesitation." Dalliah's eyes filled with anticipation. "If the spirit in the wheel realizes what we are doing, it will fight back."

Dalliah dragged a moldering cloth from the wall and exposed a small stone wheel hidden underneath. It was set deep into the wall and made up of a central circular tile—a few inches wider than an open hand—with smaller tiles arranged in a channel around its edge. Each tile carried a symbol, and the wheel itself held an imprisoned soul that had been trapped inside for centuries. It looked well preserved, apart from one tile whose symbol had been scraped away, leaving a well of deep scratches behind. Kate had seen wheels like that before, and she knew enough to treat it with respect.

"These wheels are the keystones upon which this city stands," said Dalliah. "The souls within them act as anchors, binding the half-life to the living world, while also ensuring that the two remain separate. Creating them protected Albion from the terrors of the half-life once. Destroying them will lead this land into a new age."

"I thought we were here to *prevent* the veil from falling," said Kate.

"The barrier between life and death cannot be maintained forever," said Dalliah. "These souls are tired. Many have already lost their potency. When the veil does fall, we are here to make sure it happens in a way that suits me. We will simply be hastening a natural process. You will understand when the time comes."

"And what will happen then?"

"Then my work will be complete," said Dalliah, "as will yours."

Kate did not like the way Dalliah said those final words.

To the right of the wheel, where one corner of the wall cloth still clung to a rusted pin, Kate spotted a glint of light reflecting from something in the wall. Ravik moved behind her, and she felt the shiver of a gentle hand upon her shoulder.

Dalliah opened her bag and compared the positions of the symbols on the wheel with a diagram sketched in the pages of one of her old books.

"Each of these symbols represents an old Skilled family, most of whom are now long dead," she said. "I have heard that people have learned to interpret them and communicate with the spirit trapped within the wheel. That was not why these souls were bound, but I can see why, after five centuries sealed within stone, they may have needed something with which to pass the time." She placed two fingertips gently upon the scratched-out tile. "My family's symbol has been defaced, but the wheel should still function."

From the moment Dalliah's hand made contact with the spirit wheel, the room felt colder. More enclosed. Even though there was only a staircase between her and the door to the outside world, Kate felt trapped.

She looked at the hidden light out of the corner of her eye. A cracked mirror was tucked beneath the cloth, and a shard of glass had been removed from the bottom left corner. Ravik remained close by. In Dalliah's presence, everything about him seemed slumped and defeated, but his attention was secretly fixed upon the hiding place within the mirror and a thin fold of paper that rested there in the dark.

"This wheel is one of twenty-four like it across the city," said Dalliah, pulling a collection of empty glass vials stoppered with wooden corks from her bag. "The most powerful bonemen's souls were sealed within these wheels to prevent the full energy of the half-life from spreading across Albion. That energy is already bleeding out, which means the weaker spirit wheels have already lost their link with the veil. This wheel holds one of the three most powerful spirits that were bound that day. Fume's connection will survive so long as those three wheels last. When they fall, the veil will fall."

"The Skilled should be here," said Kate. "Shouldn't they be doing something?"

"*We* are doing something."

The central stone was carved with a four-pointed star. Dalliah pressed her palm firmly against it, and the tiles around it trembled. "Few bear grudges longer than the dead," she said. "This soul resisted the procedure that ultimately saved Albion in the bonemen's time. It did not trust me in life. It will not do so in death."

Kate thought the spirit had good reason to be wary of the woman who had sealed it into stone. The atmosphere of the room had changed markedly, and now Kate recognized the cause. Hate was leaching silently from the wheel: hate toward Dalliah for what she had done.

"Five hundred years is a long time to be wrong." Dalliah was talking to the stone, keeping one hand upon the star and the other on the ruined tile that had once held her symbol. "The bloodline lives," she said. "The girl is here. Despite everything you have done and all the barriers you have put in my way, she will not save you."

The tiles around the stone circle rattled and clicked, but none of them moved.

"Bring me one of those spikes."

The only spikes that Kate could see were the collection of rusted spearlike tools. She pulled one out of the box and held it out.

"No. You will do this," said Dalliah. "Do you see the damage done to the edges of the central stone?"

The stone was worn away at four equal points around its

circumference. Kate had assumed the erosion was caused by age, but the shape of the damaged areas matched exactly the point of the tool she was holding.

"You sent Ravik here to dismantle the wheel," said Kate.

"And he succeeded," said Dalliah. "Now you will do the same. Pry out the stone."

Kate could not afford to drop her pretense, so she lifted the spike and drove it hard into the wheel.

Metal rasped against stone, and the star carving moved slightly as she worked the spike deeper into the wall. Whatever mechanism was meant to work the wheel was not attached to it any longer. Ravik may have dismantled it, but he had failed to piece it back together. The stone loosened easily. It was thin and disk shaped, with sides that tapered to a narrow edge, allowing it to spin easily within the wall.

Kate let the spike fall and held the disk safely in her hands. There were carved holes where a mechanism had once been connected, but now there was nothing left. Even if the spirit had wanted to communicate using the tiles, there would have been no way for it to move them. "Ravik was studying the wheel," said Dalliah. "The creation of these devices is a lost skill. I needed someone who could understand the mechanics behind them, as well as the veil work that infuses the finished stones."

"So you could make more of them," said Kate.

"In the beginning, yes. Unfortunately, I could not do it

alone. Ravik was talented enough, but he allowed his empathy with the soul inside to cloud his judgment. His dealings with it twisted his mind. It drove him mad." She glanced back at the shade of the young man, who was now waiting near the stairs. "I see very little has changed."

Kate saw her chance. While Dalliah was distracted, she quickly reached out, slid the fold of paper from its hiding place in the mirror, and tucked it into her sleeve.

"The past is no longer important," said Dalliah. "A new future begins today."

She reached her hand into the space left by the stone, and the atmosphere in the room darkened at once. It felt as if the rest of the world were falling away, leaving the walls swamped by the endless touch of a realm without substance, the lost place between the living world and the embrace of true death. The air became thin, and the only light was concentrated in the very center of the room, pressed in upon itself by the darkness. Ravik tried to move away from the walls, and Kate found herself stepping in toward the light, trusting it to keep her safe.

"The veil has many levels," said Dalliah. "Most Skilled eyes can see into the first level quite easily. They can share the memories of the dead and draw upon the energies of the veil to heal the physical body. A rare few can see into the second level, where wandering souls wait to die. Even fewer can see beyond that, and barely one or two of us can peer into places that human imagination would find difficult to describe. I have seen every level there is. I have stepped beyond the shallows of the half-life and witnessed what lies beneath it. Death is beautiful, Kate, but there is another place, a more distant and powerful place. Death cannot save souls who are pulled into its heart."

Kate and Ravik were forced closer by the encroaching dark. Whatever Dalliah planned to do, Kate feared that what was left of Ravik was not meant to survive it.

"The veil confuses the soul, but the darkness at its depths tears it apart," said Dalliah. "Walkers referred to that place only as 'the black.' It severs every link to the physical world, steals every memory, and leaves a soul with everything that the living mind thought it had forgotten. The unspoken lies, the regrets, the fear, and the pain. The black makes a soul doubt that the living world exists. It removes every memory of the life it once had until only fragments are left behind. Death embraces the soul. The black destroys it. That is where the soul from this wheel must go."

Ravik was so close Kate could feel echoes of fear trembling through him. Dalliah's link with the wheel drew the darkness closer. There was nowhere to go. The emptiness touched Ravik, and his soul gave out a whispered cry. Kate had never heard a sound like that before. It was a gasp of anguish and panic, the cry of someone who was used to being alone, knowing that no one would come to help. Kate did not know what to do, and then it was too late. The depths pulled Ravik in, and his spirit fell silent, dissipating into white haze.

Wherever that darkness came from, it was filled with threat. The airless force nipped like acid on her skin, exploring her flesh and stinging her eyes. It felt as if she were standing in the jaws of a creature that was deciding whether or not to swallow her. Instinct made her hold her breath, not wanting to invite any of it into her lungs. The tower contained it. The stones formed its cage. Her soul, still bound to a living body, could barely resist it, and its touch had already taken Ravik away.

Dalliah reached through the blackness and took hold of Kate's hand. Her touch felt like hot needles, pulling her toward the wheel.

"You will see what this girl can do," said Dalliah, addressing the spirit in the stones. Her voice sounded dull and strange, as though Kate were listening to it underwater. "Your time is over." Dalliah pressed her fingers firmly against Kate's throat, forcing her to breathe in the black mist; then she thrust Kate's hand deep into the hole in the wall.

Kate expected the blackness to overwhelm her, but instead everything around her slowed and hung within one silent moment: Dalliah watching her; the spirit wheel illuminated in a blaze of orange, every symbol shining with a fiery light.

"*Dalliah has returned.*" A voice spoke within Kate's mind, sad yet proud, drawing her consciousness into the veil. "*She is ending us.*"

"The veil is falling," Kate answered. "I don't know how to stop it."

"We know this."

"What can I do?"

The wheel's glow faded from every tile except one. The snowflake symbol of Kate's family. Then, on either side of the circle, two more illuminated: the bird and the bear.

"I don't know where Silas is," said Kate, recognizing the bird's meaning at once. "And Edgar . . . Edgar is gone."

"No," said the soul. *"You are three."*

"Edgar died. The Blackwatch . . . I couldn't help him. I left him there."

"He lives, as you do. His body lives on. He has returned to Albion."

"Edgar is here?" Kate could not contain the relief she felt as the burden of grief and guilt fell from her. Her energy sent a shiver through the stones.

"Dalliah knows her enemy is close by. She is ready."

"I don't know how to stop this," said Kate. "Tell me how to help you."

"We are lost. You shall live on. You will be the first and the last."

The blackness scratched at Kate's back, like ants biting her skin. "The first what?" she asked. "What can I do?"

"You will do what is necessary. Others will show you the way. You cannot help me. Let me go."

The wheel faded back to dull dead stone, and Kate felt a tugging sensation in her chest as the spirit was drawn away, into the depths. Into the black.

Kate's soul was standing on the edge of an abyss. It would take only a slight touch to send her into it. She felt the creeping hands of the dark, the horrors of emptiness, the certainty of destruction.

She pulled her consciousness back from the edge, dragging herself back into the living world. The darkness fell away. Her body ached, and her hand felt heavy as she pulled it from the wall.

"You are as ruthless as your ancestors," said Dalliah, who had not shared the conversation between Kate and the trapped spirit. "How do you feel?"

Kate wanted to say that she felt dirty, sickened, and hollow. She wished she had never stepped into that room, that tower, that city. The back of her hand had been sliced open, and blood ran freely along her arm. Kate did not need to ask what Dalliah had done. Her blood had been used in veil work before. Dalliah was not the first to recognize its power.

"I was right about you, Kate," said Dalliah, her cold eyes bright with excitement. She took Kate's hand again, and at her touch the cut healed perfectly. "Your blood is more powerful than I had hoped. You and I are going to achieve great things here."

6

TRAITOR

"Call the guards!"

"Do not waste your breath." Silas marched toward a fresh-faced warden who was guarding the chambers' main door. He disarmed the young man in two smooth moves and held the officer's own dagger to his neck. "The High Council," he demanded. "Where are they?"

"I can't tell you that."

"Where?"

Edgar winced as Silas dragged the warden's head back, exposing the beating thread of the artery in his neck.

"The meeting hall!" said the warden. "They've been there since yesterday. No one goes in without authorization."

"I do not need authorization," said Silas. He pushed the warden against the wall and walked away.

The warden watched Silas and Edgar leave, then stepped

outside and raised the alarm. "Enemy in the chambers!" he shouted. "Ring the bells!"

The sharp clang of metal echoed around the chamber buildings as warning bells were rung one by one, melding together into an urgent cacophony of noise.

"It's about time," said Silas.

He and Edgar walked swiftly through the corridors and up opulent staircases as if they had never been away. The chambers filled with servants, and wardens burst out of side corridors, hurrying to their posts. One or two looked directly at Silas, registering him just for a moment, before they lowered their eyes and ran on. They valued their lives too much to challenge him.

Silas and Edgar reached a long corridor leading down to the meeting hall. The wardens on either side of the doors drew their weapons when they spotted someone approaching and immediately lowered them again when they identified Silas, their faces filling with dread.

"Move aside," he said smoothly, before pushing the doors open with both hands and entering a room filled with raised voices.

"I don't care what you think," came a shout from inside. "You are wrong, and that is the end of it!"

The meeting hall was a vast paneled room, painted black, with huge tapestries hung upon all the walls except one. That wall was filled with a square window of clear glass that let

WINTERVEIL

moonlight stream in across a long wooden table etched with
curls of silver. The table was surrounded by the thirteen
members of Albion's High Council and their closest advisers.
Some were seated, others standing, watched over by eight
wardens, who stood silently against the walls.

An argument was raging, and there was no sense of order.
Silas doubted they had even heard the warning bells over the
sound of their own voices, but when he entered the room,
every voice fell quiet, except for one.

"It is a waste of our time, a waste of our men, and the
most laughable excuse for disobedience that I have ever
heard," it was shouting. "I don't want to see another single
person leaving this city. I don't care what they have heard
or what they *think* they have seen. All this talk of 'restless
souls.' It is the talk of children and has no place within this
room!"

The councilman realized that people had stopped arguing
back and spotted Silas standing just a few steps away from
him. "Oh," he said, much more quietly. "You. Those bells
are for you, I presume? Traitors are not welcome in this hall,
Officer Dane. I trust you are here to turn yourself in to the
judgment of Albion law?"

Silas watched the man with interest. He was the most recent
member among the thirteen—Da'ru Marr's replacement—
and still naive enough to think he had a voice and an opinion
separate from those of the council as a whole.

"Since you already know me," said Silas, "I will not waste time on introductions."

The councilman turned to his fellow members. "Why is he here?" he demanded. "Who let him get this far into the chambers? A murderer is standing a few feet away from me, and no one is moving!"

Most of the advisers whispered excuses and exited the room, leaving the council and its wardens alone with the two visitors.

"I have served this country far longer than you have worn that robe," said Silas. "You will listen to me, or this city will soon be unrecognizable. You have become blind to what is happening here. You have been so busy doubting the truth about the ground beneath your feet that you have allowed a poisonous enemy into your lands."

"And that enemy would be . . . you?" The councilman laughed quietly, looking around for others to share in his joke. Edgar watched nervously. He had never seen anyone attempt to mock Silas before.

"Dalliah Grey is here." A whisper of surprise spread around the table as Silas addressed the council as a whole. "She is here, and she intends to damage our city and our country. Those of you who were present on the Night of Souls know that the veil is not merely a superstition. Dalliah intends to bring it down upon all of us, allowing restless souls to wander through our streets, our homes, and our lives. She plans to bring chaos to Albion, and she must be stopped."

As Silas spoke, he studied every face in front of him. He was looking for clues, any sign that Dalliah's appearance came as no surprise to someone in that room. If what he had heard from his sources was true, someone had wheedled his way into power even more deviously than most. An enemy agent had infiltrated the council's chambers. One person sitting at that ruling table had been working for the Blackwatch all along.

"I am here to offer my services in defense of the city." He continued. "People are afraid, and they have good reason to be. Until you accept what is happening, you will be of no use to them. The veil will fall, and you will lose control."

"Why do you care if we lose control?" asked one of the seated men.

"Because the leaders of the Continent are preparing to move against us. Rumors have spread that Fume is weak. There is talk of sickness within its walls, and people are beginning to distrust your rule. The Continental leaders see this as the perfect time to attack. If you do not act, you will lose this city. The war will be over. They will have won."

"That will never happen. Fume is ours. We will defend it!"

"Then you must prepare. Now."

A third councilman, his confidence bolstered by the presence of the wardens in the room, stood up. "That is the most ridiculous thing I have ever heard," he said.

"It is the truth."

"I see no armies on the horizon. There has been no word of attacks upon our southernmost towns for days."

"No competent leader would waste time on smaller towns when our capital is weak," said Silas.

The third councilman raised a thin smile. "Then we are perfectly safe," he said. "Our enemies have already proven that they are far from competent."

More nervous smiles spread around the room, fueled by the arrogance of fools.

"Every battle against the Continent has been hard won," said Silas. "Their leaders will not waste this chance to strike at the heart of our lands. The wardens on the walls are disorganized and unobservant. They are not used to being challenged. When the armies come, we will need to provide greater resistance than we have raised so far. I will hunt down Dalliah Grey, but I cannot protect this city on two fronts. I need men and women who are willing to fight, and I need them to be ready. I am here because my duty is always to Albion. As is yours."

The outspoken councilman folded his arms and shook his head, raising his eyebrows in mock concern. "This is all very interesting," he said. "Unfortunately, your 'duty' extends to one action alone. You are a traitor, a murderer, and a criminal. You have no right to stand in this room and address this council as an equal. You are an insect, worthy of nothing more than being crushed under my heel."

The room waited silently for Silas to react. He unbuckled his scabbard from his belt and passed it, sword and all, to Edgar, who held it carefully and backed away.

"Then you surrender yourself?" The councilman's mouth twitched with victory, and he signaled for the wardens to close in. No one moved. "Take him!"

One warden stepped forward, sliding a silver dagger slowly from its sheath. No matter who had given the order, Edgar could not believe anyone would be foolish enough to act upon it. But instead of approaching Silas, the warden walked up to Edgar and passed him his weapon before standing to attention at his side.

"What is going on here?" The councilman's smile twisted into rage.

Two more wardens joined the first. Then five more, all placing their daggers on the ground at Edgar's feet.

"You have already lost control," said Silas. "You have lost the respect of those who serve you. You have lived in decadence for too long while your own people suffer to keep you in power. You have allowed yourselves to neglect what should have been most important to you. Without the trust of the people, a government is powerless. The greatest threat to our country is inside this very room."

"I think we can all recognize the greatest threat in this room, and I'm looking straight at him."

"No," said Silas. "I am."

Everyone followed Silas's eyes and stared at a councilman who had been content to sit quietly at the table and let others do the talking. He was middle-aged, with a neatly trimmed beard and a face that looked open and trustworthy. He was sitting back in his chair, casually making notes on a piece of paper.

"Gorrett?" said the councilman sitting directly beside him. The entire council smiled, and a few suppressed sniggers of laughter.

As an infiltrator Edwin Gorrett had been easy to overlook. He was old enough to make himself appear physically weak. His opinions, as far as Silas had ever witnessed, always ran in line with the general consensus, and he had never openly challenged anyone around that table. He wrote his notes, cast his votes, and went about his business with quiet grace. No one had anything bad to say about the man. Silas had always thought of him as a pawn used by the other members to bolster their own opinions, but Gorrett's reaction to the announcement of Dalliah's presence in the city had not been one of shock like the others'. Instead his lips had flickered with secret pride. Silas's arrival had surprised him more than his fellows, but he had been quick to hide it, forcing himself to appear relaxed while the sharp scratch of his pen betrayed his true feelings: not fear, like the rest, but frustration.

Gorrett's eyes sharpened, just for a moment, and Silas saw the heart of a soldier simmering beneath the veneer of power.

He beamed a politician's smile, but his fingers tightened around his finely nibbed pen. He kept his head low and looked at Silas, shifting his weight very slightly to his left. In trained hands, that pen could be an effective weapon, and exposed enemy agents rarely allowed themselves to be taken down alone.

"Councilman Gorrett has never served Albion," said Silas. "He has been against us from the beginning. He ingratiated himself into the life of the man whose seat he now fills. He earned his trust and now betrays that trust by passing every secret shared in these chambers on to his true masters. Gorrett is a Blackwatch agent."

"That is impossible!"

"He was posted here to undermine this council," said Silas. "He deceived us all."

Exposing a Blackwatch agent in the center of a council meeting was a dangerous move. A lesser warden would not have noticed the flex of a tendon in the back of Gorrett's hand. They would not have seen the tiny twitch of the upper lip and the furrowing of his brow that betrayed what he was about to do. To have survived undiscovered in the heart of enemy territory for so long, Edwin Gorrett had to be one of the Blackwatch's best men. His mission had been to destabilize the High Council. Now that he was exposed, there was only one way to continue that mission. He was out for blood.

Gorrett's right arm tensed and sent the pen stabbing up toward the throat of the man beside him. In the space of a second, Silas pulled a concealed dagger from his sleeve. The blade cut the air as the metal nib speared toward the artery throbbing beneath the targeted councilman's skin.

Silas's weapon struck first.

The dagger punctured Gorrett's chest with a soft, fleshy thud. His arm lost momentum and slumped onto the table as blood blossomed across the front of his robes, sending councilmen fleeing and scattering against the walls.

"No one leaves!" shouted Silas, sending the wardens to take up positions at the doors. Gorrett was bleeding badly, but the wound was not immediately fatal. Silas was not finished yet. He skirted the table as the infiltrator reached in vain for a blade hidden in his boot. Silas grabbed him by the neck, lifted him from his seat, and slammed him down onto the table.

Silas reached the blade before Gorrett could and thrust it hard into the tendons of the dying man's ankle. Whoever Gorrett truly was, he was well trained. He barely made a sound.

"Officer Dane, stop! You are killing the man."

Silas grasped the handle of the dagger still lodged in the man's chest. "Not quickly enough," he said.

Gorrett smiled through bloodstained teeth. "You . . . are too . . . late. I did . . . my duty. Do yours. Kill me."

Silas twisted the blade inside Gorrett's chest. His body

buckled with pain, and with one last shuddering breath the life in his eyes died.

The wardens were uncertain how to react. No one moved. No one dared speak.

Silas pressed his hand to Gorrett's forehead. A glut of memories spilled out into the veil as the man's spirit prepared to leave its physical body behind. Silas saw them all but ignored everything except the details of the Blackwatch plan. He witnessed Gorrett's secret meetings, the opening of letters carried in by unofficial messenger birds, until finally he found the information he was looking for. He lifted his hand away and spoke to the council. "We have less than a day," he said. "The armies are here on Albion soil. They are coming now."

"How could you know that?"

Silas dragged his blade out of the dead man's chest and pressed his palm against the open wound. The veil spread through him like trails of ice, passing into Gorrett's muscles and flesh, binding them together and dragging his spirit back from the very edges of death. Gorrett's skin flushed as he breathed in a gasping breath, choking on the blood that had collected in his throat.

"Welcome back," said Silas, holding his dagger barely a hair's breadth from Gorrett's left eye. "You are a parasite feeding off my country and killing it from the inside. I could tear your soul from your chest and send it into the darkest pit of existence that your nightmares cannot imagine. Do not test me again. You will die when these men have no more use for you. Until then . . ."

Silas dragged Gorrett down from the table and let him fall hard upon the floor. "You saw this man attempt to take a councilman's life," he said as wardens converged upon the prisoner. "Interrogate him. If he will not speak . . . force the truth from him."

"Albion will fall!" Gorrett coughed and struggled weakly as his hands were bound behind his back. "This city is ours now."

One of the wardens bent to pull the blade from Gorrett's useless ankle.

"Leave it," said Silas, remembering his own treatment during his time as a Blackwatch prisoner. "The Blackwatch enjoy causing pain. Make sure he suffers plenty of it in return."

"You should not have been here!" Gorrett shouted as he was dragged away. "You were supposed to have been kept away!"

Silas waited for the doors to close, then stabbed the bloodied dagger deep into the table and left it there while the remaining councilmen stared at it, nervously taking their seats. Even the outspoken newcomer sat down, his lips quivering in response to the brutality he had just witnessed.

"Now I have your attention." Silas tugged his coat sleeves back into place, his fine appearance giving no sign that he had almost killed a man. "We can continue to distrust each other, or we can work together and get things done. Decide quickly."

The man whose life Silas had saved spoke slowly, rubbing a hand protectively over his throat. "What could you possibly need from us?" he asked.

"I need wardens on guard in every town from the southern coast to the High North. Wherever they are posted, they need to be seen. If we have soldiers nearby, send word that we need more men here in the city. Let the enemy know that challenging us will not be an easy fight. I want every warden to man these walls, scour them for hidden breaches, and make sure every entrance to the Thieves' Way and the City Below is watched at all times. As you have seen, the Blackwatch are already here. The Continental army will not be far behind. Let us give them a fight to remember."

"And you?" asked the councilman. "You expect us to let you go free, after everything you have done?"

"I am already free," said Silas. "My loyalty is to Albion, not to you. I came here because you appear incapable of doing your duty. Do not try to prevent me from doing mine."

The warden who had been the first to stand beside Edgar stepped forward. "I will send word to the towns and recall the Night Train," he said. "The officers will do as you have ordered."

"Take the council to a safe place," said Silas. "They are our enemies' primary target, and it will do the people no good to see their leaders fall."

"Yes, sir."

"You can't do this!" protested the loud councilman. "We make the decisions here, Officer Dane."

"When you finally make a decision, perhaps someone will listen to it," said Silas. "Until then, keep quiet and you may stay alive."

The wardens retrieved their weapons and escorted the High Council out of the room, but before the new member could leave, Silas ordered the warden with him to wait. He walked up to the councilman and stood over him, a full head and shoulders taller than the frightened man.

"Nothing would give me greater pleasure than to throw you out that window and claim you jumped to your death through cowardice and fear," he said. "I had no argument with you before I stepped into this room. Speak to me the way you did here again, and I will tear out your fingernails and gut you in front of the men you seem so eager to impress."

The councilman shrank before him. He tried to speak, but fear would not let the words come out.

"A prisoner is about to be interrogated," Silas said to the warden. "I think a representative of the council should be there to witness his confession and listen to any information he may share."

The councilman's eyes widened in shock at the thought of being present at an interrogation, and the warden could not quite hide his smile. "I will escort him to the cells at once," he said.

The man was led roughly out of the room and taken in the opposite direction from the others. The doors fell closed, and Silas and Edgar were left alone.

"I think that went well," said Edgar.

Silas took his sword from Edgar's hands. "They think I am wrong," he said. "They will deny there is any threat until the first arrow flies over the walls."

"Do you think the wardens will follow your orders?"

"Most of these men have known me longer than you have been alive. They will follow my word out of respect. The others would not dare to defy me." Silas walked to the window and looked out over the eastern half of the city. "Fume is not prepared for an attack. Its people have become complacent."

From the window, Silas could see memorial towers rising over the moonlit city like giants striding through the streets. Every one of them was different, but one tower in particular caught his attention. Its stones were edged with silver and looked as though the cracks between them were belching smoke. The meeting hall's window began to rattle. Tiny cracks veined through imperfections in the glass, and the air around the distant tower filled with the shadowy forms of the dead.

Whatever was happening inside that tower, the shades of Fume were retreating from it like wolves from a fire. Their hazy forms drifted above the surrounding streets, until something powerful shifted within the veil. The air filled with sudden pressure, and the smoke blasted outward, sending the surrounding souls fleeing in fear.

"Get away from the window," snapped Silas. "Now!"

Edgar ran for the table and slid under it as the entire pane exploded inward, sending shattered glass spearing across the room. Silas had turned away, but slivers of glass embedded themselves in the side of his neck and bristled down the back of his arm. Shouts carried up from the city, and Silas heard the screams of hundreds of shades, desperate to escape the smoke. To his eyes, the streets blackened as phantom souls washed through them, pouring from the area around the tower and heading toward the edge of the city. There they collided with one another, unable to breach the boundary created by Fume's outer walls, making the stones surge with energy that reverberated through the city as a sickly whisper of terror.

"What was that?" asked Edgar, scrambling out from his hiding place, trying not to cut his palms on the glass.

Silas raised his chin and plucked shards out of his neck, already making his way to the meeting room door. Edgar noticed that his eyes had lost their usual gray and looked instead like ominous puddles of black. He had never seen Silas's eyes do that.

"Is your neck all right? Do you want me to get someone to . . ." Edgar's voice petered out; he was not expecting an answer. He couldn't tell if Silas was angry about being caught by the shattering window or about whatever he had seen happen outside it.

Silas pulled more glass out of his arm and dropped a handful of shards on the floor before rubbing a slick of blood from his neck. The cuts were healing, but his vision blackened until the corridor ahead of him appeared heavy and oppressive. It looked as if the walls were preparing to crumble in upon themselves, ready to crush anyone who passed that way. It was a feeling Silas had experienced before, but it had been years—more than a decade—since he had managed to force it to the back of his mind.

He was seeing that corridor through the eyes of his torn soul, the lost part of his spirit that was trapped within the horrifying depths of the veil. His mind was layering the horror of his soul's prison over what his eyes could see in the physical world. He felt the familiar claws of madness scratching through his thoughts, and it took a huge effort of will to silence the rising anger and terror that spread from a place no human eyes should ever have seen. He felt the creeping touch of lost souls scratching and blistering beneath his skin. The screams that never died. The vast open chill of the black. In that place, madness was the only way out, death was unreachable, and ravaged souls hoped only for oblivion.

Silas knew that place too well. Dalliah's spirit had been torn the same way his had been. If she saw the same horrors when she closed her eyes, he understood her need to bring it to an end: to tear down the veil, reclaim her soul, and hope that death would finally accept her before the black dragged her back down. Silas had endured twelve years of torment. Dalliah had survived centuries. Whatever release she needed, no matter how misguided her methods, he understood her need to escape.

Edgar could tell that something was wrong, but he waited for Silas's eyes to settle back to gray before stepping too close. "The window," he said quietly. "Was that Dalliah?"

"It is not Dalliah you should be worried about," said Silas. "This was too much, even for her. The veil is being torn apart. This is Kate Winters's doing."

← 7 →
WHAT LIES
BENEATH

While Dalliah collected her belongings in the tower, Kate slipped the discovered note safely between the pages of *Wintercraft*. The two of them descended the steps together, and Dalliah noticed immediately that the key was missing from Ravik's bones.

"Unlock the door," she said.

Kate pulled out the hidden key, and they stepped outside. The streets were in uproar. People were wandering around. Some were bloodied and confused, others simply angry at the damage caused to their homes as windows stood cracked or smashed within their frames.

"Our work may have attracted some unwanted attention," said Dalliah. "If I had known you would be so effective, I would not have used so much of your blood."

"That spirit's life did not have to end that way," said Kate.

"Its true life was over long ago."

"What about Ravik's life?"

Dalliah shot Kate a pointed look. "He should not have defied me."

Dalliah secured her bag alongside the Blackwatch package on her saddle, held Kate's horse still while she climbed up, then mounted her own horse and looped both sets of reins around her wrist.

They rode on toward the center of the city until a disturbance blocked the street ahead, forcing them to slow down. A clutch of private carriages was parked in the center of the road; each was covered with bags and boxes stuffed with expensive items that were strapped onto every piece of available space. Dozens of families were attempting to leave the city, only to find their path blocked by other carriages belonging to people who were still packing.

"Back!" shouted one of the carriage drivers, brandishing his whip and making his horse stamp. "Clear the streets!"

Angry people shouted back, many of them insulted at being told what to do.

"Petty, worthless arguments," said Dalliah. "They are too caught up in their small lives to understand what is happening around them."

Kate's horse stayed close to Dalliah's as they moved through the crowds, passing through narrow spaces between buildings where carriages could not reach. When they emerged onto a wide road covered in shattered glass, Kate's horse tugged against Dalliah's grip, and Kate struggled to stay in the saddle as it backed away from a commotion flaring up ahead.

People were staring down an adjoining street, where shouts and fast hoofbeats were echoing loudly from the walls, and a gray horse bolted powerfully out of the shadows, dragging a carriage behind it. The driver was not quite solid enough to pass as one of the living. He was dressed in brown robes, his eyes wild with terror, his mouth open in a scream as he drove the vehicle along its ghostly path. Waves of silver fire poured from the windows on either side of the carriage, but instead of passengers Kate spotted a stack of coffins inside, every one of them crackling with flame.

People fled from the eerie vehicle as it burned down the street, turned a corner in the opposite direction to the curve of the road, and vanished through the front wall of a grand house. For a moment everyone who had witnessed it just stared. Kate had become used to seeing shades, but the coach and driver were clearer than any apparitions she had ever seen.

Once their minds had caught up with the evidence of their own eyes, people burst into action, even more desperate to leave that place behind. Dalliah bullied the two horses along, not caring whom she might trample beneath their hooves as the crowd parted to let her pass, but one man was too busy staring at something behind them to move. When Dalliah's horse knocked into his shoulder, he barely noticed. Kate turned to see what he was looking at and spotted the shade of a black-robed warden standing right in the middle of the road. She knew that face. His teeth were black and twisted, his skin was stained with pale mud.

"I remember you, girlie." The warden's robes were worn and tattered, and a slit over his heart oozed with dark blood. *"I'm not finished with you yet."*

"Kalen?"

Kate's horse worried and fought against its reins as the man walked toward them. He shuffled forward on rag-wrapped feet, leaving footprints of ghostly blood on the ground behind him.

"Ya'll regret what ya did to me. I'll make ya scream before the end, just like yer daddy did."

Kate could hear his rasping breathing, even though he was long dead. Dalliah stopped the horses and turned to see Kalen for herself.

"Ya know what's comin'," said Kalen. *"Ya can feel it."*

"Leave us," Dalliah said, treating Kalen like some kind of stray animal. "Go." Kalen looked up at Dalliah as if he had not noticed she was there and stopped walking at once. "Our history can always find us in the veil," she said to Kate. "Now is not the time for unfinished business."

"Why can we see him?" asked Kate.

"Souls have long memories," said Dalliah. "Hate can feed their anger for a very long time."

"He has no reason to hate me."

"His hate is not drawing him here. Your hate is doing that," said Dalliah. "This is what drives many of the Skilled into madness when the veil is weakened. Ordinary people see random souls, but the Skilled attract those whose deaths they have touched. At least you remember him." Dalliah looked away and snapped the horse's reins. "That is a good sign."

Kate noticed the sharpness in Dalliah's voice. Kate had said too much, and she knew it.

Kalen's spirit voice echoed around the street. *"Ya won't chase me off!"*

Dalliah and Kate rode on, but Kalen kept moving. Kate saw his essence disappear from the living world and thought he was gone, until cold hands gripped her ankle and Kalen's soul tried to sink beneath her skin.

Kate screamed and kicked out. Her boot connected where Kalen's face should have been, and he twisted away, lost in a burst of writhing mist.

"Unwanted souls can be difficult to deal with," said Dalliah, stirring the horses to a faster trot. "It takes a strong will to see them off. I am impressed."

Small clusters of people were crying, staring, holding on to their children, and trying to reassure each other that what they had seen could not possibly have been real. Just a few months ago Kate would have doubted her own eyes as well, but she saw the look of triumph on Dalliah's face as they passed by.

Somehow, this was all part of her plan. She wanted chaos. She wanted the people of Albion to be afraid.

The streets surrounding the lake were in a part of Fume that was ill kempt and run down. The small district was a warren of alehouses and shops. The smell of straw and stale alcohol overwhelmed everything, and the people there had locked themselves in their homes and the alehouses to escape the commotion outside. These were the servants' streets. Litter blew through the gutters, and tattered banners hung down from every gable, each cloth roughly painted with a blue eye. The horses shied as the banners snapped in the wind, and Dalliah told Kate to dismount. It would be easier to lead the beasts from now on.

"I see people have not yet let go of their superstitions," she said. "The dead are not interested in pointless pieces of cloth."

"It's a tradition," said Kate, who had often hung banners in memory of her parents during the Night of Souls.

"It is a way for the living to calm their fears and believe they are still in control. The dead are not listening. Either they have moved on to the next life, or they are tormented by their own doubts, fears, and grief. They do not care how many candles are lit in their memory or how many whispers are shared in their name. The dead are lost. They cannot aid us any more than we can help them. It is foolish to believe otherwise."

The book hidden in Kate's coat felt heavier the farther

they walked. The pages trembled gently, as if an insect were thrumming its wings together beneath the fabric. She pressed her hand against it to make it stop and spotted movement in a window as she and Dalliah passed. She saw a figure in the glass, there and gone again in an instant, but there was something very familiar about it.

"Keep moving," said Dalliah.

They left the horses and walked down a flight of shallow steps squeezed in between two leaning buildings whose rooftops almost touched above their heads. The effects of the veil were much weaker there. Kate could not see anything out of the ordinary, until the steps led down through a low stone arch and opened out onto the edge of one of Fume's most spectacular sights.

The Sunken Lake was a huge expanse of deep, clear water. The dying light gave the appearance of gentle waves shifting upon its surface, and small boats bobbed and scraped against one another around a little dock that was crossed with old chains. The banks were gently curved and lined with gray stone, but the water level was far lower than the land around it, exposing ruined pieces of Fume's history jutting from the mud along the water's edge. The stony arms of broken statues reached out of the earth, and what could have been pieces of railway track glinted in long layers where rain had washed the mud away.

"People are rarely interested in what lies under their feet," said Dalliah. "In my time, the spirit in the next wheel was so powerful that people suffered nightmares from being too close to it. Its anger leached into sleepers' unconscious minds and tormented them. The wheel was lost centuries ago, but my people found it beneath the waters of the lake and raised it. I have not been able to study it myself. Two men died dragging it out of the water, and three more survived only a day after moving it. The spirit inside is damaged but strong. You will need to be careful. Do not touch the stones until I instruct you to do so."

"Where is the wheel now?"

"The first two men collapsed dead on the bank as soon as it touched dry land. The others fell sick almost immediately, but they managed to move it. There." Dalliah pointed to a small square building that seemed to cower in the shadow of the larger buildings nearby. While the others looked occupied, this one had long been left alone. Its small door was stripped bare, and its oval windows were glazed in blue. If Dalliah had not drawn her attention to it, Kate would not have given it a second look.

"Why did they put it there?" she asked.

"That is the records house," said Dalliah, "where the bonemen recorded the names and details of every dead body and every soul that entered this city. There were trees here once. The records house stood alone upon the bank, and it was a beautiful, peaceful place. Now it is surrounded by people and stone." She stood quietly, letting her thoughts carry her briefly into memories of a different time. "The spirit wheel used to be inside, until a new owner decided to remove it and throw it into the lake. That was during the early days of the High Council's occupation. But the wheels are not meant to be moved. Each one was placed in a particular location for a reason. My men retrieved it eighty years ago. The wheel is back where it belongs."

"And now you are going to kill the spirit in it," said Kate, trying hard to keep the bitterness from her voice.

"I sealed it in there," said Dalliah. "It is mine to do with as I wish."

Despite Dalliah's warnings, all Kate felt while walking up to that house was sadness. Movement flickered in windows as she passed, and where there was no glass a shadow that was too large to be her own crossed the empty frames. She could sense eyes watching her as she walked up to the records house, and when she passed in front of one of the blue panes, she saw the presence clearly: a man with silver eyes, too solid to be a shade, too ghostly to be a piece of Fume's history revealing itself to living eyes. The book in her pocket trembled again. She had seen this man before. He was one of her ancestors and one of *Wintercraft*'s first book bearers. Whenever Kate walked a path that he had once taken with the book, she sometimes saw him as a memory locked within the pages. Now he was much clearer than she had seen him before.

The lake behind him in the pale reflection was filled right to the edges, and the trees Dalliah had spoken of were planted in copses around the water. Few of the buildings were visible, leaving gravestones and towers stretching as far as she could see. The man glanced slowly at Dalliah, then stepped back, fading out of sight.

Dalliah did not have a key to the records house. She did not need one. The wood swung back freely, and the space beyond looked exactly as it must have looked to the men who had moved the wheel. There were shelves everywhere. Some held long boxes meant for holding maps and scrolls, while others were filled with small cabinets whose keys had been left rusting in the locks. Two thick tables stood against one wall, on either side of a blocked fireplace, and at the very back of the room a circular space had been cut out of the wall and filled with more shelves, which were stacked with the moldering remains of old ledgers so fragile that just attempting to open one would make it crumble at once.

A few feet from the door, a spirit wheel had been laid unceremoniously on the floor. The stone was at least three feet thick, and the circle was almost exactly as wide—much larger than the wheel in Ravik's tower. This wheel had been retrieved from the lake and then abandoned before it could be returned to its proper place within the wall. Kate stood over it. Nothing moved. Not even a flicker of light stirred in the spaces between the tiles.

"This one has been waiting for us," said Dalliah. "The only people alive who can free it from that stone are here in this room. It will try to tempt you. It will try to trick you. Do not listen to it."

"*Murder.*" The word filled the room, trembled from the walls, and a rush of air ruffled through the pages of the books on the shelves, scattering them into fibers that choked the air.

The wheel remained still, and for the first time Kate saw Dalliah look slightly surprised.

"I am sure the locals have found your theatrics very entertaining over the years," said Dalliah, already unpacking her bag and laying two books open on the larger table. "I, however, will not be taken in by your display. You cannot escape the wheel. You are manipulating our senses to make it appear so, that is all."

"*The dead are listening, Dalliah Grey.*"

"Yes, yes. I'm sure they are."

"*They are waiting for you.*"

Dalliah stopped unpacking and rested her hands upon the tabletop. "They will have to wait a very long time," she said.

"*This girl is not like the others. She has protected herself. You . . . will fail.*"

Those words grabbed Dalliah's attention. "How has she protected herself?" she demanded. "I have eliminated the boy. There is nothing left."

"*She is bound to another. We can see him.*"

"No," said Dalliah. "I will not listen to you."

"*You doubt the truth.*"

"I doubt *you*. Kate is under my control, and you will soon be gone. I will not listen to you."

"*That is a mistake.*"

The door to the records house closed by itself, and Kate heard the snick of a lock.

"*Did you think we would not defend ourselves? Did you think we would not be prepared?*"

Dalliah returned to her books, refusing to acknowledge the presence of the spirit she was about to destroy.

"*The wheels were not yours to take, Dalliah. You ruined us.*"

Dark liquid seeped out of the cracks between the tiles within the wheel and surged out over the symbols, staining each tile with a wash of old lake water. Trickles of it spilled down the side of the wheel and ran toward Kate's boots.

"Ignore it," said Dalliah, without turning around. "It is only trying to get your attention."

The water trailed around Kate, leaving a small patch of dry floor where she was standing.

"*Dalliah spilled our blood. She stole everything from us.*"

"Each individual spirit is a vast repository of energy," said Dalliah, her voice light, talking to Kate as if she were instructing an ordinary student in an ordinary room. "But every one of them is driven by something." She tore a page out of one of her books, lit a match from her bag, and held them both over the wheel. "Greed, love, ambition, empathy. Whatever they think is important, *that* is their weakness. You find it and use it against them, living or dead. After that, they are yours to control."

The spirit fell silent. The water receded a little, and the flame licked gently at the very tip of the torn page.

"This page contains the final prediction of a very particular seer. Someone who is connected to both this spirit and to you, Kate," said Dalliah. "It was written in the woman's blood just before her execution at the hands of the wardens fifty years ago. Her spirit is still here in the city somewhere, bound to this . . . the last of her physical remains. Burning her blood will break her last connection to the physical world and send her soul into the black. The spirit in this wheel will not allow that to happen."

Kate could not see what was written upon the paper, but the effect upon the spirit was immediate. The water dissipated, the room darkened, and the wheel on the floor began to turn. The tiles in the outer ring flipped and grated smoothly around their channeled grooves.

"That's better," said Dalliah, allowing the match to fizzle out. "You wouldn't want anything to happen to this."

"What does it say?" asked Kate.

"Your mother's family have always done things a little differently," said Dalliah. "They knew enough to see beyond their own existence and protect the future long after their own deaths. Your great-grandmother foresaw the falling of the veil when she was ten years old and went on to become one of the greatest seers Fume ever knew. These were her final words. She used her blood to allow her to connect with the living world even after death. This spirit will not risk harming her, even to protect its own existence."

"If this spirit is a member of my mother's family, I can't let you kill it," said Kate.

"Why should that matter?" said Dalliah. "Every soul belongs to somebody's family. Why should yours be spared? And why would you care? I thought you were an intelligent girl, but you were foolish enough to try to hide the truth from me. You have let your mask slip. You know too much for a girl whose memory has truly been lost. You knew the banners in the servants' quarter were a tradition. You recognized the spirit that was drawn to you in the street. You have remembered. Do not think I have not noticed. You may not be my student, Kate, but you will follow my orders. The veil has already shown me what is to come. No seers or spirit tricks of the mind can stop what we must do. This spirit will be cast into the black, where it belongs. It is a relic of the past."

"Just like you," Kate said defiantly. Anger welled up inside her, and it was a relief not to have to pretend anymore. "You are used to getting everything you want. You buy people's loyalty or frighten them into doing things for you. The men who pulled the wheel from that lake never would have risked their lives unless you forced them to. You killed Ravik because he wouldn't follow your orders. You left Silas and Edgar to die on the Continent, and now you think you can force me to do what you want. You're wrong. I don't care who you are. I won't let you do this. I won't help you."

The two women stood on either side of the spirit wheel, but neither noticed the shifting movements of shades pressing in around the walls. They did not see the wheel illuminate two bright symbols—the snowflake and the mask—or notice the pungent smell of deep water as the lake outside slowly began to rise.

"The Winters family has always been stubborn, reckless, and misguided," said Dalliah. "I expected more from you."

"No, you expected less," said Kate. "You wanted someone you could control. That person is not me."

8

BLOODIED BLADE

At the same moment, half a city away, Silas was at the reins of a carriage speeding through the dark streets with Edgar at his side when they felt the ground tremble. Ahead of them, a flock of bats exploded from the roof of a tower before its spire slipped and smashed down into the street below.

Silas forced the horses to the right, slowing down to dodge debris as it rained down upon the buildings and the people hiding within.

"What was that?" shouted Edgar.

"That was Kate resisting Dalliah."

"But the ground . . . it was like . . ."

"Thousands of souls literally turning in their graves," said Silas. "Walkers cannot breathe in this city without attracting attention."

"That felt like a *lot* of attention."

"This has already gone too far," said Silas, steering the

carriage around a tight corner and snapping the reins to gain speed. "Dalliah wants Kate to leave her spirit vulnerable. She is testing her. She wants Kate to lose control."

Edgar hooked the hatch open and leaned out as they sped onward. "Are we going in the right direction?" he asked. "I thought Kate was back that way."

"Dalliah has already moved her," said Silas, pulling the horses to a stop as they encountered a jam of people snailing through the streets. "I sent the crow to watch her. We cannot stop them like this."

"Can't you . . . *sense* where they are?"

"The veil is letting the half-life seep in all around the city," said Silas. "As it falls, it becomes harder to see clearly."

"Shouldn't it make it easier?"

"Do not make assumptions about things you do not understand. The more active the souls within the city become, the more difficult it is to sense individuals within the crowd. We will find them, but we are going to have to do it the old-fashioned way."

Silas turned the carriage down a steep, rattling slope, slowed the horses, and turned them at the very bottom, where the way was blocked by a low iron fence. There he and Edgar abandoned the carriage. They climbed over the fence and followed a narrow path between a mass of tightly packed buildings.

"Where are we?" asked Edgar. "I feel like I've been here before."

"Things have changed since then." Silas walked straight into a narrow house that had a sign nailed to its front wall.

Dangerous Structure
Keep Out

Inside, the first room looked as if someone had ignored the sign long before them. A hammock was slung across the far corner with full sacks spread around it to create a long bunker of belongings. The fire had been lit recently, but whoever was living there was nowhere to be seen.

"Can't these filthy parasites read?" Silas walked straight through to the back of the building, where rubble and broken beams were spread across the floor. He pulled open a hidden panel in the wall, and a wide section of bricks swung out into the room. The creak and heavy rattle of its metal wheels were sounds that Edgar could never forget. He knew now exactly what that place was. He froze on the threshold. His breathing became fast and shallow, and it was an effort just to stand his ground, so strong was his instinct to run.

Silas flicked a switch behind the wall, and a small fuse burned down a sloping corridor, igniting a trail of gas lamps as it went. The smell of the gas focused Edgar's memories. He had only ever seen that place in darkness, but it was somewhere he had never wanted to visit again.

"Follow me," said Silas.

Anxiety made Edgar's muscles twitch and his stomach knot. However, if this was the only way to find Kate, he was not going to run away.

The corridor was simple and straight, and Edgar walked down it like a man on his way to the gallows. He winced when the wall swung closed and concentrated instead upon what lay ahead: Silas, standing beside a plain wooden door.

"I never thought I'd come here again." The sound of his own voice gave Edgar confidence, but he was careful not to look too closely at the door. The last time he had seen it he had been eleven years old. He had walked through that door a boy and emerged as something else, something he tried every day to forget.

Silas pushed the door open and walked inside.

The cellar space was just below ground level: a wide room with grids in the ceiling that were wide enough to let light through, but small enough to make sure no one could get in or out. It smelled old. The floor was made of stones laid to simulate the city streets, and there were metal clasps set at irregular intervals near the center where wooden training dummies could be bolted into place.

It was a practice room, built for teaching and testing older children in the "art" of battle. It might have been completely empty now, but Edgar remembered the heat and the sweat, the brutal instructors, and the students who dared not get to know one another in case they were forced to fight. There had been no harmless training weapons in that room. Every blade was live; every arrow, sharp.

Eight doors leading away from the main room all hung open, with only faint patches of light seeping from those that were lucky enough to have grids of their own looking up to the street above. Edgar remembered the smell of the horses that had walked above those rooms. He remembered rain pouring in, soaking the small bed that had been his for five terrifying months of his life, and the sound of locks thudding into place as the students were sealed in one by one.

"We are looking for a metal lockbox," said Silas, his voice echoing around the empty space. "I will take the rooms on the right; you take those on the left."

The inside of the door they had entered through was stained with the dark silhouette of a sword pointing to the floor. Edgar touched it gently. Only people who had worked in that room knew what the sword represented. He was ashamed to be one of them. He ignored Silas's order and stood there looking at the sword until Silas returned, carrying a metal box.

"Do you still believe you made the right choice?" asked Silas, standing behind him.

"It wasn't a choice," said Edgar. He lowered his hand from the door, remembering the night years ago when he had smeared a streak of his own blood upon it. It had been before he had known Kate. Before everything. "Why is no one here?"

"The High Council moved the operation soon after Da'ru

claimed you. They could not risk an outsider's knowing about it. You know that."

"Then it's still happening somewhere?"

"There is no reason to change a system that works," said Silas.

"Why did we come here? There's nothing left."

"Nothing I would want anyone else to know about." Silas smashed the lockbox against the wall, and the lid cracked open, revealing a bunch of keys, each one made from dull iron. "It pays to keep a few hiding places. That is one of the first things we are taught. I'm sure you remember it."

Edgar had done his best to forget everything about the time he had spent in that room. It was the first part of Fume he had seen after being taken off the Night Train on the day wardens had harvested people from his hometown. He had never spoken of those months to anyone. Not even Kate.

"This has nothing to do with me anymore."

"Our past makes us who we are," said Silas. "You had an opportunity here. Some of our finest wardens were trained in these rooms."

"We weren't *trained*. We were *tested*. Three students died while I was here. They didn't deserve to."

"They were recruits, and they died because they were not good enough," said Silas. "When you claimed a life in the name of Albion and smeared your own blood upon that door, you swore an oath, the same oath that I did in a room just like this. You pledged your life to the protection of Albion and to the safety of this city. You swore loyalty to the wardens and therefore to *me*. Regardless of the turns your life has taken since then, you still owe me that loyalty."

"I don't belong here," said Edgar. "I shouldn't have come in."

Silas pulled the door closed, and Edgar backed away from him. "You are afraid," Silas said. "Not of me. Not of what's out there. You are afraid of yourself and what you became in this room."

"No."

"Do you think I entered warden service willingly?" asked Silas. "Few people choose this life. You were carried away from your home when you were young. I was sold by a father who needed silver to feed the rest of his family, but we are both the same. We were trained into this life. We were molded into something we never would have been had our lives taken a different path. Once it is done, there is no turning back. We survived when others did not. We were better than them."

"I didn't know what was happening!" said Edgar, his face reddening with anger. "You stole us from our homes. You took us from our families and then made us *kill* each other!"

"The recruit who died at the end of your blade died an honorable death. Would you prefer he had killed you instead?"

"It wasn't meant to happen."

"But it did happen," said Silas. "If you forget what you

were taught in this room, it will have all been for nothing." He held out the keys. "You escaped the warden life once, but you cannot hide from that part of yourself forever."

Edgar took the keys and looked at Silas with suspicion. "Why did you bring me down here?"

"Before this is over, you may need to fight," said Silas. "You have been following me around like an injured dog since we left the Continent. I know you are stronger than that. You are not the weakling people see when they look at you. I saw you during your early training. I know what you can do."

Edgar breathed in a deep breath. "It wasn't right," he said, looking around the room.

"Life rarely is." Silas stepped aside, leaving the doorway clear. "You made a choice here once; now I am offering you another. You can renounce the oath you made as a recruit, disappear into the city, and I will never look for you again. Or you can do more than just trail behind me. You can accept your past, remember your training, and reclaim the potential this room sparked within you. I need a fighter, not a servant. This is your last chance to walk away. I will not save your life again."

Edgar looked down at the keys. When Da'ru Marr first came to the training room to collect him, his brother, Tom, had already been sold into her service. Da'ru had known that their parents were Skilled. She had murdered them both during her experiments into the veil, and she intended to keep the brothers close by. If they showed signs of the Skill, she would be the first to know about it.

By council law, recruits could leave active warden training only if the High Council required their services elsewhere, so when Da'ru made her offer, Edgar, forced to choose between two equally unwanted futures, had accepted it. If he had known then that Da'ru had killed his family, he would gladly have shed more blood in that room. He remembered being young and worn down. All he had cared about was protecting his brother. In the end, he had not even been able to do that.

Without the skills he had learned from the wardens, Edgar would never have escaped from Da'ru's service. He would not have been able to help the Skilled or survive days traveling through the Wild Counties before infiltrating Kate's hometown. He would not want to change any of that. It had become easy to forget about his past and pretend that he was afraid, that he was weak. But deep inside, Edgar Rill was very different.

Edgar held out the bunch of keys. His shoulders were set a little straighter, his back was firm, and his chin was high. "I'm not a coward," he said, "and I'm not weak."

Silas clutched the keys and let the door swing shut. "I was not the one needing to be reminded of that," he said. "This city is still ours. As long as a single brick of it stands, we will defend it. Dalliah is moving quickly, and an army is on its way.

The old rules no longer apply here. It is time to make a few of our own."

Edgar had been through only six of the doors in the training room before. Silas headed straight for the seventh. The tiny room inside was completely bare except for a circular stone grate sunk into the floor. Silas crouched on one knee, and a long iron key slid perfectly into a concealed lock at the side of the grate. He swung the heavy lattice of stone open, revealing a narrow staircase spiraling down.

"The Blackwatch are not the only ones who have used agents to infiltrate the City Below," said Silas. "Wardens have walked these tunnels secretly for years. If the people down there want to save their city, they are going to have to fight for it." He disappeared quickly from view down the steps, and Edgar followed, pulling the grate shut behind them.

The tunnels of the City Below were dank and silent. The gentle flicker of a few rare candles illuminated the way, and the deeper the tunnels sloped, the more distant the sounds of the world above became. Silas knew where he was going, hesitating only twice when he came to junctions that were unfamiliar.

Deep within the narrow maze of rock and earth they crossed a wooden walkway that hung over a deep tomb cavern, and the ground beneath them gaped like a wound beneath the city, endless and black. Silas slowed his pace when they reached the other side, closing in upon a dark shape lying across the floor of the tunnel up ahead. Edgar picked a candle from the wall and kept walking until the candlelight was close enough to spread over the shape, revealing a lifeless face staring blankly into the dark.

Edgar stared at the woman, lying on her side with one of her arms outstretched, left where she had fallen. Her eyes were open, their natural color bleached with deathly gray, but there was no mistaking what that color had been.

"Black irises," said Silas. "She was one of the Skilled. The deaths have already begun."

Edgar's throat tightened. "I knew her," he said. "Her name was An'tha. Her family came from the far south. She hadn't been with the Skilled very long."

"So her mind could not cope with the onslaught of the veil," said Silas. "She will have slipped into madness before the end. It would explain why she died here alone." He stepped over the body and continued on his way.

"You're just going to leave her? Can't you do something?"

"She has been dead almost a day," Silas said, without looking back. "Nothing could bring her back from that. Her spirit is gone. Considering the state of the veil, she will no doubt haunt these tunnels until someone sees fit to guide her fully into death."

"Then help her!"

"This woman is dead," said Silas. "There will be many more. You should prepare yourself for what may lie ahead."

"Where are we going?"

"We have two Walkers up there who need to be brought under control," said Silas. "The Skilled are the only people who may have a chance of doing that. Tempting as it would be, we cannot afford to let them die off one by one. We need them to slow Kate and Dalliah's effect upon the veil as long as they can."

"Do you really think they'll be in any state to help?" asked Edgar, following him through the dark.

"They won't have a choice."

9

BETRAYAL

Edgar walked the rest of the way in silence, carefully checking the shadows of every tunnel that crossed their own. There was no sign of anyone else down here, but he was so busy keeping watch and listening for movement in the passageway behind them that he did not notice when they reached tunnels that he should have recognized.

Silas stopped at last in front of a long curtain covering a green door that marked the entrance to the only place in Albion the Skilled called their home. He tested the handle. The lock clicked, and the door swung silently open. "I was expecting more resistance," he said. "Be ready."

The cavern was lined with dwellings built partly into the walls. Their windows, normally bright with candlelight, were dark, and only a few lanterns flickered along the spaces between them, illuminating the cavern with scattered patches of weak light. The door had scraped open through a collection of sticks and daggers, the ground at their feet was stained with blood, and the smell of death clung to the air.

Bodies lay against the fences, upon the paths, and even slumped over windowsills. Some had been killed by weapons; others looked as if they had collapsed where they fell. So many faces. Edgar knew the name of every one.

"Stop there!" A man's voice broke the silence before an arrow flew weakly through the air and skidded to a halt next to Silas's boot. "State your name and your intentions or I will shoot again!" A second arrow followed the first, this time veering wildly off to the left and landing a few feet behind them. "This is your final warning."

"Meeting hall," Edgar whispered, but Silas had already seen the man. Their attacker was standing in the upper window of the meeting hall's bell tower, the cavern's tallest building. A bow was raised awkwardly before him, while his aim quivered almost as much as his voice.

"It's Baltin," said Edgar.

Silas could feel the presence of the dead lingering in the atmosphere of that place. Recent dead, and every one of them had died in fear. That cavern had come under attack, though whether it had started inside or resulted from the actions of an outside aggressor there was no way to know.

"You seem to have had some trouble here," said Silas, moving slowly toward the tower.

"'Trouble' would be a minor inconvenience. This is not

trouble you are looking at. It is horror." Baltin's eyes widened as he realized whom he was speaking to, and his clumsy fingers readied another arrow. "What are you doing here?" he demanded. "Come to finish us off?"

"If I were here for that, it appears someone got here before me," said Silas. "Sloppy work. But effective."

"Murderer!"

The bowstring snapped, the arrow flew, only this time there was real power behind it. The arrowhead ripped toward Silas, who casually stepped aside. Baltin started to ready another arrow, but his fingers were clumsy and slow. He cursed with frustration; then his shoulders slumped, and he dropped the weapon to the cavern floor. "What's the point?"

He disappeared back into the tower. A few moments later the lower door opened, and he stepped out into the open with his hands in the air. "Finish it," he said. "It's better to die at your hand than the way some of my people have gone."

"There are many dead men who would disagree with you," said Silas.

The tiny sound of boots scuffing against the floor carried from inside the meeting hall, and Baltin glanced nervously into Silas's eyes. "Please," he said. "We are no threat to the High Council or to you. Leave my people in peace."

"You weren't so keen on peace the last time I was here," said Edgar. "Last time it was *you* threatening to kill Kate and me. People like you always get what they deserve in the end."

A shadow moved behind Baltin, and a woman stepped out with her nose held proudly high. "Baltin," she said. "We are ready."

Edgar recognized the woman as Greta, the Skilled's magistrate. She was in charge of enforcing order among the Skilled. Edgar knew her as a hard woman who worked to the letter of every law the Skilled lived by. She had bracelets of dried herbs knotted around her wrists, her pale hair was loose around her ears, her feet were bare, and she was wearing what looked like a brown blanket over her ordinary clothes.

"What's going on?" asked Edgar. "What's happening in there?"

Silas held on to his shoulder, preventing him from walking forward. "Subtlety is a skill," he said. "Learn it. Use it now."

Edgar seethed inside. Something was very wrong in that place. If the Skilled had been attacked, why would they have left one of their doors to the tunnels outside unlocked? And why had no one made any effort to move the dead bodies?

Baltin's eyes were darker than usual, and he was breathing awkwardly. "This is the end of us," he said. "We have done everything we can. We should never have let Kate Winters escape. I was weak. I should not have held back. We are paying the price of my failure."

"You are a small man," said Silas. "The world does not wait for you to tell it what to do. Step aside."

"Stop!" protested Greta. "You can't go in there!"

Silas ignored her and pushed his way past.

Inside the meeting hall twenty or so nervous people were dressed much like Greta. Of the group, three were small children, eight were around Edgar's age, and the rest were elderly men and women. Greta and Baltin were the only people of their age who had survived. Silas doubted that was a coincidence.

The stage at the front of the hall was empty. Chairs were stacked around the edges of the main space, clearing the floor, and in the center a large circle had been drawn in blood. The younger children were kept to one side, while the older ones followed the directions of their elders, walking around the perimeter of the space and placing old skulls evenly around the bloodied line with their empty eye sockets staring into the center of the space. Silas did not go in any further, but all work stopped the moment people sensed him in the room.

Those who were holding skulls clutched them to their chests, and the rest looked to Baltin for some sign of what they should do. Baltin was too nervous to offer anything other than a weak hand gesture, warning them to keep their distance from the visitor.

"Is this your worthless attempt at a listening circle?" asked Silas. "Are you trying to heal the veil here or destroy it?"

"Neither," said Baltin. "We are doing what we must to stay alive."

Silas walked toward the circle and heard the whispers of

the newly dead circling it like water gushing along a channel carved through rock. He felt the soft presence of a world beyond the living, the calm silvery place of peace. The Skilled were using that circle to connect with the second level of the veil, beyond the half-life, beyond the normal reach of any living soul. They were forcing open a window into a place seen only by the peaceful dead and Walkers of exceptional ability.

No one in that room was Skilled enough to recognize the truth of what they had done. Most of them would be able to sense a difference in the air within that space, but they would still be blind to the world beyond. They would not see the souls moving across the water or recognize the current of death when it drifted close. None of them could see the damage they had caused.

Silas closed his mind to the veil as far as he could, ignoring the warm ebb of stillness that tempted him to step inside the circle. "You are dealing with energies beyond your understanding," he said. "Circles like this are old work. No one has practiced their creation for centuries."

"This is what we have been reduced to," said Baltin, sneaking in behind him. "The old ways are all that will save us now."

"No. This is an experiment," said Silas. "You have no idea what you are doing."

One of the older boys spoke up. "We are calling for the

help of the ancestors," he said with well-rehearsed confidence. "They will help us."

Silas laughed coldly. "Your ancestors do not care about you," he said. "They are not waiting to step in and undo the mess that you have caused. Many of them have needed your help for generations. It is pitiful that you expect them to listen to you now."

Baltin started to walk past Silas, but Silas drew his sword swiftly and blocked his path with the blade.

"I am not finished with you yet."

Fear spread through the meeting hall, and one of the younger children began to cry.

"You," Silas said, nodding to one of the elderly women, "take the children into the side room. The rest of you, leave everything where it is. Do not move until I order it."

"You have no authority here," said Greta, blatantly ignoring Silas's warning and stepping into the circle of blood. "Leave us to do our work."

The circle thrilled with energy when Greta stepped into it, but only Silas's eyes saw the ripple of light glow around its inner edges like flickers of lightning. The souls of the dead that were lingering in that place fled from the hall at once, but one of the shades was too slow. The circle drew the faded form toward it, and the blood line crackled as their essences connected. The shade's energy sank into the stones of the meeting hall floor, and Greta's cheeks flushed with health.

To anyone else in that room it would seem that very little had changed. Greta's mind would feel clearer, more focused, but she would not understand why. That floor may have looked like a makeshift listening circle, but the Skilled were not using it for communication. They were using it to draw energy from the veil, saving themselves while inadvertently sealing the spirits of the dead in the stones beneath their feet.

"This is how you are staying alive?" said Silas. "You are feeding from the veil, focusing your connection, using the blood of the dead."

"They have no use for it anymore," said Baltin. "It is too late for them. We are doing all we can to continue to exist."

"At the cost of the souls you are meant to protect!" said Silas. "This circle is a taint upon the veil, and that blood carries the mark of the Skilled. How many of your own people did you murder to create it?"

Baltin's face darkened. "Enough," he said.

"You killed your own *people*?" said Edgar.

"Not all of them," said Baltin. "The madness came too quickly. There were too many voices. Too many memories. We were not prepared for what our minds could see. When the first of us died, some took it badly. They did not want to die the same way, in confusion and pain. We sealed the doors, trying to keep everyone where we could see them so we could try to control what was happening to us, but a few escaped. We tried to maintain order, but the visions of the dead became too strong. It was hard to know what was real and what was touched by the veil. People began to arm themselves, and there were . . . accidents. Soon we lost control of the doors. Ordinary people touched by the sickness came to our cavern for help, looking for ways to close their minds to the veil. What they saw here was death. We could not let them leave! Some of them . . . fought back. The cavern filled with the cries of the insane and the dying, and I knew we were facing the end. The few of us who still had our minds sealed ourselves away and waited. For those who had gone too far into madness . . . it was a kindness, what we did to them."

"You murdered the weak to save the strong. How honorable." Disgust laced Silas's words, but Baltin was unrepentant.

"Do not lecture me on morality," he said. "You have done far worse."

"I did not torture the souls of those I killed," said Silas. "I did not murder those who trusted me, harvest their blood, and justify it in the name of sacrifice."

"Then you have not seen the things I have seen," said Baltin. "You have not had to make that choice."

"I am not interested in excuses. Are these the only people you decided to save?"

"I was in an impossible situation! I protected as many as

I could. Others . . . left us. There's no way to know how many of them are still alive."

"What about my brother?" asked Edgar. "Where is he?"

"Tom? He left with Artemis Winters before any of this began," said Baltin. "No one has heard from either of them since you and Kate went missing. The newly Skilled were not affected as severely as the rest of us. If he is lucky, his descent will be slow. He may not see any effects until the veil has completely collapsed. After that, no one will care anymore."

"*I* care," said Edgar. "I never should have left him here."

Silas crouched beside the edge of the circle and touched the streak of dried blood. Memories of six clear deaths played behind his eyes: four falling to blades held in Baltin's hand, two to Greta.

"You should have saved more of your people," he said, standing up. "This group alone will not be enough to stop them."

"Stop who?" asked Greta.

"Kate Winters and Dalliah Grey. They are together, in Fume," said Silas. "They will make sure the veil falls unless you stop playing with death and blood and do what the Skilled were born to do."

"We don't know how," said Baltin. "We have spent generations restraining our minds. We were not ready for any of this. We learned how to create this circle from scrolls discovered hidden within the bonemen's graves. Most were rotten and incomplete, but they gave us enough to keep going. They gave us hope, if only for a short time. We believed we could help ourselves."

"If Dalliah Grey is here, there is no hope of that," said Greta. "We are not strong enough to stand against one Walker, let alone two."

"You were willing enough to take lives," said Silas. "Now is the time to risk your own. Otherwise what did those people die for? So you could hide here for the rest of your miserable days?"

"We do not answer to you," said Greta.

"You do now," said Silas. "You will listen to me, or you will prove to me beyond all doubt the worthlessness of your kind."

"We are far from worthless!" said Baltin. "Ask the boy. He knows what our ancestors have done for Albion." He tried to grab hold of Edgar's arm, but Edgar saw him coming and moved away. "Tell him! Tell him about the sacrifices that we have made."

"You live on the achievements of your predecessors, while ignoring your responsibilities to honor their memory," said Silas. "You squirm here, down in the dark. Do you want to see where you are leading this land? Do you want to witness the darkness, the dread, and the pain that await every soul in this place?"

Baltin glanced at his followers, trying to remain composed.

"I know what lies beyond the veil," he said. "I have seen it for myself."

"You have seen only what you wanted to see."

Silas moved before Baltin had time to react. Edgar tried to step between the two men, but Silas was too quick. The energy in the room was already highly charged, and Silas had decided that there was no more time for talk. He pushed Baltin so hard that the older man fell back and scrabbled across the floor, landing just inside the blood circle, and Silas was right behind him.

"No," said Baltin, desperately trying to find his feet. "Please!"

Silas felt the sickly tug of the physical world fall away as he crossed the blood line and stood over Baltin, who raised his arms uselessly to protect himself. Traces of Kate's blood surged through Silas's veins, reacting to the broken presence of the veil. The circle was not perfect. It was a crude guess at something the bonemen might once have created every day, but it was enough to tear through the already delicate barrier between two worlds. The blood of a Walker made Silas's own connection to the veil more powerful, and the moment he looked into it he saw a flicker of an image as if he were seeing directly through Kate's eyes. He could see where she was at that moment. Water pooling around her feet and Dalliah Grey shouting, her words lost within the veil.

"I never wanted any of this!" said Baltin, flailing his arms.

"I wanted to help. I was only doing what I thought was best."

"Be silent," said Silas. "And listen."

Baltin let his hands fall to the floor and felt it tremble gently. "Wh-what's happening?"

Every person in the meeting hall pressed against the nearest wall as the circle spluttered with new life. If that circle had been a flickering flame of energy before Silas's arrival, now it was white hot. None of them wanted to go near it, except for one.

Edgar walked right up to the edge, watching Baltin's expression as it changed from panic to sheer terror and then sank into the abject desperation of someone who was looking straight into the veil's terrifying heart.

"This is unacceptable," said Greta. "Stop this." She tried to cross into the circle, but Edgar stopped her.

"You can't go in there," he said. "Silas knows what he's doing. Baltin has to understand. We are not your enemy."

"Is *that* the face of a friend?"

Edgar looked behind him, where Silas had begun pacing around the inner edge of the circle. Baltin was curled on his side, trying to block whatever Silas was showing him from his senses, and Silas's eyes shimmered white, looking like the eyes of a predator captured in the glare of moonlight.

"I know it looks bad, but he knows what he's doing."

"He is polluting the circle with his presence," said Greta. "He will attract too many souls. He will ruin everything!"

Edgar looked at her. "I thought you were worried about Baltin," he said, "not your precious circle."

"Baltin is one man," said Greta. "He is more than expendable."

"It's a good job we don't all think like you."

"Move aside!" she demanded, but Edgar held her back.

Silas took no pleasure in exposing an unwilling mind to the black, but Baltin had been quick to end other people's lives in the name of his cause. Risking his own sanity was a small price to pay in return.

Baltin writhed. His fingers clutched at empty air. "We killed them," he whispered. "We had to do it. *I* had to do it. I—" His body tensed and fell limp. Silas continued to pace.

Time passed strangely within the circle. What felt like a minute held within its influence was almost an hour in the meeting hall. When Baltin fell still, Edgar was left to calm the Skilled and reassure them about something he knew little about. Greta was determined to break the circle and disturb the process, but some of the older members of the group, worried that she would cause more harm than good, helped Edgar to keep her away from the blood line.

Only Silas would ever know what Baltin had witnessed inside that circle. Only he would remember the sight of Skilled souls trapped beneath the meeting hall. He would see them, frightened and lost, reaching out to Baltin for help the man was unable to give. When Baltin's soul threatened to break away from his body, Silas helped him find his way back to the living world, where he lay horrified by the torment that his actions had caused.

Silas reached an arm out and helped him to stand. Greta looked flustered as he stumbled from the circle, breathless, dazed and determined.

"Greta," he said, "it is worse than we thought. This effort of ours is not enough to stop what is coming. I saw the prison that lies in the dark. I walked within it. I think . . . I was dead. Was I dead?" He turned to Silas, who said nothing. "Those people we killed, Greta. They are suffering now. These hands . . ." He raised his palms in front of his face. "They are stained with more than blood. What we have done should never be forgiven. We have to put this right. I thought I knew the veil, but I knew nothing. Nothing at all."

Greta looked at him with disdain. "You are allowing yourself to be misled," she said. "Our first duty is always to protect those who are still alive. The children need us, and those who are missing may yet return. We cannot afford to risk our lives on the word of someone whose very existence in this world is an abomination against everything we know and trust about the veil. He is a bound soul, Baltin. He is less than a shade, and we cannot trust him. We cannot even be sure his mind is his own."

"I trust what I have seen," said Baltin. "Gather the ones who are strong enough to travel. We are not finished yet."

He hurried over to those of the Skilled who were still clutching old skulls and took them from them to lay each skull carefully on the floor. While he tried to rally the others, Silas scrubbed his boot through the blood circle, severing its link to the veil.

"Stop that!" cried Greta. "These circles cannot be made in the same place twice."

"Then perhaps you will listen," said Silas. "The veil is under threat, and much as I would like to leave you and your people to rot here underground, you are its guardians."

"That does not give you the right to invade this cavern and spread your soulless lies among my people."

"Yes, it does!" said Edgar, stepping forward. "We are here to help you. We could have stayed away."

"My role here is to enforce order and to protect the group," said Greta. "I have done that to the best of my ability. As a former soldier, your master should respect that."

"He's not my master," said Edgar.

"I knew the Winters girl was too dangerous to be set free," said Greta. "I did not approve of Baltin's treatment of her in the end, but we were right to contain her. If it were not for the boy"—she stabbed an accusing finger toward Edgar—"we would not be in this situation. He interfered where he did not belong."

"Nothing could have prevented this," said Silas. "Everything that has happened was seen within the veil long before Kate was even born. Dalliah deliberately created the chain of events that brought us here. She has manipulated all of us, and now she intends to finish her work."

Greta looked grim. "Do you believe she has gained some degree of *control* over the girl?"

"They entered the city together, but it is impossible to say how much of Kate's will has been lost."

"Then you are right," said Greta. "This is bigger than any history we may have shared. Baltin is good at reacting to events. Whatever you showed him in there certainly provoked a reaction, but he is like an excitable dog. When he runs out of energy, he will lose focus. I, however, will not. I assume you and I are contemplating the same solution to this mess?"

"Yes," Silas said, without hesitation. "This has already gone too far."

"Then, at last, we agree," said Greta. "For Albion to survive, the Winters girl cannot be allowed to live."

↤ 10 ↦
RELEASE

Lake water seeped slowly into the records house, spreading across the floor and into the corners, where stacks of old papers became swamped. Loose pages floated just beneath the surface as the freezing water swallowed entire books, devouring their ink and rendering them worthless.

Kate had not taken her eyes off Dalliah since she had challenged her, but instead of looking angry or concerned, Dalliah did not seem to care. Knowledge was Dalliah's greatest advantage. She was not surprised by the swelling of the lake. She knew exactly why everything was happening. She had planned for every eventuality, whereas Kate could only react to events as they happened around her.

"Your anger will only make it worse," said Dalliah, turning back to her books. "The spirits are listening to us."

"I don't care," said Kate. "This city isn't yours. You can't come here and destroy it."

"I have done nothing," said Dalliah. "*You* sent the souls in the tower into the black. Events *you* have put into action are forcing the city to react. Destroying Fume has never been my intention. I doubt it could even be done. Its stones will stand here long after every living soul has fled its walls."

The water crept up past Kate's ankles, beyond her knees, and settled around her hips, where it stopped rising and became still. The surface was mirrorlike with not a splash or a ripple to break its calm. Only a thin film covered the top of the stone wheel, trickling through the spaces between the outer tiles.

"This lake was here before any of the buildings around its edge," said Dalliah. "At its height it once covered the entire district. The water is reclaiming what should never have been taken away."

Kate waded toward the table closer to one of the windows. The cold water stabbed at her legs, and she lifted herself up, checking to make sure *Wintercraft* was still intact. It seemed untouched, so she placed it on the tabletop, out of reach of the water, while Dalliah remained next to the wheel, her dress and coat swirling in the flood. Kate's warm breath came as vapor as she spotted shapes moving beneath the surface of the water. There were shadows where shadows should not have been: fast-moving drifts of black and gray, seeping through the walls and gathering around the spirit wheel.

"Working the veil to this level takes years of concentration and study," said Dalliah, continuing to keep the spirit in the wheel under her control. "But all of that is useless without the ability to use it: the spark to trigger the first switch. Once the first step is taken, everything that follows becomes easier." She looked up at Kate. "I couldn't have done any of this without you."

"You have spent your life destroying people," said Kate. "I saw the graves around your house on the Continent. There were thousands of bodies there. All those souls, unable to enter death because of what you did to them. The Skilled are supposed to help people."

"Walkers have more important things to do," said Dalliah. "When I was away from Albion, it became difficult to connect strongly with the veil. It would not speak to me unless I called it with the souls of the dying. Now we are here in the city, I have everything I need." Dalliah pulled a twist of cloth from her bag and unfolded it to reveal a thin glass vial filled with red liquid. "I did not expect you to obey me forever," she said. "I do not need you for this. Your blood is more than enough."

"No!" Kate jumped back into the water and waded toward Dalliah as the woman unstoppered the vial. The cold snatched her breath away, but she stripped off her heavy outer robe and moved quickly across the room. "Don't!"

The center stone, loosened by the water, lifted easily beneath Dalliah's searching fingers, sending water swirling into the space beneath. Dalliah pushed the disk over the edge, and it flipped as it fell, revealing one side carved with a spiral, the other carved with a goblet. The goblet side was faceup as it sank to the floor, and the symbol flared with light before sinking out of sight. Kate struggled to reach Dalliah in time, but it was too late. The vial dropped into the wheel's open void and smashed, spilling smears of blood over the mechanism inside.

"This is not the existence I chose for myself," said Dalliah. "Once my blood would have been more than enough for this work. That strength was stolen from me, along with so much else, by your family. You should condemn them for leaving you the burden of what you must do, but I can condemn them for far more. You were born to be betrayed by your family's legacy. I was not."

Kate stood over the wheel, watching the bloodstains darken as the black crept in. She reached down, trying to fish out the shards, but the glass bit her fingers, threatening to add more blood to the mix. Shadows formed against the walls, and the water moved as if it were filled with live fish. The surface bulged and churned, and shades burst from the building as though something had physically dragged them out. Kate pressed her hands upon the outer tiles in desperation, determined to do something to stop what her blood had put into motion.

"The Winters family and your mother's family have hated each other for generations," said Dalliah. "The Winters family drove the Pinnetts' seers into madness more times than I can remember. You may hate me for what I have done, but your ancestors did far worse in search of knowledge. They would be surprised to see you trying to save the soul of a Pinnett now."

"Shut up!" Kate glared at Dalliah. She wanted to look at *Wintercraft*, but she could not remember anything inside that could be of help, and she did not have much time. She turned instead to logic.

Everything connected to the veil had a method behind it. If her blood had done something to the spirit wheel, that meant she was at least partially in control of it. She had seen something similar before, when she had been forced to open a listening circle against her will. She had been able to bring that circle under control, but this was different.

Kate did the only thing she could think of. She placed one hand on the snowflake tile, the other on the small goblet tile that matched the central stone Dalliah had removed. At that moment she did not care about history, family, or anything else. She would not allow another spirit to be stripped away.

Dalliah did not try to stop her. In her mind, she had begun something that was unstoppable, but it interested her to watch Kate try.

The mechanism inside the wheel grated into action, sending disturbed air surging up in strings of tiny bubbles to the surface. The tiles flipped, sank back, and switched places, all except for the two that Kate was touching. The snowflake and the goblet drew energy from the other tiles until all movement stopped and the only brightness came from the light bleeding up through Kate's hands, making her fingertips glow red.

There was no pattern to the final positions and no order that Kate could see. She felt the room darken, just as the tower had before, but she refused to simply accept the blackness. She concentrated upon the aspect of the veil that she knew best, the half-life, the upper level where souls still had hope of being delivered into the peace of true death. She shivered as the water stilled around her and crackles of ice began webbing across the surface, creating frosty trails that radiated out from her body.

She could no longer feel the spirit wheel beneath her palms. All she could sense was gentle heat, as if she were standing close to a fire. The tiles no longer felt solid. Something moved beneath them, and she felt warm fingertips touching her own. The spirit in the wheel was reaching out.

Kate did not dare open her eyes for fear of losing the connection, but behind her eyelids the physical world peeled away, and she sensed the shade's soft gray form as clearly as a lucid dream. It was a haunting, gentle shift in the darkness that was easy to miss until she stopped focusing upon it and let it linger at the very edges of her consciousness. It did not want to be seen. It moved like a fly in a jar, knowing the boundaries of its prison by memory. Only its eyes appeared human: the dark, penetrating eyes of one of the Skilled. Ancient, but still very strong.

Kate moved her fingers slightly. The stone was still there, but it was like placing her hands against a mirror to touch her reflection. Her world and the spirit's world were separate, but they were connecting. Kate's blood was breaking the hold the wheel had upon the soul, letting it fall into darkness. It should have already happened, but the soul, drawn to Kate's presence, was lingering.

"Distant child. We are proud of you." The spirit's voice echoed up as though from deep inside a well, and Dalliah began to take serious notice of what was happening. She put one of her own hands on the wheel, but the tiles sank away instantly at her touch.

"What are you doing?" she demanded. "Stop this. Now!"

Kate did not move. The tiles rattled once again and flipped to reveal their undersides, where letters were carved instead of pictures. They settled into a ragged order, and the lights beneath Kate's hands wandered around the circle, pausing upon letters to spell out five words.

DO NOT TRUST THE WARDEN

The light faded the moment the final letter was revealed. Dalliah looked unimpressed.

"Not the final words I would have chosen," she said.

The spirit's faded hands clutched tightly around Kate's, and the wheel burst with sudden energy. Instead of blackness, soft light reflected from the thin ice across the water. The stones singed Dalliah's hand, forcing her to back away, while Kate's fingers felt as if they had been plunged into the frozen sea.

The spirit was rising out of the wheel like a delicate swimmer standing over a mist-covered pond. Kate was drawing it up. Out of its prison, out of the stone, and into the air of the city.

Kate wanted to let go. She *needed* to let go, but her conscience would not let her. The connection binding the spirit to the wheel was splintering further the longer she held on. She would not let it fall into the dark.

The skin on her palms blistered against the energy of the deep veil. Physical life did not belong in that place. She was connecting with it for far too long, but she would not sever the link. She was intent upon drawing the spirit away from the black, carrying it to a place of peace and hope, a place where— she hoped—death would eventually come.

The spirit separated from the wheel with the lightest of sounds. A whisper, partway between sadness and relief. Only then did Kate allow herself to let it go. The spirit's essence unwrapped from her fingers, and Dalliah watched powerlessly as the soul dissipated into the veil. It was not free—not yet— but it was in a far better place than that to which Dalliah had intended to deliver it.

The wheel fell still. Kate stumbled back from the stones, her head swamped with dizziness, her hands red and sore. Her body was exhausted by the effort, her muscles would not hold her, and she sank beneath the water, letting the flooded lake carry her under. She did not have the energy to fight it. She wanted to sleep, to escape the tiredness, the cold, and the pain. It would be easy to let go, let the veil take her and turn away from the madness her world had become. Dalliah stood beside her in the water, looking down, as if she were viewing an experiment that needed to run its course.

Kate heard the echoes of the dead reverberating from the walls of the records house. Their voices were thin and weak, like a conversation captured upon the wind. The water's touch seared her injured hands, and she felt a warm presence close by. The spirit from the wheel had not left her behind. It reached out to touch her hands and heal the damage its rescue had caused, but Dalliah got there first. Solid fingers grabbed Kate's arm and dragged her back to the surface. Kate coughed the moment her face reached the air, and the spirit retreated, leaving her hunched over the sunken wheel, clutching the stones.

"Do you *want* to lose your mind?" demanded Dalliah. "Taking risks has gained you nothing, except this." She grabbed Kate's wrists to inspect her blistered hands. The flesh was raw, and every movement felt like knives slicing across the open wounds. "The touch of the black is beyond my skill to heal," she said. "Even if I could do it, I would still leave you with the pain as a lesson against stupidity." She let Kate's hands fall, and Kate pulled them protectively to her chest.

"I don't care where your soul is or what you need to do to get it back," she said. "All of this . . . it's not worth it."

"You are in no state to say what you will or will not do," said Dalliah. "You should have stayed ignorant."

She pressed her hand against Kate's shoulder, making Kate's hands blaze with pain. Any slight healing that had occurred in those few minutes was picked apart by Dalliah's influence. Blood seeped from the sores, and Kate cried out in pain. Anger flooded her thoughts, and the air trembled. The water felt as thick as oil, and when Dalliah raised her arm, tendrils of it hung from her sleeves like melting grease.

"Be careful, Kate." Dalliah's voice was suddenly serious and wary. "This is not the place for you to lose control. Not here. Not yet."

Kate was far from losing control. She could see more clearly than she had in her life. She was turning the connection Dalliah had forged between them back upon Dalliah herself. The water was as it had always been; only their perception of time had shifted, forcing the world around them to slow down. There, in that pocket of mutual existence, Kate could see into Dalliah's memories and share her most secret past. Dalliah tried to resist her, but it was too late.

"I'm not scared of you," said Kate. "You left Albion because you were afraid. You hid yourself away because people were hunting you."

"Stop this."

"You hated what you had become, but you had no real power. The bonemen feared you, the Walkers lost respect for you, and you could not manipulate the veil as well with a broken soul. You hated the people who had stolen part of you away. A

Winters made you what you are. He was supposed to bring your spirit back, but he never discovered how to do it."

"He did not try!" Dalliah said bitterly. "He was arrogant. He collected the knowledge he wanted and moved on to the next 'challenge' without a thought for what he had left behind."

"You trusted him."

"We were rivals. He stole everything that was mine," said Dalliah. "His family became the strongest bloodline while mine was slaughtered one by one. We all knew that Skill grew more potent with each generation. Families were our strength, every generation surpassing the abilities of the last. The book of Wintercraft was meant for all of us. The Winters family claimed ownership of its secrets and conspired to destroy all Walker bloodlines except their own so they would maintain control. They murdered Walkers in their beds. They stole children from their parents and abandoned them in distant towns. It was those named Winters who tempted the bonemen into destabilizing the veil four centuries ago. They are the reason I sealed these souls into the wheels. If they had not already taken my spirit, they would have sealed it in there just as swiftly to cover up their mistake. Do not tell me how I should live. The Skilled may be remembered throughout history as healers and kind fools, but there are darker undercurrents to our society that you have barely begun to recognize."

Dalliah's face was hard with anger. She reached for the table, grabbed *Wintercraft*, and held it over the time-slowed water. "This is what your family treasured most," she said. "Beyond friendship, beyond duty, and beyond any sense of morality. They studied the veil because they wanted their line to flourish, while others were expected to wither and die. They sacrificed too much for the words in this book. They did it for you and for every other sorry soul that carried their tainted blood. Look where it has led you! Those who fight the will of their ancestors become tormented by the ghosts they left behind. You have seen them. They watch from the windows and wait in the shadows, but they will never help you. All they want is for you to live like them. Those who walk the path of a Winters always carry destruction in their wake. You all deserve to die in fear. Every . . . last . . . one."

Dalliah dropped the book into the center of the wheel, and its purple cover hit the water with a sharp slap. For one brief moment Kate thought it might float, but instead the thick water clawed over its edges and began seeping into the paper. Guilt crept across her chest. She had not saved it. She had not *tried* to save it. She was just standing there, watching it. She waited for the pages to ruffle open and bleed ink, but it stayed firmly shut. No air furled from it, and it dropped like a stone, taking Ravik's note with it, settling against the exposed mechanism inside the dead wheel.

"The book is no use to your family now," said Dalliah. "Soon you shall die along with it."

11

FELDEEP

Nothing Edgar said could convince anyone that killing Kate was not the answer to Fume's problems. He argued with Greta and Baltin. He even tried to be reasonable, but in the end he was informed that the decision had been made and he was in no position to challenge it. He remembered shouting about the Skilled—telling them they had developed a taste for murder. Finally he was so appalled by the shift in their approach to life that he could not share the same room with them any longer.

He left Silas and the Skilled in the meeting hall and headed back into the open cavern. He tried not to look at the bodies, abandoned where they had fallen. He did not want to risk finding his brother among them. He needed to believe that Tom really was still out there somewhere with Artemis, protected and safe.

He walked past a row of houses and spotted a fallen dagger on the ground, still tucked into its sheath. Its unfortunate

owner must not have had time to use it before the others turned upon him. Memories of his time in the training room returned at once. He picked the dagger up, unsheathed it, and spun the handle deftly in his hand. His lower back tingled at the point where a faint scar marked his own recent near death at the point of a Blackwatch blade. Silas had saved him then. He did not understand why Silas would not give Kate that same chance.

Edgar threw the dagger at a closed door, and the blade stuck proudly into the wood. No one would listen to him because he was not one of them. They thought he could not understand the importance of protecting the veil just because he could not see it for himself. But he understood enough. He was not the one being blinded by fear. He could see more clearly than any of them.

If anyone deserved death, it was the Skilled. They had raised weapons against people who should have been as close as family to them. In the past Edgar had thought of the cavern as a haven; now it would always be a place of blood and death.

He walked past the empty lockhouse and sat down in a garden where rotting logs had been laid in rows, each one of them covered in wide mushrooms. He picked a handful and ate them raw, throwing their rubbery stalks against the nearest house. Water seeped in droplets through the cavern's brick-lined ceiling, dampening the garden. Edgar shook a trickle of liquid from his hair and looked up.

Living underground meant that people quickly became used to water leaching down from above. That water served as a lifeline to the people of the City Below. Their underground rivers and ground-filtered streams allowed them to live. The mushroom garden would have been placed there to make use of the water leaking from the roof, but what Edgar saw was more than a trickle, much more than a simple leak.

Trails of water were clinging to the curved ceiling, following it down into holding troughs placed around the walls. Edgar watched rivulets of water vein across the bricks until heavy droplets gathered at the source and dripped straight down onto the garden. The trickle of water became a spluttering pulse, and then gravity took over, sending water streaming down at a rate that was definitely not normal.

Edgar stood up. Water was seeping out of the bricks all over the cavern. Droplets became spurts, and the flow above Edgar became a stream that forced speckles of old brick down onto the log where he had just been sitting. A sudden glugging sound made him turn to the fountain that stood in the very center of the cavern. Water was bulging out of its wide stone basin. Waterfalls poured from its sides, and the ground around it glistened as it overflowed.

Edgar ran back to the meeting hall and interrupted an argument between Greta and Baltin. "The fountain. It's flooding!" he said. "Water's coming through the ceiling."

Silas was already on his feet, pushing past Edgar to see what was happening.

"That is impossible," said Greta.

A thin slick of water washed in around Edgar's boots, and Greta's expression changed from disbelief into fear.

"We have to leave," she said. "Gather up everything you can. Count the children, bring the books."

Silas returned. "The water is rising quickly. You," he said, pointing to Baltin, "take the first group to the city square. And you"—Greta this time—"take the rest to the museum, and prepare the circle there. Enemy soldiers may already be nearby. If they breach the walls, the square should be safe for a short time. If they reach the museum, do what you can to keep the circle going."

"Where is the water coming from?" asked Baltin, as people burst into action around him.

"The dams sealing the rivers from the Sunken Lake could have been damaged," said Greta. "Too much water is being released too quickly. This cavern was built on one of the old waterlines. If it floods, this entire level could be reclaimed by the old river."

A few of the older Skilled were looking up at the meeting hall ceiling, whispering their good-byes to paintings pinned there of people who had died before them.

"We do not have time for superstition," said Silas. "Move."

The water in the cavern was already ankle deep. The Skilled waded through it, carrying crying children in their arms, heading for the green door. Silas and Edgar stayed to make sure no one was left behind.

"Do you think they can make a difference?" asked Edgar.

"The children are useless," said Silas. "Greta and Baltin rely more upon what they think they know than what they can actually do. The elder women and the freshly discovered Skilled are the city's best chance to slow Dalliah's work, but that chance is still small."

"What good will opening the circles do?"

"Possibly none whatsoever, but it is better than leaving them down here to drown or kill each other. If more of them had lived, we would have had a greater chance. We have done all we can do here."

Water fell from the ceiling like rain. The fountain was so full it looked as though a large bubble were sitting on its surface, but even that would be swamped if the level rose much higher. The flood was showing no sign of receding as water spread down through the cavern's tiny cracks from saturated channels that ran between ancient layers of rock and earth.

Silas moved through the knee-high water as smoothly as a rat. The cavern's rear door was open, and he could hear shouts from nearby tunnels as the water spilled down into the deeper levels.

"What do we do now?" asked Edgar, shouting above the

noise of his own legs splashing through the wet. "Shouldn't we get out of here?"

"The water will follow its natural channels," said Silas. "You are in no danger."

They reached the exit, and Silas chose the nearest turning heading down. From there they followed a thread of tunnels until they heard someone giving orders to people up ahead. Silas led Edgar away from the voice and squeezed into a narrow passageway hidden in the wall. Edgar could hear him scraping sideways between two walls of solid earth, and he stopped at the opening, unable to see any light at the other side. He hesitated, his heart quickening; then he forced himself in.

The narrow space made it impossible to breathe freely. The wall was so close to his nose that motes of earth tickled his nostrils with every breath. All he could do was concentrate on his feet as his squelching boots picked out a curve of long, shallow steps. He counted them silently as he went—sixty-seven . . . sixty-eight—until the wall fell away and he squeezed his way out into the relative freedom of a pitch-dark tunnel.

He took in some deep breaths and listened for Silas nearby. With no sound to give him away, and not daring to speak in case Silas was being quiet for a good reason, Edgar ran his hands along the tunnel wall and headed in the direction that made his instincts tremble with primal fear, a sure sign that

Silas was nearby. He found Silas twenty paces away, his eyes shining in the dark.

"Good," said Silas. "You are learning."

"Tell me we didn't walk through that for nothing," said Edgar.

Silas struck a match and held it out before letting it fall. The tiny flame fell to the ground and kept going, passing through a tightly latticed grate and casting its glow over a ladder hanging down the side of a steep shaft. Edgar took the matches and lit another, crouching down to look closer. Below the grate, a band of tarnished metal circled the inner edge of the shaft with words etched into it.

BY ORDER OF THE WATCH, ANY OFFICER ENTERING THIS

PLACE DOES SO AT HIS OWN RISK.

"Where does it go?" he asked.

"Into a place most people on the surface would like to forget," said Silas, pulling the keys he had taken from the training rooms out of his coat. "No one can be ordered down here. If you choose to come with me, stay alert and avoid eye contact with people unless absolutely necessary. They have more right than anyone to wish both of us dead."

Silas unlocked the grate, and it swung open in perfectly oiled silence. He descended the ladder, and when Edgar finally joined him at the bottom, the glowing embers of a slow-burning torch flickered up ahead. Directly above it, letters had been scorched into the stone, creating black words at least three feet high.

FELDEEP PRISON

Dozens of small crates were stacked neatly beneath the sign, leading toward the looming shape of a large arched door. Edgar had seen one like it before, only that one had been chained and marked with a warning: NO ENTRY. NO ESCAPE. Silas dug a long key into the lock. "Be ready."

Heavy locks clicked and creaked within the door, and the ratcheting sound of a chain and pulley mechanism clunked into action, pulling the door inward to reveal a fiery light. The smell of burning caught in Edgar's throat, and he could hear people shouting to one another farther in. The corridor they had entered was perfectly straight, and Edgar's boot sent a loud metal twang reverberating from the walls as his foot connected with one of two rusted rails running along the ground.

"Coffin rails," said Silas. "They were here long before the prison. Nothing runs on them anymore."

Edgar already knew more about Feldeep Prison than he would have liked. During his time working for the councilwoman he had been present at trials when prisoners were sent there and had overheard conversations between wardens about the kind of life people lived locked away underground.

The prisoners kept down there were not murderers, smugglers, or thieves. The High Council dealt with people like that in a far more direct way, often involving a rope or a sword. Feldeep was reserved for a different type of threat. Its cells were populated with people who the High Council believed could be of use to them someday: collectors who had disobeyed orders or whisperers who had stumbled upon secrets not meant for public ears. If Councilman Gorrett had protested his innocence, he might have been sent there after a short trial, but following his open confession Edgar knew that all he had to look forward to was a bloody death.

Feldeep was a holding place for people who found themselves in the wrong place at the wrong time. Edgar could not imagine what spending years down there might do to a person, but Silas certainly could. The two of them followed the passageways with the steady walk of condemned men, neither of them admitting to the other the extent of their hatred for the place they were about to enter. Whatever reason they had for being there, Edgar hoped it was worth it.

"The prisoners will try to attract your attention," said Silas. "Some of them have been down here for decades, and they are not the same people they were when they were first sent here. Do not listen to them. Stay quiet and let me speak. I was responsible for sending some of them here, but for two years of my life I was one of them. They will know me."

Silas's keys allowed him and Edgar to pass easily through barred gates that restricted entry into the prison's inner sanctum. Compared with the city it served, Feldeep was not a huge prison. It had once served as a repository, protecting relics taken from the estates of the most revered people in Albion. Jewelry, statues, diaries, carvings, and other precious items were taken there whenever a person of historical interest died, but all that was long gone. The cavern now housed almost a hundred prisoners within its walls, but it was still home to some of the most impressive architecture in the City Below.

Edgar could not help looking up. It was like standing beneath the hull of an upturned ship, a vast mausoleum created using craftsmanship that had long died out within Albion. Its inner caverns had vaulted ceilings that tapered up to points in some places, all paneled with slats of ancient wood stained black and mottled with age. The wooden beams reached up into narrowing clusters that looked like starbursts when viewed from below, and the entire place was centered on one far-reaching hall that magnified every sound, with smaller paths leading off from it on either side.

It would have been beautiful if still used for its original purpose. In its time that magnificent chamber had been filled with Albion's cultural treasures. Now its small side rooms were home to a very different aspect of Albion's history. They had been adapted into a series of sealed cells, their old arched doors replaced by barred iron gates, and almost every one of them was occupied.

Candles flickered behind the doors, and shadowed faces turned to look at the newcomers as Silas and Edgar walked by. Whispers spread quickly along the halls, trailing them to the nearest crosspath and spreading out until the entire chamber hissed with hushed words. The prisoners were thin and wary, their bagged eyes betraying the tiredness that came from years of being locked away underground. Edgar felt uneasy. "What if the wardens see us down here?" he asked.

"Then things will become interesting," said Silas.

"Are you sure about this?"

"No one in Feldeep is permitted to know anything about events in the City Above," said Silas. "Even the wardens are forbidden to communicate unnecessarily with people outside these walls. With luck, they will not know what has happened in Fume in recent weeks. We can use that ignorance to our advantage."

Edgar located the source of the burning smell when he spotted two prisoners working within a barred kitchen, stewing something for the other inmates' next meal. Whatever it was, it smelled as though they were boiling old boots.

Footsteps echoed ahead of Silas and Edgar along the hall. They were too heavy and purposeful to belong to any of the prisoners. Edgar's instincts bristled at the presence of a potential enemy, but Silas was already taking control. He stepped out into the path of two approaching wardens, saw that their weapons were already drawn, and floored one of them with a sharp jab to the throat. The officer fell to his knees, struggling to breathe, and the second man had just enough time for fear to register on his face before Silas did the same to him, only this time he did not let go. A few of the prisoners in nearby cells cheered, before Silas glared them into silence.

"I am here to talk," he said, tightening his grip on the older man's throat. "You will listen."

The warden on the ground recovered himself enough to speak. "Officer Dane," he said, his voice strained. "If we had . . . known it was you . . ."

"Drop the daggers," said Silas.

The men let their weapons fall at once. Silas released his grip. The younger of the two, not much older than Edgar, stood up but was unable to look Silas directly in the eye.

"Don't tell him anything," said the older warden.

"You have been in contact with the surface," said Silas.

"We heard what you did. About the men you killed. You are a traitor who deserves nothing but the noose!"

A glint of a hidden weapon flickered in the warden's hand, and Edgar looked away. He heard the gentle crack of bone and the slump of a body dropping to the floor. When he looked back, the older man's body lay still on the ground, and Silas was talking as if nothing had happened.

"How many wardens are stationed here?"

The younger officer's eyes met Silas's just for a second before he lowered them. "Twenty-five, sir." He looked down at the body by his feet. "Or . . . twenty-four."

"Gather them together. Tell them their orders have changed. I want the name and cell number of every prisoner who is strong enough to walk or wield a weapon. The Continental army is coming. I need people to fight for this city."

"They won't let the prisoners out," said the officer. "Our orders—"

"You have new orders," said Silas. "Tell your associates that I would not be here wasting my time if I were deceiving them. This is not a test. It is a command. Anyone who challenges me on this will meet the same end as this man. Go."

The young warden nodded smartly, stepped over the dead man, and hurried back the way he had come. It was only then that Edgar noticed the staring faces peering from the walls. Prisoners, looking out through their bars, had seen everything. Most were stunned into silence by Silas's words, and some did not believe what they had heard.

"Is it true?" A woman's hand reached out beside Edgar, making him stumble away in fright.

"Yes," said Silas. "The enemy is coming. This is your chance to earn your freedom. Every one of you."

"Why should we care about the City Above?" asked an old man, who blinked through large spectacles. "Fume is dead to us. It cast us aside. Now it'll get what it deserves."

"The High Council sent you here," said Edgar. "The people of the city have done nothing to you. Now trouble's coming, and weird things are going on up there. You must have felt the changes that have been happening. Haven't you seen things? Heard things you couldn't explain?"

"We've seen things all right," said the woman beside him. "No surprise really, being locked down here. Bodies hanging from the ceiling, eyes watching us while we sleep. We've all seen it. That's what this place does, see? It watches you. Makes you see what isn't there. Sends you insane."

"And we've heard plenty, too," said the old man. "Scratching. Whispering. More than we'd tell you."

"Then know this," said Silas. "What you are seeing is real. Our ancestors have been disturbed. The veil is falling. The dead will soon walk again within these halls."

Prison whispers relayed his words throughout Feldeep, and as they reached the farthest reaches of the cells, a rattling sound rang through the walls as prisoners clutched their bars, listening.

"These souls are showing you the truth," said Silas. "They are sharing the story of their deaths, trying to find peace. This city was built to honor the dead and rescue those who had become lost on their way into death. We all have failed them in some way. The dead are trying to be heard. They have been sealed away from the world, forgotten, for too long, just like you. If we allow Fume to fall, the Continent will bury all of us beneath their twisted version of history. Albion will be forgotten. Our families will live under the flag of a new nation, the dead will walk alongside us, and no one will know peace again. I am giving you the chance to reclaim what was taken from you. Take back the freedom that the High Council denied you and fight by my side against an enemy that will never expect it. You all were sent here because of your beliefs, your skills, or your histories. You can stay here in the dark and wait for the Blackwatch to slay you like rats in a trap, or you can trust me."

The prisoners' whispering fell silent, but the steady rattling grew louder as weak fists shook the bars of their cells, rising into a steady rhythm as those who could not see Silas signaled their solidarity with his cause.

No one wanted to be left down there. Silas knew that any prisoner would do anything for even the slightest chance of escape from that place. But for his strategy to work, those prisoners were not the only ones he had to convince.

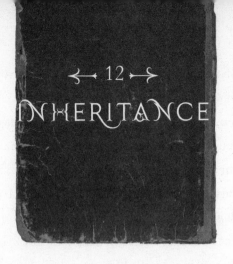

← 12 →
INHERITANCE

Kate left *Wintercraft* in the water. Part of her was glad to see it sink. She was tired of carrying the responsibility of something she had never wanted in her life. She wanted to be free of it. It had clung inside her coat like a heavy weight ever since she and Silas had discovered it in the ancient underground library. She had thought she was its protector, but instead it had claimed her. Her life was no longer her own. She was trapped in a cycle of events that had threatened to overwhelm her many times. And for what?

Dalliah had studied every word within the book's pages and knew all of them by heart. She would not care that her enemies' work was being destroyed. She hated the Winters family, perhaps with good reason, and that hate extended easily to Kate herself. But Kate was not a direct reflection of her ancestors. She was her own person, with her own thoughts and plans for her life. She was not responsible for carrying on what they had begun. *Wintercraft* was not her burden to bear.

Kate wanted the water to wash away the ink her parents had tried to protect. She wanted to see the pages disintegrate into fiber, catch upon the water, and wash out into the city to be lost in the gutters. She wanted more than anything to take back the events of recent months, to go back to the way life had been with her uncle in the bookshop. She missed Edgar. All she wanted was to be back home.

The book sat in the water, as still and solid as a stone. Kate might not have trusted Dalliah, but it was hard to believe that the way the woman had spoken about her family was anything less than the truth. Artemis had kept most of their history from Kate. He had even lied to her about the way her parents had died. He had known enough to hold back the truth. Maybe now she was hearing it for the first time.

"The final wheel will be of interest to you, Kate." Dalliah had returned to her favorite technique, manipulation. "If you want real answers. You will find them there. Your ancestors do not want you to think for yourself. If you want to challenge the fate they have delivered to you, follow me to the wheel. I will let you ask the spirit there anything you wish before the end. He will speak to you, just as this spirit did because he, too, once shared your blood."

"You've found the Winters wheel?" said Kate. "Where is it?"

Dalliah pointed out of a blue window. "Their memorial tower was built on a rise at the edge of the lake before it was drained. You can see its walls from here. What is left of them, at least."

Kate looked back at the sunken book and was sure she saw the silver glint of spirit eyes watching her from the water. "Take me to it," she said, turning away. "I want to end this."

Kate and Dalliah left *Wintercraft* behind and stepped out into the predawn hours of a freezing morning. It was still dark, but Kate no longer felt the cold that was chattering in her bones. She did not care about the scattering of snow that had settled on every surface. She did not listen to her aching leg muscles, which prickled like shards of glass, chilling her blood and tiring her body as her pulse began to slow. Her physical body no longer felt important to her. The pain in her veil-burned hands was worse than anything she had ever experienced, and it stole all her attention as she tried to lock it away.

Kate and Dalliah walked through the flooded waters and climbed the steps up to the bank's highest point, where people were gathering to see if the water would rise any higher. The lower rooms of a few buildings that stood too close to the water had been flooded, but they were long abandoned by everything except rats. People stood huddled with coats over their nightclothes, arguing about what they had seen and trying to guess what the rising water could mean, but they all fell quiet when Kate and Dalliah walked by.

Kate was soaked through, but her face was set with such determination and her hands were held so close to her chest that no one dared ask if she needed help. They avoided Dalliah completely, stepping back to make way for her as she followed the water around to the opposite bank.

The splintered remains of a memorial tower scratched the sky up ahead, surrounded by smaller towers that huddled around it like a group of whisperers sharing their secrets. Kate fixed her eyes upon the central tower. She was shivering and pale, but even if Dalliah had offered to heal her injured body, she would have refused her help. This was her journey. Her fate.

Every step felt heavier than the last. Kate's breaths were too shallow to feed her body the oxygen it needed, but she did not care. If the spirits in that city wanted her to do something, it would be on her terms and by her own choice. She would not be led into anything against her will. Not anymore.

If Kate had looked back, she might have seen a face watching her from the center of the small crowd: a boy, no older than eleven, who waited for Dalliah and Kate to turn off into the streets leading toward the broken tower. Once he knew which direction they were heading in, he pushed his way back through the gathering and ran toward a man who was hunched in a doorway with a blanket wrapped around his shoulders like a cloak, waiting for him.

"Artemis," the boy whispered, "it's her."

The past few weeks had been unkind to Artemis Winters. He struggled to his feet and reached for the stick that Tom held out for him, trying to see through the crowd. He was barely forty years old, but his body was weakened by worry and grief. It had taken days to find his way out of the City Below, where he had searched for any word of Kate and her whereabouts only to be threatened into silence whenever he had mentioned her name.

Finding food had been difficult in the tunnels, and he had been forced to rely upon Tom's skill at thievery to feed the boy and himself down there in the dark. When they first left the Skilled cavern, Artemis had been fit and confident of finding Kate within a day. Now he was nursing an injured leg, caused by a fall from the edge of one of the City Below's vast underground caverns. He had been lucky to fall only part of the way. Tom's increasing healing ability as a fledgling member of the Skilled was all that made walking on what had been a broken bone bearable.

Artemis did not like relying on the boy to help him. He had failed Kate, but he was determined not to do the same to Tom. During their journey together, he had hidden the boy from a wandering Skilled who had clearly lost her mind and shielded him from the woman's rage. When Tom had been caught stealing from a traveling trader near the surface, Artemis had taken the blame and suffered a black eye in return. They had walked through a dangerous world, and Artemis had barely survived. Life in the upper city had not been any better.

"Do you want me to follow them?" Tom walked restlessly beside Artemis as the older man hobbled to the lake edge, where people were already starting to disperse. He pointed to where he had last seen Kate and Dalliah, and Artemis immediately recognized the jagged shard of the tower that they were heading toward.

"No need," he said. His voice was empty, as if he were already defeated. "I know where they are going."

Artemis's stick splashed in the water as he slowly followed Kate's trail, but the farther he walked, the more uncomfortable he became. Pressure squeezed in upon his temples, and his eyes blurred until it was difficult to see. He stopped walking, and the pain faded until he started moving again. His stick lost its footing in the damp, and he fell forward, plunging his hands into the shallow water, where a face that was not his own looked up at him.

Artemis cried out in fright and scrambled backward. Tom tried to help him up, but Artemis was pointing at the water with terror in his eyes. "Did you see that?"

"There's nothin' there," said Tom. "You haven't slept much. Maybe that's it."

"No," said Artemis. "No . . . I was warned about this. It's happening again." He managed to stand and took a careful step forward, only to double over in pain. This time he looked down at the water and refused to look away when silver eyes emerged in what should have been his reflection near his feet. Logic and reason fought against the evidence of his eyes.

"What are you lookin' at?"

"I—I've seen him before," said Artemis. "I've dreamed about that face. I should be seeing my reflection, but it—it's someone else." He took a step back, and the face moved with him. As long as he was moving away from the tower, the pain did not return.

"Artemis?" Tom whispered to get his attention as he continued to back up. Artemis looked up and discovered that the two of them were far from alone.

Dark figures had gathered around the lake's shore. They looked like shadows when viewed straight on but took almost human form when seen out of the corner of the eye. Every one of them was still, looking not toward the water but to a partly submerged building near the shore.

"I can see *that*," said Tom.

Artemis instinctively pushed the boy behind him.

"Shades can't . . . they can't harm people," said Tom. "That's what the Skilled said. That's right, isn't it?"

"Yes. Yes, that's right." Artemis hoped Tom would not hear the uncertainty in his voice. "There's nothing to worry about." He glanced down and winced. The silver eyes were still there.

"What are they doing?" asked Tom.

"Just . . . letting us know they are here."

The two of them moved back along the bank until they were forced to wade into deeper water, and Tom bumped into a wall set with a blue window.

"All right," said Artemis, talking loudly, trying to sound authoritative. "Tell us—tell us what you want."

Some of the shades left their places on the banks and drifted across the water, heading straight for Artemis. "Go inside," he said, pushing the door open for Tom. "Quickly." The moment the two of them were inside the building, the shades stopped moving, content to watch them from a distance. Tom stayed by the doorway, looking back at them with nervous fascination.

"Climb out of the water," said Artemis. "You'll catch your death in this cold."

Tom scrambled up onto a table at the side of the room and sat there shivering. Artemis waded deeper into the room and bumped into something solid that was hidden under the water close by. His hands found what felt like an open circle made of stone.

"Artemis . . ."

Tom sat up straight. Artemis put a shaky hand upon the edge of the circle, and the stone tiles trembled beneath his fingers. A symbol—a snowflake—glowed in the water, flickering as though lit by a submerged flame.

"I—I don't . . . ," he stammered nervously, looking back at Tom. "I can't . . ."

". . . book bearer . . ."

"No. That's not me," said Artemis, talking to the symbol, not knowing what else to do. "My niece, Kate. She's the one who—"

". . . she abandoned us . . ."

"I don't know what she did. I'm looking for her. I want to help her."

". . . Kate will see in the darkness. She is not strong enough to resist us . . ."

"Who are you?" demanded Artemis, his voice quivering. "How can I hear you?"

". . . we have claimed this wheel to speak with you. These stones are ours now. We are your past, your blood, and your bones. We gave you life through the centuries. You carry our name, but you deny our ways. You and Kate are nothing without us . . ."

"I don't believe that," said Artemis. "If you are Kate's ancestors, you would try to help her."

". . . you let her go . . ."

"I was protecting her!"

". . . from us . . ."

The stone tiles became colder than ice, but Artemis refused to lift his hand away. "Was Kate here?" he asked. "Did you speak to her?"

". . . she will finish our work, then she will die beside us . . ."

"No. Your time is over. This is her life. *Her* time."

"*. . . no Winters walks alone . . .*"

Artemis pushed himself away from the spirit wheel, and the light in the symbol died. "I am talking to the air!" he said furiously.

"Shades were alive once," said Tom. "They still are, just in a different way."

"I don't care," said Artemis. "I don't care about any of it! I want Kate out of this city and back where she is safe. With me."

"*. . . your chance has passed. You have a new role to play.*"

Water drained swiftly from the center of the wheel, sending droplets spluttering into the air, and Artemis spotted an object hidden in the space it left behind. The purple cover of *Wintercraft* was damp but not soaked through. The edges of its pages were discolored, yet the papers themselves had survived. Artemis reached in carefully to lift it out. He inspected the book on all sides, ran a hand over the silver studs speckling its edges, and opened it carefully to the first page, which bore the inscription he already knew so well.

THOSE WHO WISH TO SEE THE DARK, BE READY TO PAY YOUR PRICE.

Those words had never seemed more true. That book had already cost him and Kate their family. Now its legacy was threatening to claim Kate, too.

Artemis turned gently through the pages, and faint whispers spread around the room. Halfway through, the pages were parted by a loose note that had been slipped in between them. For a moment Artemis hoped that Kate had left something behind. The paper was dry and fragile, and when he unfolded it, he found a letter signed with a name he did not know.

"What's that?" asked Tom.

"I'm not sure," said Artemis, before reading the letter out loud.

My name is Ravik Marr and these shall be my final words.

"Ravik Marr?" Tom suddenly looked even more interested. "Da'ru used to talk about him. He was her grandfather or great-grandfather. A powerful Skilled in his day."

"I don't think he lived very long after writing this," said Artemis, continuing to read.

My work in the Fourth Tower has come to an end. Dalliah knows I have turned against her. I have refused her final orders and found no way to escape. It is only a matter of time before her agents come for me.

During my imprisonment, I have spoken with the spirit sealed within the wheel. It has offered glimpses of a future that shall occur less than one century from my death. If the visions are correct, a book bearer will find this note when the bonds upon the veil begin to fall. I only hope it is not too late to share what I have discovered.

Wintercraft was already an uncomfortable weight in Artemis's hands. Now it felt like a stone.

You cannot prevent what is happening. If I am right, the lake will have risen, the old city will begin shaking off the stones of the new, and the souls within the walls shall awaken. The old families placed safeguards within the city to help balance the chaos of what is to come. You, book bearer, are one of those safeguards.

Artemis's hands were shaking a little, but he read on, keeping the next lines to himself. The final section had been written much more carefully, its letters formed with great precision.

You must carry the book with you. It cannot be left behind. The soul within it must be returned to its resting place. The Winters tower is where the past must be put to rest.

Tom waited to hear more. "What does the rest of it say?" he asked.

Artemis let the note fall closed. "It says I have to follow Kate." He tucked the note back into the book and closed it gently, not wanting to let the spirits in the room see Ravik Marr's final words. Artemis's idea of what was and was not possible had shifted greatly in recent months. He had worked with books all his life, and the idea of a soul's being locked inside the pages he was holding, while certainly disturbing, did not seem as unlikely as it once might have.

The surface of the water rippled with tiny waves, and Artemis made for the door, carrying *Wintercraft* with him. "It's too cold to stay in here," he said. "We need to go."

"*Artemis . . .*"

The voice chilled him. He did not have to look down to know that the silver eyes were still close by.

Tom dropped down into the water and beat him to the door. A drift of warm air passed across their faces, and the lake receded slowly, its waters dragging at their legs until they were walking on relatively dry ground.

"I've never seen water do that before," said Tom.

"Nor have I," Artemis said warily.

The shifting water had exposed part of the upper lake edge, allowing them to climb safely back to the streets. The shades were still standing around the water, but Artemis made a point of not looking at them as the lake surged in to fill the path behind them.

"What do we do when we find Kate?" asked Tom.

"We find out what is happening and we get her out of it. *I'll* get her out of it. You will be hidden somewhere so that I know you are safe."

"Like out here, you mean? With them?" Tom raised his eyebrows, unimpressed by that plan.

The lakeside was certainly not a place anyone would want to be alone in the dark. There was something disturbing about the way the shades watched them walk by. They were distant but alert, and their forms faded smoothly into the water whenever Artemis limped close to them.

The Winters tower loomed up ahead, easily dwarfing the other towers around it, even in its broken state. His parents had told stories about it when he was young. They had talked about the pride of the Winters family and the secrets they had hidden away, not only in the book of Wintercraft, which had been missing for many years in his parents' time but in other places, like that tower, where his father believed time lost all meaning to those of Winters blood.

Artemis had never taken those stories as anything more than fables, but believing in them was what had eventually led his brother to his death. Now, standing within sight of the tower itself, Artemis wished he had paid more attention to his parents' words.

When the two of them reached the point where Kate and Dalliah had headed into the streets, the sky in the east glowed with soft orange light. Artemis ignored it, believing it to be the first light of sunrise. When the sky faded unexpectedly back to black, he glanced at the rooftops, where another fiery glow soon followed the first. This one was higher up, like an orange star that rose straight up before sinking back down into the city. A faint sound echoed from the towers: a heavy sound that reverberated like a beaten drum.

Artemis kept walking, not knowing what he had just witnessed.

The walls of Fume were under attack. The battle for the city had begun.

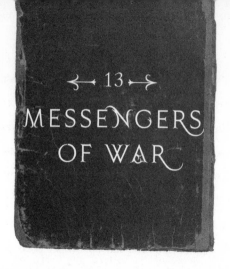

13
MESSENGERS
OF WAR

In the east, a street was licked by fire. The air filled with the smell of foul smoke, and a fiery mass smoldered where it had become embedded in the side of a tower. Plumes of smoke rose like fingers from the city's surrounding walls. The narrow walkways within them flickered with firelight, and flames spread along them like sparks along a fuse wire, forcing night servants and slaves to run down the spiral staircases into the city, fleeing for their lives.

Distant screams carried across the city, and wardens moved through the streets in packs, their black robes sweeping back to expose the leather armor beneath. Every one of them was heavily armed as they forced their way up onto the burning walls, passing the servants streaming down.

Beyond the walls, organized ranks of Continental soldiers had gathered out of arrow shot. The network of watchmen stationed along Albion's coast had failed. No birds had carried messages of an incoming enemy attack, and the Wild Counties were vast enough for any number of soldiers to pass through unseen. The High Council would never have expected more than a thousand men to appear at the gates within the space of a day. Silas was the only one who had ever planned for such a direct assault. Now he had been proved right.

The black-clothed enemy had reached the city before the wall guards could raise the alarm. The wardens were vastly outnumbered, but the officers listened to Silas's warning as word of it carried through their ranks. The order to prepare for battle had spread quickly through the city, calling every warden into his defensive position. During his time as warden leader, Silas had ordered the wardens to train for a city attack twice a year, and that training sharpened every officer's mind now that the enemy truly was at the gates. Even though Silas was not there in person, the wardens followed his orders as diligently as if he were shouting them from a tower top:

Five men to a battle group.
Secure the section of wall under greatest threat.
Send teams to the gate farthest from the attack, and
    defend in case of possible infiltration.
Execute, imprison, and contain.

Runners lit beacon fires at strategic positions on rooftops across the eastern city and scattered copper filings upon them whenever an enemy was spotted within their lines of sight. The copper-tainted flames burned green, allowing lookouts to identify the section of the wall most under threat.

As the wardens advanced, the city's remaining residents fled through the besieged streets, leaving their protectors to fight for their homes. Not one of them chose to pick up a weapon and defend himself. They were used to having people serve them. Now they expected wardens to die for them, as well.

The yellow moon moved behind a bank of heavy cloud as Continental soldiers converged upon the walls, bombarding the buildings beyond them from horse-drawn siege weapons loaded with fiery ammunition designed to tear into buildings and scatter destruction across the ground below.

Hot streaks cut through the air as arrows speared over the walls. The wardens took cover, and warden bowmen posted on the battlements soon returned fire. A handful of men fell, but most officers were practiced enough to hold their positions until the flurry of arrows gradually lessened and a loud thud announced the arrival of a battering ram at the eastern gate.

That sound was every Fume resident's nightmare. The gate shuddered, sending shivers through the mighty walls. The noise carried through the streets and was heard as far away as the central city square.

Thud.

Thud.

The gate groaned upon its hinges and resisted. It had been

built to repel anything that was hurled against it, but this was its first true test. One sharp-eyed warden took up a position along the gate's approach, drew back his bow, and shot arrows cleanly between the bars, taking down three of the six soldiers operating the ram, while more wardens closed in upon the gate to help defend it.

The once-quiet city was alive with the sounds of battle. Spilled blood stained the ground and trickled in rivulets between the cobbles as more wardens fell. The sky became a hailstorm of arrows. Using their sheer numbers to their advantage, infantrymen used ropes to scale the walls and swarmed over the warden bowmen. Blades flashed along the battlements as the enemy killed their way along them, and buildings were cracked and torn by pitch-slicked boulders, lacing the streets with flames.

Worried that Silas's warning had come too late, lookouts stationed high above the action could not help glancing toward the northern horizon whenever they had the chance. The Night Train and its promise of reinforcements was still out there somewhere, but as the battle raged on, its bright light did not cut through the darkness. There was no sign of the engine, no sign of any assistance.

The wardens were alone.

In the deeper levels of the City Below, Silas felt the veil tremble as souls were delivered into it one by one. Death had spread across the streets above, but those whose lives were ending were not accepted easily into the peaceful unknown of the next world. The instability of the veil pulled them into the half-life instead.

Silas's connection to the veil allowed him to feel the final moments of every man slain above him. The more the veil weakened, the more the half-life shifted to overlap the living world—and the longer Kate and Dalliah were left to roam unchecked within the city, the worse it would become. Silas tried to close his mind to that part of his awareness and concentrated upon the task ahead of him.

The wardens of Feldeep were glad to have any reason to return to the surface, and when Silas told them of the impending attack, many of them had looked relieved. He had expected more of them to challenge his plan, but the current guards had been stationed there for months without relief. They were tired of the dark and more than ready to return to the city. Prisoner or guard, Silas knew what it was like to spend too long in that place. Officers were not meant to spend longer than a month at a time belowground, but these men had clearly been neglected by the council. Silas could understand their eagerness to be relieved of their posts.

After seeing the body of the dead warden, the remaining officers listened to Silas's orders without question. Although most were reluctant to allow the prisoners out of their cells, they still retrieved the keys when Silas demanded them, and a sense of anticipation moved through the prisoners sealed around the edges of that mighty chamber.

The siege had already begun. If there was to be any chance for the city, and for Albion, Silas had to move quickly. These people had been incarcerated for a long time. They wanted to breathe cool air and see the open sky. He had to convince at least some of them to do the very opposite of that. He hoped they would become fighters, but first they would be messengers.

The young warden handed Silas five iron rings, each hung with twenty keys. The other wardens stepped back and stood between Silas and the nearest cells as he walked around the chamber, surveying the men and women imprisoned there. They were quiet, but they were strong. When Silas spoke, he did not need to raise his voice. Everyone in the place was silent, attentive, and cautiously hopeful, listening for what he was about to say.

"You are one of Fume's greatest secrets," he said. "Every one of you has been locked away by order of the High Council because they needed to keep you under control. There are trespassers among you, whisperers and thieves. But I am not interested in your stories. I do not care what your lives were before this day. Some of you know me as the officer who brought you to justice. Others will know of the cell hidden on a deeper level beneath us where I spent two years of my life 'serving' the High Council with my blood and my bones."

Edgar saw some hands shrink back from the bars as their owners remembered the days when Silas, too, was a prisoner: the echoes of torment and pain that filled the endless nights, the smell of seared flesh, and the terror of long months spent wondering if they would be next. Stories of Silas's time in that place were among the first shared with new prisoners. The denizens of Feldeep Prison could not fail to respect him for what he had endured.

"The High Council sent you here to forget who you are," Silas continued. "Even when they planned to let you go, there would have been no escape. They promised you freedom when your sentence ended, but no one who leaves these walls ever returns to the life he left behind. The council would take every one of you and send you off to war rather than let you back into society. I have seen the hopes of 'free' men and women fade when they are sent from the city to die upon an embattled shore. You are not waiting for freedom. You are waiting for death. I can offer you something different."

Silas threw one of the key rings to the floor, and the sound echoed around the prison walls. "The High Council wants you to forget who you are. Now I want you to forget what you have done. Many of you have families within the city. Remember them now. The Continental army is here. Enemy soldiers are threatening our city, and I want you to help me stand against them. If Fume dies, everything you have lived for will die with it. I want you to fight. Not for the High Council. Not for the country that let you suffer in the dark. You must fight for yourselves, for the lives of the people you left behind, and for the streets you once called your home."

A small voice seeped from one of the rear cells. "What about the army?" it asked. "And the wardens?"

"The army is not coming," said Silas. "The wardens will fight to their last man, but it will not be enough."

"And the people on the surface?" said a woman's voice. "Will they fight?"

"Many have already fled from the city," said Silas. "They did not know about the attack. They were driven out by visions of the dead. I doubt those who are left behind have either the strength or the inclination to protect what is at stake."

"Why come down here to us?" asked the woman. "Why should we fight if they won't?"

"Shut up!" a prisoner shouted a few cells away from Edgar. "Do you want him to change his mind?"

"I want him to be honest with us."

"I need you to spread a message," said Silas. "The people of the City Below can help us in this fight. They do not know what is happening above us. I need messengers to bring the people of the understreets to the surface. We need numbers. We need strength. The residents of the City Below will not listen to me. Your voices will carry far farther than mine alone."

"And what happens after all this?" asked the woman.

"The wardens got me once. How do I know they won't come after me again?"

Silas walked up to the woman's cell and looked in through the bars, forcing her to step back, any confidence she had shrinking away.

"You don't know that," said Silas. "I am not here to pardon you for what you have done. I am here to recruit you. If you do what I ask, you have my word that no warden or collector will hunt you down until this crisis has passed. Beyond that, your life is your own responsibility. You will earn a short reprieve. I am not offering you protection. I am allowing you the chance to take responsibility for your own lives beyond this prison. Some of you will find your way back here, but others who embrace this opportunity will continue your lives in freedom. If Fume survives, you will live on knowing that you have earned every breath of clear air you breathe. If you continue to respect your country, the wardens will have no reason to come for you." Silas found the ring with the woman's cell key on it and separated it from the rest. "Or you can turn down my offer, and I can remove your key from the ring along with that of anyone else who chooses to stay. Your cell will remain closed, and you will regret this night for the rest of your life. If the Blackwatch find you down here, I doubt you will have many hours left."

The prison fell silent. No one moved. No one spoke. The

wardens stood quietly, and Edgar saw the prisoners' nervous eyes wandering along the corridor. They had learned to be suspicious. None of them had any reason to trust anyone outside the boundaries of their own cells. The silence allowed the cries of the dying to creep back into Silas's mind. His fingers tensed, but only Edgar noticed the tiny glimmer of distraction in his eyes.

At last one voice spoke up as a prisoner pressed his face to the bars and asked the question Silas had been waiting to hear: "What do you want us to do?"

"These officers will unlock your cells," said Silas. "Those who are strong enough will make their way out of here and head to the City Below. Once there, you will spread the word. Warn everyone you see that Fume is under threat. Call them into action. Tell them it is only a matter of time before the enemy reaches their home. They will not stop at the surface. They will seal off the tunnels and leave every soul down here to die. You will rally the people of the understreets to fight, and then you will join them. Lead them to the surface. Tell them to protect this city with every ounce of energy they have. This is no time for enmity between ourselves. We must fight as one, or we shall die as one. Tell them the wardens will stand with them. Fume needs us now. We will not let her down."

For a short time no one spoke, and Silas felt the creeping fingers of the black spreading into his mind. His eyes darkened in the shadows as the veil edged closer to the living world, letting him see through the part of himself that was sealed away. Horrors bled into his mind like poison, but only Edgar noticed the change in him. When Silas's eyes became dark, Edgar knew something was happening, and he stepped forward. He took the keys from Silas's hand as if he had been ordered to do it and handed them out to the nearest wardens.

"You heard Officer Dane," said Edgar. "Those who are with us, stand at the front of your cells or sit and raise your hand. Anyone who wants to stay here, turn away when an officer approaches. Take your positions now!"

The chamber exploded with the sound of desperate voices.

"I'll fight!"

"I'll go!"

"I'll do whatever you ask!"

The prisoners' shouts rang from the walls. Bars shook. Feet stamped. No one wanted to be left behind.

The wardens did as Silas had commanded and opened the cells in groups of ten, allowing the prisoners to filter out into the chamber in manageable numbers. Some of them stepped awkwardly out of their cells and took a few moments to take a last look around their prison before heading toward the door. Others collected tiny belongings that reminded them of their past before scuttling out, and those who were not strong enough to walk far unaided were helped along by others who had not yet been physically ravaged by their time in the dark.

The wardens escorted each group to the ladder that led up into the shallow levels beneath Fume's streets. A warden positioned at the top of the shaft directed them to the tunnels leading to the deeper understreets, but most headed the opposite way, fleeing straight toward the surface. For them, the promise of freedom was too potent to resist, but there were at least two dozen who chose to do as Silas asked. His words had earned him temporary allies in the most unlikely place.

Those men and women spread out through the tunnels, following directions that were carved high upon the walls, heading for the most populated areas of the City Below. Word of Silas's fears for the city spread through every cavern and trading post, down through the Shadowmarket and along the underground streets. No one knew who the messengers were, but fear of war was enough to make them take their news seriously. In less than an hour whisperers had spread the word so far that leaders of the different cavern communities were called to make decisions for their people. Guards who kept order within the settlements announced their willingness to fight, and soon the original messengers were forgotten.

The City Below was rallied by thoughts of its own self-preservation, and the people of Feldeep soon became as invisible as they had always been. Their identities would not be remembered by history, although their actions were set to shape everything that was to come.

The wardens headed to the surface to join the battle for

the eastern gate, leaving Silas and Edgar alone in Feldeep. Silas would have gone with them, but he could no longer trust his own eyes. The connection to his broken spirit was lasting longer than it had the first time in the council chambers. Even if he had trusted himself to join the fight, his responsibilities lay elsewhere.

"Give any man or woman a good enough reason to fight and they will fight," he said. His eyes were distant, and his words were clipped as though he were in pain.

"Why don't you sit down?" Edgar gestured to a low bunk in one of the cells. Silas's eyes fell briefly upon the bars of the open door serving the small room.

"No," he said. "The Skilled are taking their positions, and the wardens will soon have the reinforcements they need. Now is the time to play our part." He stood tall, rolling his shoulders back and managing to look more fearsome than ever.

"Do you know how to find Kate?" asked Edgar.

Silas looked down at him, his eyes still blackened by the veil. "Kate is everywhere," he said. "The city is listening to her. It is reacting to her. It knows where she is. Now so do I."

He walked the length of the prison chamber like a phantom. Terrors surged like bloodied masks at the edges of his vision, leaching from a place where nightmares became real and horrors felt by one soul could bleed into others close by. He recognized the screams of one spirit in particular, his former mistress, Da'ru Marr. He had dragged her soul there and left it. He was responsible for the wrenching horrors that twisted her soul, but he pushed her aside, refusing to be distracted by her cries.

He spoke quietly as they reached the ladder, so Edgar was not certain whether he was talking to him or not.

"No one deserved to be sealed in this place," said Silas. "No one.

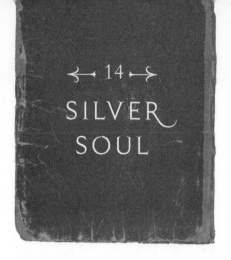

← 14 →
SILVER
SOUL

Silas's crow ruffled its feathers against the cold and looked down from the jagged point of the Winters memorial tower. The outer walls were all that was left of the old structure, and the lower floor was exposed to the sky through a surround of stones that reached high enough to be among the tallest structures in Fume.

With wintry wind and brief flurries of snow swathing the city, that tower was not the most pleasant of places for a bird to be. The crow was not interested in the distant fires or the sounds of human battle. Its attention was fixed solely upon two figures that were approaching the tower, one tall and strong, the other slow and uncertain. The crow's feathers bristled at the sight of the taller woman, and it lowered its head, remaining still. It knew the girl who was walking behind, but there was something unusual about her.

The taller woman disturbed the veil as she walked, driving back any souls that passed her way. The girl's energies were very different. The veil around her was usually calm and controlled, attracting the dead rather than repelling them. That night Kate Winters's energies had much in common with those the crow usually saw around Silas. She was a tightly held bundle of energy just waiting to find a release. Silas often found that release through aggression, violence, and death. Kate's spirit looked ready to do the very same thing.

The crow cocked its head, uncertain. It had the uneasy feeling that it had followed the wrong girl, but beneath the volatile haze of anger and hate the crow still sensed the human it knew underneath. She was preparing for something. She was closing herself off from everything around her, losing herself within her own thoughts. The crow had seen Silas do the same, but only during his darkest times. There was nothing to do until its master arrived, so the crow settled down to watch and wait.

Kate hung a few steps back from the other woman. She seemed reluctant to approach the tower yet still maintained a determined pace. The crow shifted a little, attracting the girl's attention when it knew the other woman could not see. Kate glanced upward. The crow had no reason to hide from her, but when she noticed it, her energies changed. Her spirit crept momentarily from the dark place it had sunk into and directed all its concentration toward the crow.

If Kate had been anyone else, the crow would have swooped as far away from those eyes as it could get. This was a girl of great interest to his master, a girl who had saved the crow's own life more than once, but something had changed inside her. Something dangerous lurked where a peaceful soul had once been. This was no projection from the woman beside her. Kate was creating it all herself. The crow lowered its head again, sinking its beak out of sight.

Silas pushed a fallen stack of wood aside and forced his way out of a hidden passageway into a tumbledown house. Edgar was right behind him, and the two of them stepped out into Fume together, both sensing the same thing at once.

"Fire arrows," said Edgar, recognizing the smell of black powder. "Burning wood. Lots of it."

"There." Silas pointed between the closely packed buildings to a patch of orange sky where sparks leaped up to puncture the perfect black of the clouds.

"Do you think they'll breach the walls?" asked Edgar.

"They would not have attacked if they were not confident of victory."

Silas turned away from the ongoing battle, following a quiet instinct that was drawing him in the opposite direction. His crow was afraid. Fear was the most potent emotion to carry through the veil, and it reached Silas as clearly as if the crow had screeched from the rooftops. Silas's eyes still flickered between the living world and his soul's prison, but when he concentrated upon his crow, he became aware of two living creatures that existed within both worlds. Dalliah Grey's soul was trapped in the black, just as his was; that he already knew. But there was another soul close by, sinking more deeply into the darkness surrounding Dalliah with every passing second.

Silas's palms seared with old pain, and the scar Kate had once healed felt exposed once again. His hands felt blistered, his skin tight and raw, as if it had been slashed with knives. He looked at his scarred palm, expecting to see the old wound open and sore, but nothing had changed. The skin was still intact, and when he pulled away from Kate's consciousness, the pain faded away.

"Silas?"

Silas had continued walking, but Edgar's voice came from a few steps behind him, where Edgar had stopped and was staring at something in an alleyway that joined the street where they were walking.

When Silas followed his eyes, he saw that Edgar had good reason to stop. Shades were pouring out of the alleyway. Hundreds of them were moving swiftly across the street between him and Edgar. Some bore the human forms they had taken in life, while most moved like solid shadows, their silvery eyes betraying the secret suffering of their drifting souls. They spread silently between the buildings, each still captured in the half-life, yet visible to the living eye. It was a fast-flowing river of souls. A spiritual stampede.

Edgar would not have minded being close to so many souls if they had just been passing through, but the way their eyes lingered on him a little too long made him feel vulnerable. They were not simply going about their business and moving on. They were watching him. Instead of continuing on toward the center of the city, he caught glimpses of them gathering in the buildings nearby, surrounding him.

Silas had never seen shades behave in that way. Edgar should have been of no interest to them, yet they were close enough to give Silas cause for concern.

"Stay still," he ordered.

The shades were behaving more like predators than wandering souls. Silas's presence should have been enough to drive them away, but their attraction to Edgar was greater than any fear they had of him.

"What's happening?" asked Edgar. "What are they doing?"

The flow of souls settled into a quiet mist, keeping a short distance between themselves and Edgar. Shades gathering together often showed a pack instinct, acting upon the movements of more dominant souls among them. All it would take was one soul to make its move, and the rest would follow.

Remembering a conversation he had shared with Dalliah Grey during his time upon the Continent, Silas stepped toward them. Dalliah had spoken of a connection between Kate and Edgar that transcended the living world and crossed into the next. If Kate's soul was suffering, it would send tremors of energy throughout the already highly charged city. Her anguish would be magnified and spread to every soul for miles around.

To save itself, Kate's spirit would seek out the one person who had kept it grounded in the past, Edgar. That made him a danger: to Kate and to himself.

Kate's spiritual connection with Edgar was confusing the shades. Hundreds of souls were being drawn to that place, and the proximity of the half-life was bolstering their energy, giving them strength. If they overwhelmed Edgar in their desperation to find release, his soul did not have a chance.

"These souls cannot reach Kate," said Silas. "They believe you are the next best thing."

"Me? But I'm not even Skilled! What do they want?"

"You are close to Kate. She has used you to anchor her spirit to the living world more than once. She may be trying to do the same thing again."

"What?" Edgar struggled to keep the fear from his voice. "She's never done that. I can't feel anything."

"Only because you are used to it," said Silas. "Think of yourself as a living listening circle. Circles are used to create and stabilize tears in the veil. Kate may not have done it consciously, but the same thing is happening inside you. She is channeling her own energy toward you."

"That . . . doesn't sound good."

"Kate's connection to you may be the only thing that is keeping her sane," said Silas. "You are descended from a Skilled bloodline with no natural ability of your own. Your blood has always been ready to accept the energies of the veil, but you have never known how to make the connection. Kate has torn the veil too deeply this time. She has done something new."

"So do I have to stand here until she is finished?" asked Edgar. "I don't think these people want me to go anywhere."

"Most shades are confused by their time in the veil. They do not see the living world the way you do. To their eyes, you are a potential doorway into death."

"I'm not, though, am I?"

"That will not matter very soon."

Silas stepped through the crowd of souls as if they were not there. Only those he threatened to contact directly moved out of his way. The rest were transfixed upon Edgar, who remained standing in the very center of them all.

Silas looked up. Churning swaths of gray were descending quickly across the rooftops, smothering everything in a fog of souls.

Edgar did not dare move more than his eyes. "I'm not in a listening circle," he said, recognizing the danger he was in. "I'm not protected, am I?" His palms began to sweat with nerves. "What should I do?"

"You must break the link with Kate."

"I can't *feel* any link! Even if there is one, you said it was helping her."

"If you do not break the link, those souls will do it for you. Forget about her. Focus upon a memory from your past, before you had ever heard Kate's name. Think of anything except her."

"I can't do that."

"If you do not listen to me, you will die," said Silas. "The city is awakening, and the shades do not yet know their own strength. Normally, they would have no effect, but things have changed. If they move, they will overwhelm you and drive your soul from your skin. I have seen it happen during the council's experiments into the half-life. It is no way to die."

"Shades can't harm people," said Edgar. "The Skilled always said that."

"The Skilled also killed their own people to drain energy from their blood," said Silas. "Are they the kind of people you want to trust?"

Two shades moved closer to Edgar, testing the air between them and drawing the others a few steps toward him. Silas stood beside him like a wolf guarding a kill, but the dominant souls stood their ground.

"Edgar," he said, "break the link."

"What will happen to Kate if I do?"

"Far less than what will happen to you if you do not."

One shade broke away from the rest and darted through the air, heading straight toward Edgar. It moved lightning fast, but Silas saw it coming and pulled Edgar out of its path, forcing it to collide with him instead. The moment the shade made contact, Silas's consciousness plunged straight into the heart of the veil, dragging the shade down with him.

***

Darkness swamped completely over Silas. The shade twisted around him like a frightened snake, and he saw the city as it appeared to the shade's eyes. Walls became shadows, windows became shimmering shapes, and the souls of every being—living and dead—appeared as specks of silver light within the black. The city had become a galaxy, and the spirits were its stars. They were all around him, spreading out to the distant walls and filling the ground beneath his feet. Thousands upon thousands of Albion lives, abandoned and forgotten in a place living eyes could not see.

Beside him, Edgar's energy was duller than most. Silas could see tiny trails of light leading away from the boy, toward a bright distant soul that was growing dimmer by the moment. He looked down at his own hands and saw them as they were in life, except that his fingertips were touched by the same silver light. His veins shimmered with it.

The energy spread through the air and wrapped around Edgar like tiny silver chains, encircling his body and reaching all the way up to his neck, but with Silas the connection lived inside him, carried within his blood. Kate Winters's soul echoed within him, sharing the void his own soul had left behind. It acted as a reminder of Kate's presence, connecting him to her when she was in spiritual distress, but Kate's link with Edgar was very different. Her soul had latched onto his life energy, and it was draining him.

The only thing preventing Silas from losing his connection to the living world and falling completely into the black was the shade that he had carried there with him. It was pulling back toward the upper levels of the veil through sheer will, fleeing from the terrors screeching in the dark. Silas resisted the pull. He knew what it was like to stare into the black for the first time. Kate's soul was on the very brink of that place. If there was any chance her spirit could be saved, Silas had to try.

Moving through the lowest levels of the veil was like moving through a nightmare where everything was familiar yet horrifically altered. Silas's mind forced what he could sense into the most logical explanation it could create. It gave the formless solid form, and emptiness became a cage that seared against the soul. In that place nightmares were given a voice, and the living world became a doubted memory. It stripped away everything that made people who they were. Kate did not belong there.

Silas's consciousness carried him through the altered streets, witnessing every horror that had filled them throughout history. He saw cobbles stained with blood that flowed like tar and dripped globules upward into the air like raindrops on a windowpane. It felt as if the streets were moving past him while he remained still, anchored by the terrified shade, until the jagged shape of a tower stood before him. The tower's presence pierced through every level of the veil. Its stones looked alive. The veil twisted them into a writhing wall of souls before Silas's eyes, like bees swarming around a hive.

Silas tried to clear his mind and see the truth, but the shade's fear was seeping into the veil, coloring everything beyond the reach of reason. Silas could see Kate and Dalliah at the base of the tower: *one soul shining strongly, the other barely there, shrouded in a gathering of black. And at the very top of the tower, he saw the spirit of his crow, perched loyally upon a building that looked as if its stones could devour anything that came too close. He could not let Kate step inside that building. No matter the cost, she had to be stopped.*

Silas stopped resisting the desperate pull of the shade and allowed his consciousness to travel back through the upper levels of the veil. Memories flared and surged through his mind until the shade fled and Silas's mind retreated from the veil, returning to the living world.

When he saw through his own eyes again, the street looked as it should have been, except for the persistent gathering of shades still standing around him. Silas's fingers were still embedded in Edgar's shoulder from when he had pulled him aside, and frost retreated from his skin as he released his grip.

Edgar was pale with fear and relief. "They haven't moved," he said. "Whatever you did, I think it stopped them."

"I have done nothing," said Silas. "The connection between you and Kate is real, and it is strong. I doubt you could break it. You cannot stay here."

Edgar was about to speak when the entire street jolted violently. Windows shattered, roofs collapsed inward, and cracks began to thread across the ground. The shades reacted with fear, screaming and plunging in toward Edgar. Silas tried to protect him, but it was no use. The souls struck both of them, surging into their bodies like ink into water.

Whatever Edgar had expected, he was not prepared for the reality of what happened. His body fell immediately into shock as his soul was overwhelmed. Voices and memories exploded in his mind, louder and stronger until all he could hear were the cries of the dead. He tried to move, but his body would not answer him. He tried to shout, but no sound came out.

His dormant blood ran thick with the energies of invading souls, and he fell to the ground, smothered by lifetimes of torment and agony. His body could not bear it, and his soul tried to tear away, freeing itself from the onslaught, but in the midst of the madness Edgar felt the link between himself and Kate powerfully for the first time, and he refused to let go. He stared blankly at the sky, suffering in silence as the souls plunged into him again and again.

Silas was still standing, his body heavy with the burden of writhing souls. He took two slow steps away from Edgar. The third was slightly easier, and the farther he walked, the less the souls were interested in him. All they wanted was the boy.

Silas's entire body felt bruised. His muscles burned with every step. He looked to the rooftops, where the tip of the living tower was just within sight. One thought sent his crow gliding down from the stones, away from the dangers of that place, and the white feathers streaking its chest glimmered as it answered its master's call.

The crow settled on a nearby rooftop, flicking its black tail and calling out aggressively to the nearby shades. Silas pointed toward Edgar. "Watch the boy," he commanded.

He turned away from the bird and ran through the streets without looking back. There was nothing he could do for Edgar there. Kate had condemned him. She could have broken the link the moment she sensed Edgar's pain. Instead she was allowing him to suffer. He had been too slow. He had allowed Dalliah to take Kate too far into the darkness.

The veil trembled around him as he moved, anger seeping from him like oil, dripping terror into the air. He found an empty warden patrol house and broke down the door just before another tremor rattled through the earth. He crossed the room and headed straight for the weapons cache hidden beneath the floor. The rusted lock cracked under his heel, and he dragged out two items, a crossbow and a hip quiver containing a single bolt.

He slung the crossbow over his shoulder and left the patrol house, his eyes set with the focus of a soldier. He paid no attention to the endless stream of souls flowing past him along the street. He ignored the echoes of Edgar's voice carrying through the veil as the boy's soul struggled to hold on to life. One bolt would be enough. One bolt would finish it all.

← 15 →
THE LIVING TOWER

Kate stood outside her family's memorial tower and immediately felt as if she had returned home. The stones welcomed her. The arched doorway was narrow and thin, three times the height of an ordinary door, and when she looked up, her sight shifted between the broken shard that stood there in her time and the grand, beautiful edifice that it had once been.

Its walls were hexagonal, with straight sides that reflected the snowflake symbol of the family, and its very top was crowned with a black stone parapet edged with leaning gargoyles. Its past beauty made the stark emptiness of the true sight before her fade in comparison. Other towers had survived the centuries intact. Why had her family not protected theirs? Kate stepped into the stone archway, and a soft white glow emanated from the floor inside.

"They are waiting for you," said Dalliah. "You wanted to speak to them. This is your chance."

The floor inside the tower was covered in grit, washed down from the walls by centuries of wind and rain. Dalliah waited outside, watching Kate walk into the true home of her ancestors, but she was not the only one whose eyes were upon the girl. The entire inside wall of the tower was lined with skulls, row upon row of staring empty sockets. Each layer was separated by a horizontal row of bones, and the rows kept on rising, right to the very top of the tower's exposed shard, where empty spaces left by fallen skulls now yawned jagged and black. Fragments of bone crunched beneath Kate's boots, and she stood still, not wanting to show disrespect toward the remains of the dead.

The air hung with expectation. Kate could hear the wind cutting through the tallest stones, bringing with it a fine rain that glistened in the light seeping from the floor. There, in the middle, was a large sunken spirit wheel, its tiles perfectly level with the floor. The symbols were well worn. The edges were chipped by centuries of weather chewing into them and making their mark, but the wheel itself was well preserved.

Beneath the layer of grit and dirt, the floor was laid with an old mosaic of soft blue and white tiles depicting a perfect snowflake with the spirit wheel set into its very center. The delicate arms of the design pointed exactly to the points of the compass, but the tiles stopped a short distance from the surrounding wall, leaving bare stone in their place. Kate realized that the bones she could see must once have been sealed behind an inner wall, but that someone had taken the bricks away, exposing the skulls within.

Despite the gruesome surroundings, Kate still felt welcome in that place. Within its walls, life was simple. She no longer felt the tension of the veil invading her senses or the gentle whispers of the city's souls that followed her constantly wherever she went. Even Dalliah, standing outside, felt far away. She could not have been more comfortable if she had found herself back in her old bedroom with nothing but the peaceful predictability of an ordinary day stretching ahead of her. It was an intoxicating feeling, but Kate was wise enough to see through the lies that were so carefully laid before her. The pain in her palms was enough to remind her of the danger she was in. She was not there to be accepted by her ancestors. She was there to be used by them.

Kate stood next to the spirit wheel but would not go close enough to be touched by more than a faint glimmer of its pulsing light. It was easy to believe that nothing existed in the world outside, that there was no city, no people, no green land hidden beneath a blanket of white snow.

"I'm here to talk," she said out loud. "I want you to listen to me."

The bones in the walls shivered enough to shake fragments of dust from their resting places.

"You wanted me to come here," said Kate. "I want to know why."

"*Speak with us . . .*"

The harmony of the collected voices seemed gentle, but the hidden energy carried with their words was tinged with malevolence. The feeling of welcome Kate had experienced faded back a little.

"Dalliah Grey brought me here," she said.

"*. . . she ended many of us. She freed us . . .*"

"This is not freedom."

"*. . . we have been waiting . . .*"

"*. . . the city is ready . . .*"

"*. . . the veil must fall . . .*"

"How many of you are here?"

"*. . . we are many . . .*"

"Let me see you."

The tower shifted back to its original state, and Kate saw a thin staircase curling up around the intact walls, reaching up toward another perfect mosaic that was pressed into a vaulted hexagonal ceiling. Beneath it, hundreds of silver lights shimmered down the walls: spirit lights, every one of them a soul, listening to her.

"Are my parents here?" Kate did not want to ask the question, but she could not escape the possibility. She had to know.

"*. . . they are gone . . .*"

"*. . . taken into death . . .*"

Kate was relieved that their souls had not become trapped within the veil, but part of her was disappointed that they had moved on, leaving her behind.

"... *the younger generations have fallen away* ..."

"... *they do not follow the cause* ..."

"What cause?"

"... *the only cause that matters* ..."

"... *knowledge. Truth* ..."

"Did you *choose* to exist like this?"

"... *we are waiting. We knew you would come* ..."

"... *you will be our end and our new beginning* ..."

"You had your time," said Kate. "You lived your lives. Why did you not go into death?"

"... *we would leave behind too many questions. Too many days unseen* ..."

"... *history needs us.*"

Dalliah entered the tower. The walls settled immediately back to their decrepit state, but the souls remained. "Every person has her purpose," said Dalliah. "Yours was to come here with me and finish the work of the Walkers. You could not resist that fate any more than your ancestors could resist theirs."

"Life doesn't work that way," said Kate. "We make our own choices."

"I brought you here. You did not come by your own free will."

"I knew what I was doing," said Kate. "I belong here more than you do."

"You had no choice in this, despite what you believe," said Dalliah. "No person can change her fate. Most souls live and die exactly as they are meant to. Others, like you and I, are destined for something else."

"What about the souls in the wheels?" said Kate. "Were they destined to be sent into the black, or was their fate *your* choice?"

"The strong must control the weak or the world will crumble into chaos," said Dalliah. "Walkers have always been the strongest minds, the greatest souls. We have spent generations trying to drag the world out of the hole that ordinary people would like to see it languish in forever. *Wintercraft* represents only one small aspect of our history. Our ancestors were thinking beyond this world long before the first drop of ink touched its pages. We were here when the first body was laid in the ground that would become this city. Fume was built to explore the mysteries of death. This was our laboratory. People sent their dead to us to find peace, and we learned from their memories in return. The city is ours, and it will give us what we need once again."

Kate walked around to the other side of the spirit wheel and felt the consciousness of hundreds of spirit eyes following her as she moved. "No," she said. "You weren't there. You didn't do any of those things."

"I know my history," said Dalliah. "I know what I have seen."

"You know what the veil has shown you," said Kate. "I have seen your memories. I have seen the final moments of the bonemen who were sealed into these wheels, and I know that Walkers do not know nearly as much about the veil as they think they do. Including you."

The spirits in the tower flickered with agitation.

"The Walkers experimented upon one another," said Kate. "You may have lived a long life, but you and all the rest discovered most of your knowledge by accident. You stole it from the souls of others as they died. Some of you murdered to keep your secrets or to cover up your mistakes, but if you all knew so much about the veil, you would not be trapped on the wrong side of death, holding on to lives that should have ended long ago. The Walkers did not even exist until the bonemen's time, so do not pretend that this is your city. I understand that you are trapped, but you do not represent all the souls here. You only serve yourself."

"You do not know anything," said Dalliah.

"I know that you did not have to help the bonemen repair the veil the first time it began to fall. You could have ended it then, but you didn't. You had already lost your soul by that time. You could have let the veil fall and claimed your spirit back centuries ago. Instead you fixed the veil the only way you could. Why wait until now to change your mind?"

Dalliah looked up at the surrounding souls. There was no reason to lie, so she answered honestly. "I was naive," she said. "The bonemen came to me for help. I helped them. I did not have the same sense of conscience that they held at the time.

They never forgave me for what I made them do. The ones who survived could not overcome the grief of turning against their own people, and when the High Council claimed Fume as its capital, the bonemen refused to fight. Those who lived through the wardens' attack abandoned their work and fell back into the edges of ordinary life. I have paid the price for what I did then, but none of it would have been necessary if the veil had not been tested to its very limit. That is something you would need to ask your ancestors about. Having their souls bound to a tower, gradually being forgotten by their own blood, does not even begin to compare with the world that I have seen. It is time one of the Winters family realized what true suffering is like."

The ground shook violently. Two skulls tumbled from the upper reaches of the walls and smashed to dust between Kate and Dalliah.

"This is where it will happen," said Dalliah. "The veil will fall here. I have seen it. You cannot prevent it."

Kate had been given plenty of time to consider what she was going to do in that tower during her journey there, but now that the moment had come to announce her decision the words were harder to say than she had expected.

"Why would I want to prevent it?" She was surprised by the steadiness of her voice. "I am a Winters. These souls are my family. This is my cause now."

She stepped onto the spirit wheel, and the central tile rocked slightly beneath her boots. When she walked into that tower, she had known she would never leave it. The need to be there was too strong. She did not know what Dalliah had "seen," but she knew her only defense was to take control. Silas had once told her that intention was everything when dealing with the veil. If Dalliah forced her to manipulate it against her will, her connection would be erratic and weak. She had to step forward. She had to face whatever was to come with a clear mind, to retain as much influence over it as possible.

Her eyes blackened as she stood on the wheel. She could already feel her soul ebbing away, thread by thread. It was like falling asleep, only instead of exhaustion her body felt as if it were sinking into icy water, numbing her senses from her toes to the tips of her fingers. The outer tiles flushed a deep dark red, and the souls around her dimmed to barely the faintest glow. Dalliah looked on, surprised. She had not expected Kate to participate willingly.

"The city is under attack," she said, excitement shining in her deathly eyes. "The blood of battle will draw the veil even closer."

"I know what to do," said Kate.

"This is the final wheel to break. The bonemen and I *prevented* the veil from falling five hundred years ago. There is no way to know what will happen when it truly does fall."

"Then we should get on with it," said Kate, "and find out."

She made sure her feet were firmly upon the central tile. Her mind was racing, warning her that it was not too late. She could still run. She could take her chances and break free from the fear that Dalliah might actually be right about the course of her life.

Kate did not believe in destiny. As she stood there, surrounded by souls that had once shared her blood, all she believed in was chaos. No one could predict the path her life would take. Nothing was that simple or that cruel. People were free to make their own choices and react to events in their own way; otherwise what was the point in life? So long as the veil was in turmoil, everything was under threat. This was her only chance to stop Dalliah from damaging the fragile balance that had existed across Albion for centuries. It was her only chance to put right what her ancestors had got so terribly wrong.

"I'm ready," she said.

Dalliah opened her bag of papers and pulled out a cloth-wrapped package. It was the package the disguised Blackwatch agent had given her at the eastern gate, and inside it was a blade that Kate had seen before, a sharp dagger made of pure green glass. The same blade Da'ru Marr had used on the Night of Souls. The memory of that night haunted Kate as the glass glimmered in the spirit light.

"I gave this to Da'ru when she first began to serve me," said Dalliah. "I thought she would be standing here with me tonight. Your presence is far more than I had hoped for."

"The veil obviously does not get everything right," said Kate.

Dalliah let the bitterness pass. "Your blood alone will not be enough for this wheel," she said, standing at the edge of the tiles, holding the blade in her right hand. "The process requires a living soul, a powerful soul, to focus the veil's collapse, right here in this room. For that to happen, your body must die."

"I know," said Kate. "Do it."

She looked into Dalliah's eyes and saw a flicker of hesitation. Dalliah was about to conduct the ultimate experiment. She was preparing to tear apart the threads of the veil and expose the whole of Albion to its secrets, and she had no idea what to expect. Dalliah had lived her life with complete confidence in the veil's predictions, but in that moment Kate saw that she had doubts. This was her final chance to regain her soul. If it failed, she would have nothing. She would be forced to live on, without hope. Kate's blood would either set her free or condemn her. All she had to do was strike.

"Kate!"

Kate looked away from Dalliah's blade and saw Artemis standing hunched in the doorway. His clothes were tinged with frost where they had been soaked and frozen by the night air. He was leaning heavily on a stick and holding a book at his side.

"Don't do this, Kate." Artemis was out of breath, but he was strong enough to cross the tower floor and tall enough to stand beside Dalliah eye to eye. "Not her," he said to Dalliah. "It doesn't have to be her."

Dalliah assessed the shabby-looking intruder carefully. "You are the uncle," she said.

"Artemis Winters, yes. It doesn't have to be her." He held the book up, and Kate saw that it was *Wintercraft*, dry and untouched by the water that should have ruined it. "She is not the book bearer," said Artemis. "I am."

Any hesitation Dalliah might have felt filtered away as she smiled at the man.

"This is not her job," he said slowly. "She has to survive."

"You are not one of us," said Dalliah, checking his eyes for any sign of the Skill.

"No. But I am a Winters. Kate's blood is my blood. She has risked too much for me. I should be the one standing there."

"You are not what I need," said Dalliah.

"Please! Listen to me. I know what you are. I know you have a connection to something I can never understand, but I have tried to protect Kate all her life. I have made bad choices. I have put her in danger, and this . . ."—he held *Wintercraft* in front of him as if its pages were on fire—"this has led her here, to this place. To this—this shrine to everything that should have long been forgotten. This is my burden, not hers. That blade is mine."

Kate stepped off the circle and placed herself between Artemis and Dalliah. "No," she said firmly. "I know what I'm doing."

"I watched the wardens attack the bookshop the night

they took your parents away," said Artemis. "I left you hiding in the cellar—a five-year-old!—and I ran. I ran when I could have helped them. I *should* have helped them. I should have been there for our family. I won't leave you now."

"That was years ago," said Kate. "It doesn't matter now."

"And when the Skilled wanted to lock you away, I said nothing. I let them do it, Kate, and I'm sorry. I didn't know what else to do. Let me do this for you. I know this is right."

"How touching," said Dalliah.

Kate had not heard Dalliah move, but she was already behind Artemis. In one long horrifying second, Kate realized that something terrible had happened.

Artemis dropped his stick and grabbed Kate's arm as his face began to fall. Kate managed to hold his weight until his knees buckled. Dalliah stepped back and beads of blood trailed along the floor from the green glass blade.

"I'm sorry," said Artemis, the words catching in his throat.

Kate reached out to the healing energies of the veil to help him but found only emptiness. The influence of Dalliah and the vicious souls within the tower prevented the veil from answering her.

"Help him!" she shouted, partly to Dalliah and partly to her ancestors, who were watching impassively as Dalliah claimed another Winters life. "He's not one of the Skilled. He doesn't believe in *any* of this."

"He does now," said Dalliah.

The souls of Kate's family were whispering around her, distracting her, calling Artemis's spirit into their stony prison. Kate tried desperately to stop the bleeding, but the wound was too deep. He had lost too much blood, and she could feel the final fluttering beats of his dying heart as he lay on his side with *Wintercraft* still in his hand.

There was no way to help him, no way to stop the horror that Dalliah had caused. Artemis's blood seeped into the cracks in the spirit wheel as Kate rested his head on her lap, clutching him gently as his soul lifted away.

"Any Winters blood can open the wheel," said Dalliah, holding the still-dripping dagger at her side. "Now you will do as you promised and finish this." She leaned down and dragged Kate up by her hair and forced her onto the spirit wheel. "Your family has sacrificed one to finish their work; they will gladly sacrifice another."

Kate searched for Artemis's spirit among the others, but there was no way to know where it had gone. She could feel his blood winding beneath the stones, burning through the connection between the soul in the wheel and the binding that kept it in place. Tendrils of shadow reached upward, darkening and choking the wheel beneath her and forcing Kate to step back.

The Winters spirits watched in silence.

The black was drawing in.

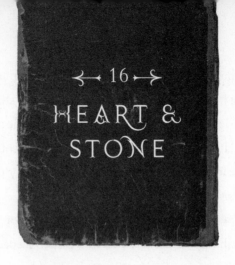

16
HEART & STONE

"And the last wheel shall be broken," said Dalliah, quietly reciting memorized words out loud. "Winters blood shall stain the stones and the veil will crack. Thunder will call across the wild lands. The dead shall walk free, and the lost shall find their way. The eyes of the living will open. The worlds of soul and bone shall become one."

Kate felt numb. She looked down at Artemis's body. "Please," she whispered to him, "please don't go."

The destructive energy of the black spread around the spirit wheel, rising up to claim the soul that was sealed inside. Kate's senses deadened as it emerged. Everything sounded hollow; her sight became blurred. The black smoke swirled around the outer tiles of the wheel, absorbing sound and light, reflecting nothing but emptiness back into the living world. But instead of sinking away when it was done, the cloud lingered. The soul was resisting.

Dalliah swept her coattails behind her and knelt down over the wheel. "This is no time for your family to be stubborn," she said. "The last soul must die!" She pulled Kate down and pressed her hand into the center of the wheel, but nothing changed.

"You killed Artemis for nothing," said Kate, backing away.

"His blood is strong, but his soul was weak," said Dalliah. "He gave his own life willingly."

Kate's grief twisted into rage. "He is dead because of you. You can help me bring him back!"

"I won't do that."

"And I can't let you do this," said Kate.

"You are here to serve me," said Dalliah, standing up, unconcerned by Kate's defiance. "Your family and I have an understanding. Your spirit will free us all. I will get what I want."

"These souls are not my family," said Kate. "Families do not abandon one another when they are needed most. They fight for one another. They protect one another. They do not do *this*." She pointed down at Artemis's body. "They may have once shared my blood, but they are *not* my family."

"Be careful, Kate. The dead are listening."

The force of Kate's anger seeped into the walls. Her spirit reached out and connected suddenly with the soul that was still inside the wheel. An image flickered behind her eyes, and she saw through the spirit's eyes at the moment of its physical death. *He was lying on his back with a brown-robed boneman standing over him, and a blade stabbed down into his chest as a younger Dalliah looked on. Kate felt the man's spirit sink into the wheel, but part of it was torn away. He resisted the full binding and tore his own soul in two, sending half of himself into the stones and half into the purple-covered book that would be carried through his family for generations. The book pulsed with energy as his body died, but no one present had known what he had done.*

Kate let the memory fade and glanced at *Wintercraft*, lying in Artemis's fallen hand. His wrist lay in a pool of blood, and the edges of the book's pages rested in the patch of perfect red, letting it leach slowly into its fibers. Winters blood was the only thing that could affect that book, and its curse was inescapable. Even Artemis, who had shunned the ways of the Skilled all his life, had been claimed by it in the end.

Noticing Kate's interest in *Wintercraft*, Dalliah picked it up and turned it in her hands. "Books can be powerful things," she said. "The dead can speak to us through their pages. We can learn from the successes and failures of the past by reading what has gone before us. Mistakes were made, Kate. I do not deny that. When the Walkers created this book, we could not have known the bloody path our future would take. We gave everything for knowledge. We looked into the darkest places, and some of us did not return; but sacrifice is an essential part of everything we do. The soul is infinitely more precious than physical life. We understood that. Silas Dane understands it, and I believe you are beginning to see the truth as well."

Dalliah's hand glistened with frost as she tapped her fingernails against the cover of the book. Kate now knew that it was far more than just a collection of paper and ink. A soul was alive within its pages. If the energy of the veil could restore a broken body when it was injured, the pages of a spirit-bound book could be protected just as easily.

"Everything here has its part to play," said Dalliah, holding *Wintercraft* out to Kate. "If you had not abandoned this, your uncle would not have been called to bring it here. His death is on your hands, not mine."

Kate took the book and felt the cool touch of the spirit lurking inside. It had protected the book, even after death. It had resisted Dalliah, torn itself in two, and left part of itself to guard the knowledge it had worked for in life. When Kate touched *Wintercraft*, she could feel the soul's presence secretly surrounding her. It had been alone for too long to still hate Dalliah for what she had done. It was a strong and decent soul, very different from the darker shades that lingered within that tower. It had lived long before any of them, and it did not like being in their presence any more than Kate did.

The pages ruffled in her hands, and Kate felt the trapped soul's need to reconnect with the half of itself that was still bound within the spirit wheel.

"The spirit in these stones must be destroyed," said Dalliah. "If you want your uncle to enter death and find peace, you will help me now. Death cannot gather souls when the veil is unstable. Destroy this spirit. Call down the veil and embrace the legacy your family left behind."

Kate could not leave Artemis trapped forever within the veil. His final act had been to bring the book to her. There had to have been a reason. She could not turn away from him when he had given so much to try to save her, but she did not know what to do. The souls in the tower fell silent, except for one. The soul that had been divided between the book and the wheel passed a clear thought, like a whisper in her mind.

"What is broken can be rebuilt. The old must fall for the new to rise."

At those words, all of Kate's doubts fell away. She made her decision, walked over to the spirit wheel, and placed the book carefully on the central stone. The silver studs on its cover nestled perfectly within secret hollows in the snowflake carving, the blood in the pages linked with the blood in the wheel, and the silver-leafed title blazed out as light burned up through the darkness.

The tower rumbled against the force of the soul stirring within it. The book fluttered open as the spirit from the wheel pulled back from the darkness like a silvery thread, weaving into the paper and becoming whole again. The ink glistened with new life as the soul's presence restored the book, replenishing its luster and absorbing Artemis's blood. The pages ruffled softly together, and the book fell closed, its silver studs glinting with the spark of hidden life.

Dalliah watched the pages settle. The last spirit wheel was empty. The final barrier holding the veil back had fallen.

"We are ready," she said, listening to something deep within the veil that Kate could not hear. "He is coming."

"Who?" asked Kate.

"A man who has a country to save."

Dalliah's eyes hardened, and her smile was tinged with malice. She grabbed Kate by the throat, returned her to the wheel, and kicked *Wintercraft* to one side. "Silas Dane is here, in the city," she said. "He has seen enemies close in upon the gates and shades emerging within the streets. He knows I cannot bring down the veil alone, yet he has witnessed pieces of it chipping away as you walk free. Each time a soul was torn from these wheels, he has felt the veil's heart pull a little more strongly at his soul. Who do you believe he blames for that?"

Kate could not answer. Dalliah was holding her so tightly she could barely breathe.

"Silas has seen the horrors that hide within the dark," said Dalliah. "He will not let his country share the nightmares that he has known. He believes he can stop everything, right here, with one simple act. Silas is a formidable soldier, Kate, and he has identified a new enemy. *You.*"

Outside in the city, Silas approached the group of smaller towers surrounding the Winters tower and entered the first one he reached. He forced the door inward and climbed the inner staircase with the crossbow slung behind him. The windows offered plenty of vantage points, and he climbed until he was in a position with a clear sight down onto Dalliah and Kate.

He pulled the window open and slid the crossbow from his shoulder, focusing upon what he had to do. He held the bolt between his teeth, pointed the weapon to the floor, and drew the bowstring back into position. He slid the bolt smoothly into place, then raised the weapon and steadied it, directing it straight through the open window and down through a narrow archway of stained glass set into the side of the Winters tower.

As one of the High Council's men he had performed the duty of execution many times. He cleared his mind of every distraction. Nothing mattered except for the task ahead. His hands were as steady as stone, his heart silent, his lungs still. His finger touched the trigger. Waiting.

At last, Dalliah released Kate and took a step back, leaving the girl exposed. Silas saw his opportunity. His sight was practiced and perfect. His finger squeezed. The crossbow sprang. The bolt soared.

Silas watched it fly. Its silver point glinted as it flew, and in that second Kate looked up. Her eyes met Silas's, and the blood connection between them burned strongly in his veins. He felt the raw grief within her: the memory of witnessing Artemis's death and anger toward the woman who had claimed his life. He saw the bright light of Kate's soul, wounded but strong.

The bolt punched powerfully through the arched window, shattered the glass, and plunged into Kate's chest. She stood her ground for a few slow moments, closing her eyes against the pain, and Silas stumbled back in surprise. He had felt the bolt strike her body as if it were piercing his own. His hand went to his chest and came away wet. His slow heart beat twice, spilling blood from an impossible wound.

The connection between him and Kate was enough to tear Silas's skin in sympathy with the girl whose soul was even closer to him than his own, and his consciousness saw the world through Kate's eyes as her body crumpled down onto the spirit wheel. Dalliah was standing over her, waiting for the last of her life to slip away. She looked up to the window from which Silas had taken his shot, and when she looked back at Kate's face, Dalliah saw something very different living behind the eyes.

"Silas," she said. "You arrived later than I expected. I almost had to kill the girl myself." She placed her hand upon Kate's chest, and Silas felt her manipulating the veil as he pulled away.

He severed his link with Kate and opened his own eyes to find himself hunched upon the tower's upper floor, struggling to control the bleeding from his chest. It did not make sense. His link to the veil should have stronger than ever in the city, yet now the link that had sustained his body for twelve years was tearing it apart.

He made his way to the stairs and half walked, half stumbled down them and drew his sword before stepping out into the night air. If his body was refusing to heal itself, there was a good chance that Dalliah's body would be weakened, too. Whatever fate awaited him, he could not let that opportunity pass.

He slumped against the lower door as Kate's pain stabbed deep into his heart. The veil was in turmoil. The barrier between the half-life and the living world was the thinnest it had ever been, but it was still there. He pushed himself out into the open air and staggered across to the Winters tower. Dalliah would not win this battle. As long as the veil held, he still had time to finish it.

Kate could feel the bolt embedded inside her, but it felt cold and distant. Her thoughts passed between the different levels of the veil as she lay there, bleeding and still.

Dalliah had moved away, but Kate's body would not move. Kate focused instead upon the spirit lights in the tower, upon her ancestors and the spirit wheel, illuminated by the energy of her own soul threading down through it like a needle piercing into the black.

"It is not easy to cheat fate," said Dalliah. She kicked Kate's arm, sending pain exploding from the wound in her chest and making her cry out. "It is better not to try." She looked up through the broken tower and watched the sky with eager eyes, waiting for the first tear to open and the first soul to fall. "Your spirit has pierced the world," she said. "Albion will soon see the truth it has denied for too long."

The darkness of the veil's depths throbbed within the spirit wheel. Kate could feel it dragging at her consciousness, stripping away pieces of her soul. She had already glimpsed the terrors that waited there. She had seen the horrors that drove the Skilled into madness and tormented Silas every day of his life. She knew what was waiting for her.

"*Artemis!*" Kate called out in desperation. She thought she was shouting, but while her throat barely made a sound, her cry carried powerfully across the veil.

Every living person within Fume's walls felt Kate's cry as a wave of sadness. Edgar's brother shivered in his hiding place out in the street, still waiting for Artemis, who would never return, as Silas pressed a bloodied hand against the tower door.

Fume echoed with torment. The shades screamed with Kate, filling the air with the anguish of the dead and the dying. Soldiers fought and died by the eastern gate. Wardens fell in defense of the city, and every soul lost became caught in the space between worlds. The current of death was nowhere to be seen. Those who were not fighting stopped what they were doing and looked toward the tower. Even people without Skill could see a change in the atmosphere surrounding it. Drifting souls were pressing against the air of the city, like smoke upon glass.

Kate's spirit bled down into the stones, down into the warm earth beneath, spreading through the city until she could feel every soul, every heartbeat, and every shade within the walls. Streets away, laid out, dying in the cold, Edgar stopped fighting against the shades. He let them sink into his body, freeing his soul, as he concentrated only upon Kate, helping her to hold on.

Kate felt as if she were standing upon a huge, tightly bound drum. Every movement in the city created vibrations that translated into a map within her mind. She could see the Continental army along the eastern wall and frightened residents fleeing the city any way they could find. She could feel stirrings toward the very center of the city, where the veil was shifting unexpectedly above the city square.

A small group of the Skilled was there, attempting to manipulate the enormous listening circle that Kate had used on the Night of Souls, but they were taking too long. They knew they were standing at the center of the largest listening circle to have been activated in living memory, and Kate could feel their fear, both of the circle itself and of being on the surface, exposed to the open sky. Most of them were kneeling on the ground, translating the symbols on the stones, trying to decipher their meaning, and searching for the way to unlock the circle's power. They had not been working for very long when the circle thrummed with energy beneath them, and the symbols began to glow.

"Stop," said Greta immediately. "Stop now. We are too late."

The magistrate glanced across the city square, watching the symbols burst into life. So long as they remained in the center of the circle, they should have been safe, but there was no guarantee that it would behave in the same way as any of the circles she had used in her time. This one was being worked by spirit, not by the living. If she and the rest of the Skilled crossed it, the risk of being captured in its influence was too great.

"Sit down!" she ordered, as veins of white energy scribbled across the empty square. "Stay away from the edges. Stay as low as you can."

The Skilled held on to one another and with a sound like screeching metal, energy thrust suddenly out of the stones, whipping their hair and toppling the rows of wooden seats around the square like falling dominoes. The Skilled screamed, and the great doors opening into the amphitheater slammed back with a thunderous clap. Shades were pressing in all around them, waiting for the first tear to form within the graveyard city. Greta was the only one who dared stand and watch, and she whispered to herself, "What have we done?"

← 17 →
REMEMBRANCE

Kate lay upon the floor of the tower, silent and still. She had lost too much of herself. Her mind had been drawn too deeply into the black, and she could hear nothing except her own thoughts becoming stranger and more foreign to her by the moment. Memories of her past tangled together. Dreams, fears, and nightmares all fought for dominance within her mind, until it was hard to make sense of what was real and what was imaginary.

Wintercraft was still beside her. The book that had seemed so cold and dangerous to her such a short time ago now felt like the only thing she could be sure of in the world. It felt solid and safe. She rested her fingers against it and felt the gentle touch of an unseen hand upon hers. Artemis was still there. She could smell the familiar scent of ink and paper that always clung to his skin and feel the touch of rough fingertips that had been worn by years of working with old books. She could sense his spirit as strongly as if he were sitting right beside her.

"I'm sorry," she said.

Artemis did not answer her, but the longer his hand remained on hers, the clearer his spirit became. He carried Kate's thoughts into a memory held within the city, taking her consciousness toward a patch of bare land some distance away from the main streets. Old headstones were left broken upon forgotten graves that were choked with ivy, and trails of bramble thorns scratched across the ground. Any paths in that place had long been claimed by the creeping hand of nature, and she found Artemis standing close to two dark figures that were leaning over a grave and digging down into the earth beneath.

He looked as real to her as he had in life, but he was not wearing the torn traveling clothes his body had died in. He was wearing his favorite ink-stained trousers and a woolen jacket that had always been too big for him. It was the Artemis she had known before the wardens and *Wintercraft* had come into their lives, the Artemis who had tried to keep her safe and trusted her to help keep him safe in return. There were times when they had been happy in the bookshop, and throughout all of them he had looked exactly as he did at that moment.

The headstone serving the open grave was cracked and broken in the living world, but Kate could see it intact and new within the veil as time overlapped to let her see what Artemis needed her to see. Kate recognized the people they were looking at: the councilwoman Da'ru Marr and Kalen, the warden whose soul she had seen wandering Fume's streets. They were talking to each other and looking into the grave, pulling shovelfuls of soil up from the earth.

"This is where *Wintercraft* used to be hidden," said Artemis. "It lay in that grave for more a century until that woman dragged it up. She should have left it to rot. It should have been forgotten." For once Artemis was in no mood to temper his words. "According to family history, your great-grandfather recognized the danger of *Wintercraft* and wanted to rid himself of it. He tried to sell it; but it always returned to the family, and its pages could not be destroyed. Having it buried with him was the only way to be sure it stayed out of reach. My father told me stories about our family and the book, but the half-life is not my world. I don't understand it the way you do."

Artemis's eyes looked troubled but determined. "I wanted to keep you from all of this," he said. "I thought *Wintercraft* was just a book, but I had heard enough to know that just holding it ruined lives." He looked over to the figures that were lifting the book from the open grave. "It infects people. It makes them forget about what is important, but I never forgot. Some of our family wanted to follow the Skilled path; others turned away from it. I should not have tried to make that choice for you."

The vision of Da'ru and Kalen faded as they left their

tools behind and carried the book back into the city. Artemis moved toward the grave and read the inscription written upon the stone:

In Death—Wisdom.
In Remembrance—Life.

"I didn't realize how important these words were," he said, as Kate looked down into a shattered coffin where the bones of one of her ancestors lay exposed to the sky. "This saying was one of your great-grandfather's favorites. He always said: 'Death is the final question. It is the one piece of knowledge that no one can possess until it is his time, and remembrance is how we keep the past alive.' Even though people leave us, we remember them, share their stories, and trust they are at peace."

Kate moved as close to Artemis as she dared, and his spirit slid its hand into hers. She felt the warmth of his touch, and sadness swept through her.

"Everything you have suffered began in this place," said Artemis. "If I had done things differently . . . if I had brought you here and let you live with the Skilled from the start, you might have been safe."

"You did the right thing," said Kate, finally trusting herself to find her voice and keep it steady. "I wouldn't have changed anything."

The gravestone crumbled back to its ruined state as Artemis let the memory fall away. "I am proud of you, Kate," he said. "Something has changed inside you. You can feel it. You are not going to die today."

Kate thought that Artemis must not have seen the bolt strike or realized how perilously close to death she was herself. Her heart fell still.

"You are not finished," said Artemis, holding her hand a little tighter. "You have to survive. This place . . . it lets you see what you didn't see in life. None of this has happened by accident. You and the warden. That is what you need to concentrate on now. He is the answer."

"Silas?" Kate's hand went to her chest, where the crossbow had struck.

"I know he did this to you, but there is more at stake here than you've seen. The veil will not stop here in the city. The Skilled remained in Fume for a reason. There must be people here who can balance the worlds of the living and the dead. Fume cannot function without them. Most of the Skilled are dead, Kate. Without enough of them to channel the veil, no one will survive. Thousands of lives will end before their time. There will be nothing here for the Continent to claim. Albion will be a country of ghosts."

"I can't stop it," said Kate. "Not now."

"You have to take control of this, Kate. You have people who care for you. Trust them. There have been cruel people within our family. Too much blood has been spilled for too long, but not all of our family are as bad as history makes us seem. Trust yourself to do what is right."

Kate could feel the veil pulling her in. She wanted to be free from the worry and the pain, and she did not want to be left alone. "Take me with you," she said. "I don't want to stay here."

Artemis pulled her into a hug, and she felt the soft delicacy of his spirit pressing against her own. "This is my time," he said. "You are not finished here yet."

Kate sank against her uncle, her heart burdened with grief.

"Don't worry about me," said Artemis. "So long as you are safe, that is all that matters. Think of Edgar now. He's a good soul. He will help you find your way home."

Kate felt Edgar's presence close by, and something tugged inside her. Artemis's spirit fell away, her vision of the city died, and her consciousness returned to her body in the tower. "No," she whispered, opening her eyes under the gaze of the skulls and plunging back into the pain of a body on the very edge of death. She tried desperately to reconnect with Artemis. She tried to touch his body, but her fingertips could barely reach his hand.

"*Good-bye, Kate.*" Artemis's voice spread like a whisper beside her, and she let her hand fall weakly to the floor.

"Good-bye," she said, her voice a trembling sigh breathed through tears.

She lay still. The last of her family was gone. Silas had

turned against her, and her connection to Edgar was only bringing him pain. All Dalliah wanted was to use her as she had used everyone else in her life. Everything that was precious to her was being taken away. She could simply lie there and give in, or she could fight. All her sorrow, all her pain crystallized inside her. She could not let Dalliah have what she wanted. Artemis was right. She had to take control.

Every movement set spikes of agony streaking through her body, but she managed to wrap her fingers around the bolt, and before she could think about what she was doing, she pulled hard. Torturing pain ripped within her as the silver-tipped weapon slid cleanly from her chest. She screamed out loud. The shaft of the weapon was slick with blood. She could feel the wound oozing beneath her coat, and her body shivered with cold as the blood seeped away.

She should have been dead. The pain alone should have been enough to finish her as soon as the bolt hit, but something else was happening. Her blood felt like rivers of ice, and as she looked up at Dalliah, she felt Silas standing outside the door. She sensed him there, even before the door swung back and he burst inside.

Dalliah turned on him the moment he entered the tower. "Do you still doubt me, Silas?" she demanded. "Look at her! A Winters soul has been broken upon the final wheel. This is the start of everything I have seen and that which is yet to be."

"No," said Silas, pointing his sword at Kate. "She should

be dead. Death should have taken her."

"What good would she be to me then?" said Dalliah. "The girl is already bound to you by blood. You have done half of my work for me, Silas. She is not the only one skilled in Wintercraft." Dalliah held out a hand that was dusted with veil frost. "I needed to break her spirit, but your actions have given her soul the final push. I thought you might enjoy that. Welcome to a new world."

Kate breathed in a shallow breath, and her soul sank through the wheel, anchoring down into the very heart of the veil. She felt its darkness creep across her mind, but she refused to let it engulf her. She closed her thoughts to it in the way she would try to forget a nightmare, never letting them dwell too long upon the torment that was waiting to snatch her away.

Dalliah lifted her hand, and veil energy spread swiftly through Kate's body as Dalliah's use of Wintercraft took hold. Kate's torn muscles fused, her skin healed, and the blood around the wound dried to a fine dust, preserving her physical life for the small part of her soul that had not yet been claimed by the black.

Silas was used to the veil's influence and barely noticed his own wound knitting together at the same time. He watched Kate struggle to her feet. Her silver-tinged eyes were flooded with the milky gray of death, but her face was still and focused. Dalliah had expected her to act as a passive channel when the veil fell, but she had not seen Kate work the veil before. Silas had witnessed Kate's abilities firsthand, and she was not an energy source to be bled. She was instinctive and strong. Her connection with the veil was more powerful than Dalliah could have anticipated. Dalliah had underestimated exactly what Kate could do.

Kate focused the energy around her and concentrated upon the spirit wheel beneath her feet. The Winters soul that had been trapped there for centuries had been enough to hold back the veil's fall; now she would see if another could bring it back under control.

The skulls in the walls began to tremble. The outer tiles of the spirit wheel began to turn, and the Winters tower rocked suddenly within its foundations. The floor cracked and shuddered. The air felt dense and heavy, like the calm before a thunderstorm. Vibrations pulsed like a heart underground and the surface of the Sunken Lake rippled outward, sending thin waves lapping in circles toward its shore.

A high-pitched noise sounded from the distant walls of the city and spread inward, growing louder all the time, until it reached the tower in one almighty eruption of sound. The tower broadcast it like an explosion, as if someone had struck the center of the city with a weight, sending a deep wave of noise sounding through the streets.

Silas and Dalliah were slammed back against the wall as energy exploded up through the floor. The wheel flared with light, its central tile burning brightly with the carved symbol of the Winters family, and the walls tore into darkness, letting the half-life spill across the living world. Swaths of spirits moved across Fume like smoke rolling across the ground, but these were not only the surface-dwelling souls of the restless dead. Among them moved the dark and tortured souls claimed by the black. They all were rising up, and they were listening to Kate.

The veil's collapse spread like a sheet of ice splintering into pieces across Albion's sky. Energy splintered like violet lightning, snatching at the clouds and splaying out across the city's memorial towers. Fume was the central point of impact, opening the eyes of the living to the world of spirit that existed barely a breath from their own. As the veil fell there, so it followed right across the whole of Albion, crackling out to the far shores of the Taegar Sea and the slopes of distant mountains in the High North.

In Kate's hometown of Morvane, shades that had wandered the streets unseen now moved clearly in the darkness, drawing shouts of fear from early traders working in the market square. Alleyways and roads flickered with spirit lights wrapped in shadow, and souls that would normally be glimpsed only as movement out of the corner of a person's eye now stood like fragile reflections caught in the firelight. People locked themselves in their houses and peered out at the moving figures from behind the safety of their windows, but the dead had no interest in the living. Phantoms moved swiftly through the streets, swept out past the town's barricaded walls, and traveled away into the far-reaching wilds, heading for Fume.

Kate was drawing in all those who had died in torment, attracting thousands of wraithlike souls from the forests, down the rivers, and across forgotten valleys. The shades passed through areas of Albion not seen by human eyes for generations, racing toward the graveyard city like an avalanche speeding across the ground. Firelit villages were swamped by swaths of gray and black. Animals stamped, howled, and bayed. Lanterns blew out, and those who had been woken by the noise looked out their doors to witness a wall of souls rumbling through their streets. The cries of the dead were heard by everyone, either awake or in dreams, as lost ancestors finally made their presence known.

Baltin's group of Skilled crossed Fume and arrived at the Museum of History just before the listening circle in the main hall activated with more power than ever before. His people were running up the museum's outer steps, heading for the door, when spirit energy rang through the walls, shattering the green windows and sending the Skilled stumbling back down to the street below. Baltin shouted a warning and pulled his coat over his face as souls poured out of the museum like a swarm of bees, surging out over their heads and spilling between the houses.

"Don't look at them!" he shouted. "Let them go. Let them go!"

Deep beneath their feet, tomb caverns rumbled into life, raining fragments of earth down from their vast ceilings. Old bones rattled in their graves and wild souls swept along the winding understreets, gathering together and rushing upward, breaking for the surface and the open air.

"It worked," Dalliah said quietly.

Kate concentrated everything she had upon the city, but the veil was too strong for her to rein it in completely. Buildings fractured, and entire streets became veined with cracks as huge sections of the city split apart. People closest to the city square ran for their lives as houses crumbled and chasms opened up within the roads. The memorial towers stood strong. The ancient buildings, gargoyles, and statues that had been placed to honor the dead remained untouched by the devastation, but anything new, anything that had been built solely for the comfort of the living, came crashing down.

Dalliah stared upward, and Silas flung open the tower door to watch as havoc spread across the city. Fume was shrouded in devastation. Dirt choked the air, and rubble covered everything in a mantle of gray. The upper levels of the City Below were bathed in moonlight as the streets built over them collapsed, revealing passageways, carriage tracks, and sunken houses that had not been seen since the bonemen's time. Fleeing people were caked in stone dust, and some of them had to hold one another back, preventing themselves from falling into the yawning chasms opening around them.

Fume was shaking off the legacy of the living. As the surface of the city was scratched away, more listening circles, buried and forgotten, were revealed within the streets: expanses of intricately carved stone—some many meters across—that had once been integral to the city's work with the dead. No one had seen those circles work for hundreds of years. Now, under Kate's control, every one of them thundered into life, casting off layers of earth that had covered all of them for too long. Entire streets shuddered, their cobbles crackling as ancient symbols beneath them flared with light.

"Kate," Silas shouted above the noise, "stop this."

Kate was not listening. Her soul was injecting fire into Fume's heart. The ancient city had come alive.

As the energy of the circles spread, shades bled up from every stone, every building, and every grave in the city. Kate's influence spread into every inch of the embattled streets, drawing out souls that had been trapped within the circles and setting them free.

Dalliah pressed her back against the tower wall, waiting for her own soul to emerge. "This is what we have been waiting for, Silas!" she shouted. "You will thank me for what I have done."

With the veil gone, the half-life smothered the living world. All across Albion, nightmares walked free. Souls from the deepest depths, altered forever by centuries lost in horror and insanity, screamed in the light of the living world, while souls from the upper levels congregated wherever there were people, seeking out loved ones they had lost and sweeping over buildings like ghostly spiders wrapping webs around flies. Albion became twisted by the memories of the restless dead as the past mingled with the present. There was no way to escape it. The shades' fear, emptiness, and regret were infectious. Soon people could not even be sure their thoughts were their own.

Inside Fume's city square, the Skilled cried out in fright when the ground beneath them started to turn. Stone grated against stone, and ancient grooves appeared where none had been visible before. Struggling to hide her own fears, Greta tried to keep everyone calm. It was there, standing beneath a lightning-lit sky, that she realized the extent of her ignorance about things she thought she understood. She had learned just enough of the ways of the Skilled to serve among them, but she had not prepared herself for anything like this. None of the Skilled had dared look deep enough into the veil to understand the extremes they might one day have to face. For all her past confidence, Greta and the others found themselves completely at the mercy of the circle's intent.

The magistrate knelt down to touch one of the tiny trails of carved words that snaked across the ground. Her fingers sparked with energy, and she recognized Kate's influence at once. A flash of Kate's spiritual suffering burned through her for barely an instant, but that brief connection was enough to make her regret everything she had said or done to the Winters girl. Greta did not know anyone who could have survived even seconds in the place where Kate's soul now lay without losing every sense of who she was.

That tiny glimpse into Kate's spirit willed Greta to look in the direction of the distant Winters tower, and what she saw made her stand up and stare, not certain if what she was seeing was real or not.

"Stay away from the carvings," she said, absently gesturing for the other Skilled to stand beside her. "And look up."

Thin threads of cloud were gathering above the city and winding together in a tight spiral tinged with violet and silver. The sky was caught in a clockwise twist of clouds and shadows that stretched for miles around.

"What is that?" asked one of the older boys.

"A maelstrom of souls," said Greta. "I never thought I would see one in my lifetime."

"What do we do?"

The boy's words were snatched away by a screeching rush of air that powered over the city square, and a wall of racing souls rolled over their heads, blotting out the light. The circle protected the Skilled from their influence, but being so close to so many unleashed shades was a truly breathtaking experience.

"This is not our fight," said Greta, as the souls surged eastward. "Not anymore."

⟵ 18 ⟶
MAELSTROM

The Continental army had come prepared for a fast, decisive attack upon Albion's capital. It had been given information confirming that the bulk of Albion's army was out of practical reach and had expected to take the core consignment of wardens guarding the city by surprise.

Councilman Gorrett's information had proved invaluable in planning and executing the attack, but everything depended upon the battle's reaching a quick resolution with dead wardens, frightened people, and a captured High Council to deliver to the leaders across the sea. The army had aimed to overwhelm Fume's defenses within a few hours. What it got was a well-trained city defense and wardens who were confident enough to mount coordinated counterattacks, forcing their enemy into a siege.

Breaching the walls had gone smoothly as planned, but once inside, the Continental soldiers were at an immediate disadvantage. The wardens were working with firsthand knowledge of the streets beyond the gates and were employing deadly strategies that their informant in the council had known nothing about. The attacking army's leaders were losing more men than they would have liked to ambushes, traps, and concealed bowmen positioned in places not even the sharpest spotter could detect.

Fume had been an all-or-nothing target, victory or death. No one had expected the odds to tip so drastically against them.

Runners were ordered to scout the perimeter of the city for concealed entrances, but not one of them came back. There were reports of ghostly figures standing upon the walls, causing bowmen to waste arrows firing at something only to watch their target disappear moments later. Some soldiers reported the earth trembling beneath them, but the army's leaders put such stories down to fatigue, and to the natural superstitions that any stranger might hold when approaching a city that held the bulk of its country's dead.

The people of the Continent knew to respect those who had died before them. Stories of Fume's restless souls had spread far beyond Albion's borders and even beyond the Continent itself. It was no surprise that the soldiers thought they were seeing things, but every mistake they made was a mistake too many. Every false story and misplaced arrow had the potential to cost a man's life, so when one of the spotters turned sickly pale beside him, the lead general thought he was about to have his time wasted once again.

The spotter did not speak. He did not need to speak. He pointed to the walls of the city, and neither he nor his leader had words for what they could see.

At first, the general thought they were birds, but birds did not skim rooftops in such a fluid way, washing around the towers like liquid, blackening everything they covered as they surged toward the city gate. They had to be weapons, but they were like nothing he had ever encountered before. The closer it came, the more detail he could see, and, despite his skepticism, he could have sworn that there were eyes within the darkness. Were they animals of some kind?

"Orders, sir?"

A voice close beside him reminded him that he had a job to do.

What orders could he give? There was nothing to fight, and retreat was not an option; but they had come too far to waste their chance now.

"Maintain positions!"

As the Continental army pressed on, a cold blue light pierced through the dark to the north of Fume. The Night Train had been recalled from its work in the High North, arriving late but carrying enough wardens to reinforce Fume's city guards. The huge engine sped along its tracks, pushing its mighty grille ahead of it as the patched metal carriages creaked and shook. The cages and chains slung within them should have been filled with people taken from distant towns, but the order to return had arrived before the wardens had had time to begin their gruesome work.

The train's twisted iron skeleton came within sight of the city. The wheels thundered beneath a vast head of steam, traveling at full speed, pushing their way under a row of tall stone arches that marked the engine's approach into Fume. The city's burning fires illuminated the night sky in patches beyond them, and the wardens on board prepared their weapons, ready to defend their capital the moment the train pulled into its station.

That moment did not come.

The Continental general studied the choking darkness that was spreading over the city. It could have been a trick designed to prey upon the superstitions of the invaders, but inside the walls, Fume's wardens were taken equally by surprise as a wave of shades plunged through the streets. In fear, men swiped at the shades as they would at human foes, but their blades sliced through nothing but empty air, forcing the wardens to retreat. A host of shades swarmed past their forward ranks and raged against the outer walls, making Fume echo with a sound like thunder as a maelstrom of spirits slammed into stone.

The impact created a shock wave that punched through the veil and across the living world. Horses fled. Siege weapons splintered. Soldiers outside Fume's walls were knocked off their feet and left dazed and disoriented. Even far-flung towns and settlements felt the vibration strongly enough to make horses worry in their stables and wake people from their sleep.

The grizzled driver of the Night Train was the only one on board who witnessed the shades overwhelming Fume's upper rooftops and smashing into the walls, before two stone arches crumpled across the track ahead of him. Eyes white with terror, he heaved on the brake lever, and when the shock wave struck the mighty engine, the effect was unstoppable and devastating.

The force of the half-life slammed through the iron frame, forcing the wheels to lock and spark as the great train encountered the veil's resistance. Carriages jolted and rocked until one near the center of the train lost its grip and jackknifed from the tracks. It crashed straight into one of the arches, sending stones crushing down on top of its open roof, dragging the carriages behind it out to the left, and wrenching the forward engine as it struggled to slow down.

The engine screamed and smashed into the rubble of the first fallen arch. Stones scattered. Sparks poured from the wheels like liquid fire, and the sharp blue light that had been a source of terror across Albion for so long flickered and died. The furnace scattered coals into the driver's cab in a haze of hot sparks, illuminating his face for one last time, and the huge wheels tore, screeching, from the track. Momentum carried it some way across uneven ground, dragged the crippled engine onto its side, and sent it scraping forward through the frozen earth.

Wardens on board who had survived the initial devastation clung to the inside of the carriages as they ripped a scar across the ground, churning the earth until the engine scraped deeply enough to counter its own power, and the Night Train's final journey came to a slow, twisted, and juddering halt.

The train lay crooked and buckled within a choking fog of smoke and dirt. Some of the central carriages had collapsed completely into a mangled mass of metal, and steam hissed from the engine's broken mechanical veins. Bloodied limbs reached from the wreckage as the wardens clambered out to pull injured officers to safety and gather in the shadow of the ruined train. The driver had not survived to tell his story, so the only cause the wardens suspected was enemy sabotage.

Those officers who were strong enough to walk regrouped to lead their horses from the stable car near the back of the wreckage. The animals' breaths clouded the cold air. Their eyes were wide, but they all were highly trained battle horses and quick to settle under their handlers' protection once immediate danger had passed.

With no information about the city's situation other than the evidence of their eyes, the wardens mounted the horses, abandoned the Night Train and rode hard toward the point of battle, oblivious to the chaos raging within Fume's walls.

***

In the middle of a shattered street, far from the fighting, Edgar breathed in a shuddering breath. He could not sense Kate anymore. The shades that had surrounded him lifted away, drawn up into the mass of souls churning overhead. He stayed perfectly still, but his eyes scrutinized every shadow, every movement, every breeze. The sudden emptiness of his own mind was disorienting. Once he was absolutely certain he was alone, he allowed his fingers to wrap around the cobbles, desperate to feel the solidness of the living world.

The vibrations of the devastated city echoed through his palms, but he could not hear anything beyond the pulse of his heartbeat in his ears. His skull rang with pressure, and his body felt as if it had been thrown down a flight of stairs. He pulled on the cobbles and sat up, trying to get his bearings. The shades had left him, but they had left parts of their memories behind. Edgar could remember places he had never seen and people he had never known. He tried to stand but soon regretted it and sat back down.

Silas's crow swooped closer and stared at him from an extinguished lamppost. If a bird could smile, Edgar was sure that the feathered beast would have a mocking grin on its face, and that made him even more determined to stand. He needed a plan, but so far it was a struggle to think beyond his next breath. He did not want to look at the souls overhead.

He decided to give the cobbles another try, but something made him stop partway to his knees. A pair of eyes was watching him from inside one of the buildings: deep yellow eyes that were neither shade nor human. Knowing he did not have the strength to run, Edgar stayed still. The eyes moved out into the street together with a long, pointed muzzle, alert ears, and powerful paws that carried a large animal with ease.

Edgar was crouching only a few feet away from a wolf, a lean, muscular beast that walked out onto the cobbles and stared straight at him. Edgar had heard of wolves being kept by a few people in the City Below, but he had never seen one so close before. It looked away, uninterested in him, before a second wolf followed behind it, tailed closely by a man who was thin and reedy, like a plant left to grow in the dark.

"All right, boys," he said. "Let's see what we've got."

The building they were emerging from was the same one Edgar and Silas had used to leave the understreets, and where the wolves and their master had stepped out, a trail of people followed. Every one of them immediately looked up at the sky, mesmerized by the shades that had gathered there. Some of them had to be pushed out of the way by others emerging behind them, until at least a hundred people had joined Edgar in the street.

Edgar spotted a man and a woman he had seen in Feldeep Prison walking with the group nearest him, ready to fight, but they all took their time standing outside the building and breathing open air for the first time in years. It was only when one of the wolves padded close to Edgar, making him scramble weakly backward, that anyone noticed he was there.

"Looks like an injured one," said the wolf handler. "Where'd they go, lad? Where's the enemy?"

Edgar tried to speak, but his throat felt burned and dry. He pointed instead, raising a finger roughly to the east.

"Right, then." The man whistled his wolves to his side and led his group of underground militia in the direction Edgar had indicated.

For people living on the surface, it was easy to forget the hordes that made their homes in the tunnels beneath the city. Once they had been convinced that their land was under threat, many of them had proved willing to set aside their distrust of the people above and rally around the word of a man whose name had once brought fear. Silas's call to arms had spread among the people of the City Below, and they were answering. Hundreds of men and women were rising up through hidden passageways all over the city, armed with any weapons they could find, ready to protect their homes.

Fume's abandoned streets filled again, its ravaged roads walked by forgotten citizens who had already proved themselves to be fighters and survivors. If the city needed help, they were more than ready to provide it. Where only a few weeks ago rich residents had paraded through the streets in celebration of the Night of Souls, dressed in masks and finery, a very different parade now wound its way east. The people of the understreets had spent their lives close to silence, and they moved through the burning city in the same way, undetected by the enemy. They had lived in the dark for so long that being out in the open made them stick near to one another, missing the encompassing closeness of the tunnel walls.

Most of the shades were now concentrated around the eastern wall, where the next wave of enemy soldiers was thinking twice before moving in. Any invaders already inside the city were being forced to flee for their lives as shades closed in around them, swamping their minds with memories so terrifying they drove many of them back to the gate.

Soon only the hardened officers of the Blackwatch remained fighting. Teams of them had infiltrated farther into the city than the ordinary soldiers, and they were moving stealthily behind the main action, picking off wardens one by one. They did not allow the shades to influence their minds. The Blackwatch had helped Dalliah gain entry to the city, and she had been more than willing to share what tactical knowledge she could in return. She had taught the agents how to seal their minds from the shades' influence, so that when the souls passed by, the Blackwatch were not distracted.

Each enemy that fell to a Blackwatch blade reduced the barrier between their leaders and success. Gradually the Blackwatch threatened to turn the tide against the wardens, regaining ground that its routed army had lost. Dalliah had prepared those Blackwatch officers for everything— everything except the people of the City Below.

The first sight the wolf handler had of his enemy was a Blackwatch agent dragging his blade out of a dead warden's chest. The handler walked along with his wolves prowling beside him, and when the agent looked up, arrows from two hidden archers hit him squarely in the chest. More agents fell the same way, as the tunnel dwellers moved in unpredictable groups, finishing the work the shades had already begun.

The Continental soldiers were paralyzed by their fear of the unknown. No orders could persuade them to attack walls that were teeming with the souls of the dead, and the residents they had expected to be weak and defenseless were quickly gathering a body count as high as any of the wardens'. The wardens from the Night Train moved in and took the Continent's right flank by surprise. Most of them were already bloodied and injured from the crash, so it was hard for the enemy to know if they were true men or phantoms riding across the land. The deadliness of their arrows and blades soon dispelled any doubt.

Fume was not an old relic of a broken civilization that was ripe for capture. It was what many of the Continent's people feared it to be. A place of secrets. A bastion of power.

"Pull back!" The general leading the invasion shouted the one order that every one of his men was happy to obey.

Every man in Continental uniform withdrew from Fume's walls, following the bolted horses back into the wilds, retreating toward the distant coast and the country the army had failed. They left their dead and their pride behind, and none who had witnessed the events of that day ever wanted to see those walls again.

The people of the City Below stood side by side with the wardens who had protected the walls, but none of them celebrated their victory. The shades were still present, creeping around them like predators. Every living eye watched the souls warily as the survivors tended their injured and counted their dead, but none of them felt that success was truly theirs. The fallen veil gave the towers a living presence, and every street followed a slightly different course from the one it had had the day before. Fume's people felt like insects riding on the back of a giant beast that could brush them off at any time with a flick of its tail. They had repelled one threat, but a greater menace still had to make its intentions known.

The people of the City Below, already standing under an unfamiliar sky, felt unwelcome in the streets, and the wardens, once masters over every movement and every life within Fume's walls, felt powerless for the first time. Albion was in the grip of something against which it had no defense. A cloud was still hanging over the stricken capital. The night was far from over.

Kate remained on the spirit wheel in the Winters tower, watching the resurgence of the listening circles through the eyes of the half-life. Fume's builders had known how to work with the veil. They had raised the city in an age when the body and the spirit were seen as two separate aspects of one whole. It was a time before superstition, before people learned to close their minds to the truth that surrounded them. Fume belonged to the dead. They were what mattered there. All they truly needed was for the living to stay out of their way.

The shades settled above the city in one vast spiraling mass, but not all the souls there had been trapped against their will. Some truly had been in Fume since long before the first stone had been laid, and they would remain there long after the last stone crumbled to dust. These old souls stood peacefully around the waters of the Sunken Lake, gathered together near the few lanterns still burning in the streets, and congregated in the oldest shallow graveyards, where large patches of earth were still exposed. They were the city's oldest guardians, overlooked by history and time, whose own stories reached back further than the written word. Silent watchers who were willing to watch history unfold.

Kate felt the attention of those souls upon her, as well as the potent presence of the Winters spirit that was bound inside the book, waiting for her to finish what she had begun.

Silas turned away from the ruined city and looked back at Kate, who met his eyes with a look that was as dangerous as it was dark. She reached out a hand, inviting him to the spirit wheel, but he did not move. He feared that she had become corrupted by the veil. Dalliah's work had already torn her soul away. There was no way to know how much of Kate was left within the shell that she had left behind.

Kate kept her hand out. Her skin was white with frost, and despite his fears, Silas was sure he could see a glimmer of something familiar in her eyes. The blood connection between them had been overwhelmed by the turmoil overtaking the veil, but it was still there. Silas had to choose between standing and watching Fume fall to ruins around him or taking the hand of a powerful young woman whom he had just attempted to kill. His need to take action overrode everything else. He crossed the room in four strides. Kate clasped his hand in hers, their energies became intertwined, and their slowed hearts began to beat as one.

Kate could read the lives of all the souls around her. She could have shared their stories and recounted their deaths. Such powerful connections had overwhelmed her in the past, but she had learned how to listen to the shades without sacrificing her own mind, and just like Silas and his crow, she found she could communicate with them without words.

Kate called out across the half-life, bringing the shades together in a common purpose. One vital aspect had been missing from the manifestation of the half-life on its way across Albion. It was the one thing that the lost souls sought more than any other, and Kate had the ability to give it to them. She was a student of *Wintercraft*. She had read from the book, learned from it. Now she was putting her knowledge to a dangerous test. Kate called out. The shades echoed her thoughts. And death answered.

A rush of warm air spread around the tower as a glistening shimmer of silver rose from the floor, filling the room and snaking upward like a creature winding its way up into the light. The current of death formed the same way as a bolt of lightning, pulling energy up from the earth and down from the atmosphere, before enveloping the tower in a glow of energy that could be seen for miles around.

The current flowed up past Kate's body and trailed out through the ruined roof. She could feel every soul that was attracted to its power, and the joy they all shared as they passed eagerly into its surging tide. Standing within the current was like becoming weightless. The pressure of her physical body faded away, her mind became unburdened by the troubles of physical life, and she wanted more than anything to let go and allow the current to take her.

But death had not come for Kate. Unable to claim souls that were anchored so deeply into the black, it washed straight past her and Silas. Kate felt death drift past her rather than accept her, and she felt forgotten. Thousands of shades funneled along the current, streaming smoothly around her and Silas as though touching them might poison death against them, too.

Dalliah retreated from the wild current in fear and pressed her back against the skulls lined up around the wall. She did not need to fear death, but Silas knew why she was so desperate to stay away from its influence. If her soul did return to her, the current would draw her in instantly. If she wanted to survive beyond that night, Dalliah could not risk being caught within the current when she and her soul were reunited.

With Kate's hand clutched around his, Silas was standing right in the center of the current. If Dalliah's plan worked, Silas would be drawn into death just as easily if he did not move from its path. It would be the release he had been waiting for, the culmination of twelve years of waiting, searching, and studying the veil, when all he had wanted was to be free of it. He had hunted death, tempted it, and coveted it. He had secretly envied every soul he sent into it at the end of his blade. Now it was his turn.

Dalliah no longer looked as confident about her plan as before. Silas could see her desperation to regain what she had lost and the fear that her one chance to find it might be snatched away from her forever. The veil was out of her control, but she clutched in hope to the words and images it had shared with her. Dalliah whispered those words to herself, taking comfort from them, and Silas heard her voice clearly through the current.

"The lost will find their way," she said. "To all those waiting, an end shall come."

Beyond the constant stream of souls rushing past him and Kate, Silas sensed two heavier presences that were moving across the city more slowly than the rest. That tower held the only three people in history whose souls had been torn away, and now two of them were coming back.

Two shades pressed in through the tower walls and slowly circled the floor. Dalliah's soul moved in and lingered beside her. With her spirit so close, Silas could see her true nature. He saw the twisted wisp of a soul that existed inside her and the ravages of hundreds of years of repairs that the veil had done to her physical body.

Dalliah's experiments into the veil had not only involved unwilling souls. She had also experimented on herself by drawing blood, trying to take her own life, and attempting to bind various souls to her own fragmented existence. Every wound had left a silver mark where the veil had healed it. Every drop of blood that had been restored to her was less potent than the blood she had lost. Her body was a patchwork of so many repairs that there was barely anything left that had not been touched by the veil. It was like looking at a living version of the Night Train. Dalliah had been patched and strengthened for so long that she was only a shadow of the living woman she had once been.

Dalliah's soul sank into her body like a healing breath. Her skin flushed with life, and she embraced the moment, becoming restored, rejuvenated, and complete once again. Her eyes were no longer lifeless gray but flooded by the darkness carried by the Skilled, with only an edge of blue hinting at what they might once have been. "It worked," she said quietly as her soul settled, barely believing it herself.

Silas did not want to care about Dalliah Grey's fate. Her entire life had brought torment to the people who crossed her path, but her twisted spirit and the ruin that was her physical body told their own terrible story. Dalliah had suffered far more than any soul she had encountered. She had destroyed many lives, but she had been driven by the most primal need a living creature could possess: to become whole again. Now that she had finally found herself, Silas could not begrudge her that release. He could not imagine spending five centuries the way she had: living every day working toward an impossible goal yet giving every part of herself completely to it. It had taken centuries, but her visions had been accurate. The veil had shown her the truth.

Dalliah held her hand out into the current of death, mesmerized by its call, then withdrew it just as quickly. She had seen her situation through the eyes of only one part of her soul for a long time. Now that she was restored, she could see both sides of her suffering. Her spirit did not want to live on. It was tired and worn from its time in the black. It was ready for death. Dalliah had not anticipated that, and she looked into the current, confused by her sudden compulsion to step into its flow.

"Do it," said Silas. "Do not waste your chance."

Dalliah looked at him, torn between the years that she had left to live and the call of the unknown realm that she should have entered centuries ago.

Silas saw her body relax as she made her choice. Dalliah could not resist the call any longer. She took one step forward and allowed her full spirit to rise up and be accepted by the current. She smiled as her soul joined the others. Her body fell gently to the floor, and she was gone.

Standing there, just a few feet from the lifeless body of a woman who should not have been able to die, Silas recognized the finality of what was about to happen. To not live, to be gone, forever, from the world, was a far more daunting prospect than he had imagined.

He could feel the welcome draft of his own soul preparing

to settle into his bones, and he saw the imminence of his own end. The deep survival instinct that he had neglected for so long stirred within him, beginning to reassert itself.

Kate held his hand a little tighter. "This is what you wanted," she said as his spirit closed in, almost within reach. "Was it worth it?"

Kate's words immediately claimed Silas's attention. When he looked at her now, he saw a broken soul. Dalliah would never have found her if Silas had not gone looking for someone Skilled enough to undo what had been done to him. Da'ru Marr had torn his soul to help further Dalliah's plan; now his actions had led Kate Winters to the same fate. Kate's spirit was not returning to her. She was going to be left behind, suffering as he had suffered for far too long. Silas had paid the price for Dalliah's freedom, and now Kate would pay the price for his.

Silas felt his spirit press against his body and filter through his skin, imbuing his blood and his bones with the spark of life that he had been denied. His lungs breathed freely. He could feel his pulse pumping through his muscles, and the current of death brushed like soft feathers against his skin, stimulating every follicle like fine prickles of lightning.

Kate let go of his hand as his eyes darkened. His gray pupils filtered back to their natural black, and his irises flooded with a deep iridescent blue. It was a perfect feeling. As his soul returned to him, it felt impossible to ever be without it again, but Kate's question still burned in his mind. Was it worth it?

Dalliah had learned to live with the harm she had caused in the name of her own self-interest. Every cost was worth the success of her final goal. Silas had once believed that any price would be a fair one to reclaim what he had lost.

Silas was the one who had ordered the wardens to Kate's hometown before the Night of Souls. He had exposed her mind to parts of the veil she was not ready to see and placed her and everyone she cared about in danger. The last of her family was dead because of the world Silas had pulled Kate into. Because of him, even the Skilled had turned against her, Blackwatch agents had dragged her across the sea, and one of the most dangerous women in Albion had stolen her memories and forced her to send trapped souls into the emptiness of the black. Silas's crossbow bolt had ended Kate's old life. His blood link with her had bound her soul into the depths of the veil, and now, despite all that, she was allowing him to pass over into death.

Silas had been a poison in Kate's life. His search for peace had been no better than Dalliah's. He had left behind his own trail of destruction. He had set fires within many lives. He would not leave and let them burn.

He could feel his soul settling into his blood. Death began to wrap its welcoming light around him, but despite its gentle touch, its calm, and its beauty, he resisted. He moved in front of Kate, pressed his hands to the sides of her head, and fixed his eyes upon hers, exactly as he had done the first time he had helped her see beyond the veil. The blood connection between them flared, and he could feel the tether holding Kate in the black. Silas could share her thoughts, running through the pages of *Wintercraft*, recalling everything she had to do to restore the veil.

"It needs a soul," said Silas, repeating what he had seen upon the remembered pages. "The veil needs an anchor. One soul, bound between the depths and the living world. Give it mine."

"No," said Kate, forcing Silas from her mind. "It is already done."

"This is not your burden!" said Silas. "This is my fight, not yours."

"You made this my fight! You tried to kill me, Silas. You have what you wanted. Death is here for you. Why don't you just go?"

Kate's eyes were filled with anger but tempered by tears for the things she had seen. Silas knew that she was using everything she had just to keep the veil under control. Arguing with him was a distraction. He could not let her risk herself anymore.

"You have already given me everything I need," he said. "I thought my future belonged here, but I was wrong. I am not ready for death. Use me. Offer my soul to the veil. It is the right thing to do, Kate. The best thing. I choose this. Let me fight."

Kate was not ready to let Silas cast his spirit away. He was not a naturally Skilled soul. He might not even be able to take her place within the dark. She could not take that chance. Artemis had given his life for her, Edgar had risked his soul, and even the shades in the city had slowed their passing into death, just to help her defend it. She would not risk everything their sacrifices had earned to save her own life, but during the brief moment that she spent considering it, Silas took his chance.

His soul overwhelmed her. She felt his spirit flood through her, chilling her blood and spreading down into the stone circle beneath them. There, in the black, their torn souls wound together, side by side, until Silas's spirit moved deeper into the darkness, severing the connection between Kate and the veil and sending her soul rushing back into her physical body. Kate breathed in a full living breath and pushed Silas away. Silas fell back, unconscious, to the tower floor, and the current of death dissipated, leaving the tower room still and dark.

Fume plunged into darkness. Shades still left inside the city faded from sight as the veil swept up like an invisible curtain, blotting out the half-life all across Albion from the mountains to the surrounding seas. The Winters souls within the tower screeched with frustration until their voices died. Kate did not listen to them. Her soul had been released from the torment of the black, but grief chilled her heart in its place.

She knelt by Artemis's side, part of her still holding out hope he might breathe again as she tried calling his spirit back to life one last time. Even with the veil restored, he did not answer. He had already entered death. He was at peace.

Kate stood up and picked up Silas's fallen sword. Holding it with the point pressing down into the floor, she stood over him as he opened his eyes. Silas looked up along the blade, his eyes touched by their old, cold gray.

"You brought me back," said Kate. "You could have freed yourself, but you brought me back."

Silas stood up. Kate held the handle of his sword out to him, and he slid it back into its sheath. "Some things are more important than one man," he said.

"I don't know how you survive in that place," said Kate. "Every day. Every second. The fear, the pain, and the dark. Why didn't you go?"

"My mistakes sent you into the black, but I have lived with the veil long enough to know its ways. I can endure it. I have already taken too much from you. This burden is mine. You have your own to bear."

She took hold of his hand. "Thank you," she said sincerely. "I will never forget what you did, and I will find a way to help you. One day you will be free."

Silas covered Kate's hand with his, then slowly pulled away. Few people had ever touched Silas's hands in friendship. Kate's hands were the delicate tools of a healer, born to restore life, while his were stained with the blood of too many deaths: trained to hold a blade and nothing more.

Silas walked back to the tower door, and as the veil strengthened once again across Albion, he and Kate could feel the energies of the people in the city shifting from fear into relief.

"The people need something more than the High Council's empty words to carry them out of this night," he said. "If you are willing, there is one last enemy for us to face today."

20

RUIN

Edgar pushed his way through devastated streets touched by the growing light of dawn, heading for the place where he had last sensed Kate while the veil was down. The road was riddled with cracks. The front walls of the houses he passed had been buckled by the force of the ground shivering beneath them, but the most ancient buildings among them stood strong and proud. As newer buildings had collapsed, old ones had been revealed like whales breaking water, standing upon stepped stone platforms that had once raised them above the level of the understreets.

Any shades that remained in the city had faded from view, and any memories imprinted upon it by the veil were swiftly undone. Towers that had appeared intact returned to their aged state. Ruined houses leaned against each other across the streets, and underground pipes spewed water as the night's true devastation revealed itself. The movement of the spirit wheels had peeled back layers of recent history and let the past dominate once again.

Edgar stumbled past ancient places that had long been forgotten. He picked his way along paths that had once been pristine but were now scattered with building debris, people's belongings, and gaping trenches where old paths had been uncovered underneath.

He coughed in the stone dust, placing his hands on fallen walls as he clambered across them, making his way toward the Winters tower. Silas's crow flapped nearby, keeping a close eye upon him as it moved effortlessly through the air, and as Edgar passed into a street relatively untouched by the devastation, a voice called out to him.

"Ed?"

Tom peered out of his hiding place inside the doorway of an empty house. Edgar took a moment to recognize his face and then hurried to meet him. He picked his protesting brother up in his arms, not caring about his aching muscles or Tom's futile demands to be put down, scuffed his brother's hair, and hugged him tight.

"I didn't know if I would ever see you again," he said, finally releasing him. "What are you doing here? Where's Artemis?"

"He went up there," said Tom, pointing up to the Winters tower. "I can't feel him anymore, Ed."

"He'll be fine," said Edgar. "He's stronger than he looks." He saw the doubt in his brother's eyes.

"Death came to the tower," Tom said. "It took him. I felt it."

Edgar rested his hands on Tom's shoulders. "Artemis kept an eye on you for me," he said. "Whatever happened, he kept you safe."

"I don't need looking after," said Tom. "You're the one who looks like he's been trampled by a pack of dogs."

"Fair enough." Edgar could not deny that Tom was in a far better state than he was. He smiled and looked out into the street, where people who had hidden from the night's madness were gradually emerging from their houses.

They were the servants the rich had left behind, the unseen undercurrent that made the city run smoothly. Most of them had been stolen from their homes by wardens years ago, but as soon as Fume was under threat their masters had abandoned them. Now they walked through the streets, many of them holding makeshift weapons to defend themselves, as curiosity drew them toward the place where the events of that night had begun.

In the east, the smoldering remains of enemy weapons were still embedded in the rooftops and walls of buildings the Continental army had attacked. Edgar could hear people shouting to one another as they tried to reconnect in the dark. Just visible by the light of the fires reaching from their tower tops, the High Council chambers burned in a searing crown of flames.

The crow wandered along the spine of a nearby roof, then swooped to the ground and strutted up the steep hill that led to the tower, sensing its master close by.

"Where's that bird going?" asked Tom.

"Can you see Kate in the veil?" Edgar asked. "Or Silas? Are they still in the tower?"

"I can't work it like that," said Tom. "It comes and goes."

Edgar weighed up the dangers of leaving Tom near a crowd of confused servants or taking him up to the tower, before accepting that his brother could obviously take care of himself. He followed the crow up to the tower steps, where the door was already ajar. There were voices inside, and he recognized Kate's at once.

Looking through the crack in the door, he could see a woman's body slumped in the shadows. He signaled to Tom to stay outside and then burst in, ready to face whatever was inside.

"Kate?" He recognized the fallen woman as Dalliah and saw Kate standing in the center of the room with Artemis's body behind her. "What happened?" His voice was so small and his expression so devastated that Kate crossed the tower and threw her arms around him, holding him close.

"Artemis is gone," she said. "He's—" She could not say the word, but Edgar could see for himself. He didn't know what to say.

"I felt you in the veil," said Kate, lifting her cheek from the dirt of his jacket. "You were there. You stayed with me."

Edgar held her gently. Terrified by how close he had come to losing her, not wanting to let her go, he felt his eyes prick with tears. He did not care what else had happened to him in the last few days. His brother and Kate had survived Albion's most terrifying night. That was good enough for him.

Silas stepped silently outside, and his crow hopped up onto his shoulder. When Kate and Edgar followed him, Kate saw the stripped-back streets with her own eyes for the first time. Dalliah Grey had brought her twisted vision of the future to Fume. So much destruction, so many lives threatened, all for the sake of one soul.

Kate was not the same girl she had been just a few weeks before. Her spirit was strong, but it had been changed. There was something not quite right about the way her senses now saw the world. Colors were different—everything looked paler than before—and the healing the veil had worked on her body did not feel as strong as she would have liked. Her breaths were shallow, and her heartbeat was slower than it should have been.

She still held *Wintercraft* in her hand, and she could feel the spirit within it as strongly as she could feel Edgar's spirit beside her. Artemis had had no choice but to let himself pass safely into death, but one of her ancestors had never left her side. The silver-eyed man was still with her, his energy alive within the pages. She would protect his book. She would keep his spirit safe.

"This wasn't supposed to happen," said Kate. "People are afraid."

"Fires can be put out," said Silas. "Buildings can be repaired. Sometimes the greatest struggle is simply to survive. These people still have their lives. They will be thankful for that."

The group walked down into the street to where a small crowd was gathering. The people parted as Silas walked straight through it.

"You still have a job to do here, Mr. Rill," he called back to Edgar. "We require transportation. The fastest you can find."

"Where are we going?" asked Edgar.

Silas turned, the stare in his eyes matching that of his crow. "To make history," he said.

The servants on the streets were happy to help them find what they needed. Under Edgar's watchful eye, two black horses were brought forward and harnessed to an old taxi carriage bearing the High Council's blue seal on the door.

Silas had not found the peace he was hoping for, but his experience within the veil had offered him a new path. The High Council did not deserve the service of people who had been stolen from their homes, the assistance of the people of the City Below, or the loyalty of the wardens who had given their lives in its name. The city had fallen in the most destructive and devastating way Silas could have imagined, but those who had risen to protect it had earned their place within its streets.

The High Council would never recognize what those people had done. In time, it would cast them out and call back the cowards who had fled. It would reshape that night's victory as one that belonged to its members, not to the men and women who had faced two terrifying incursions into their ordinary lives.

Silas had not left orders for the wardens to imprison the councilmen. They would be allowed to go about their normal duties, and in the aftermath of such a serious crisis Silas knew where they would be. It was time for Albion to hear something other than their usual platitudes and lies. The government of the High Council would not survive that day. It was time for his country to change.

He climbed into the driver's seat and took the carriage reins while Kate, Tom, and Edgar seated themselves in the back. Silas spoke out, addressing the people around him. "These streets are yours," he said. "What has happened here will bring great change to Albion. No one will hold you against your will again."

A loud cheer rang out from the district surrounding the Sunken Lake. The old shades standing around its edges settled back into their watchful role, and word soon spread across the city that Silas Dane and Kate Winters had been instrumental in stopping the nightmare that had gripped its people and its dead.

As Silas drove the carriage over ruined roads and between cracked buildings, he passed people crying in the streets, comforting and helping one another. Some of them had gathered in nervous groups and were looking down at the exposed listening circles. Most of the circles appeared dormant, but Silas could see Kate's energy still rippling through their carved words. For all his efforts, Kate's soul had not separated completely from the half-life. His spirit had taken her place within the black, but she was still bound to the veil in her own way. The edges of her soul were touched by the upper reaches, and while Silas did not know what effect that connection would have upon her, so long as she was spared the torment of the depths he considered his soul a welcome exchange.

The carriage wheels crushed wanted posters bearing Silas's and Kate's faces into the ground and rattled loudly over fallen chunks of stone. As they approached the surrounding walls of the city square, Silas saw that the grand black carriages belonging to the High Council were already outside, and all the doors leading into the amphitheater were open. People were filtering into the square, drawn in by news that the councilmen were going to address the people. Silas, Kate, Edgar, and Tom climbed from the carriage and joined others who wanted to hear what the High Council had to say.

Most of the wooden seats had been pulled back into position; but the square was barely half full, and all nearby eyes turned as people felt Silas's cold presence. They knew him at once, and many of them recognized Kate's face from the council's posters. Kate's group took their seats as whispers of their arrival rippled around the square.

A councilman was already standing at a podium in the middle of the central circle, speaking about the battle that had taken place at the city walls. It was the outspoken councilman, the one Silas had sent to witness Edwin Gorrett's interrogation. He looked smaller now and far less confident. His voice was wavering as he relayed edited versions of the wardens' reports to the people around him. With the rich residents gone, the only people left to hear him were the traders and the servants and a good number of representatives from the City Below who had decided to stay to make their own voices heard.

". . . and we should be thankful"—the councilman continued—"for all the, er, all the efforts that the esteemed High Council has made in order to bring this conflict to its final resolution."

"Liar!"

"The council are cowards!"

"We want the truth!"

Dissent rang from the crowd. No one wanted to hear the council's lies. They had been emboldened by their experiences. They had looked into the eyes of death, had fought against their Continental enemies, and had won. The wardens guarding the councilmen looked on silently, refusing to quiet the crowd, but some of them were standing guard over a small group of prisoners who had been caught within the square. Greta and her group of the Skilled were kneeling on the central circle with their hands bound behind their backs. Prisoners of the council.

"And we must—we must all remember the brave actions of the late councilman Edwin Gorrett," said the councilman, wincing even as he spoke the name, "without whose selfless actions and sacrifice Fume would, er, Fume would not have survived this day."

"Go back to your chambers!"

"Hide like rats!"

"Where is Silas Dane? Let him speak!"

The crowd fell silent. No one knew who had spoken those last words, but enough of them had noticed that Silas was present in the crowd. Many looked around nervously, unsure whether the former warden and current "traitor" to Albion could truly have been instrumental in helping them that night.

Silas did not move, but some members of the crowd did not give up.

"How exactly *did* the High Council save the city?" demanded someone near the front. "How did *they* calm the souls of our ancestors? How did they drive back the enemy and clear the sky of souls?"

Unsure how to respond, the councilman lowered his head. "Clearly . . . ," he said after some thought. "Clearly the attacks upon the city were severe enough to cause certain residents to see things that, perhaps, might not truly have been present."

"Are you calling *us* liars?"

"I know what I saw!"

"The Skilled were right!"

The councilman raised his hands in peace. "No one can be certain of what has happened here tonight. All we can do is set the city back to rights. There is a lot to do before our residents can return."

"We *are* residents!"

"The capital must return to its usual operations," said the councilman, "as a symbol of endurance and perseverance across Albion. We will make sure our lands are clear of the Continental invaders. Let our enemies see that we can rebuild Fume to be as grand as it was before."

More shouts rose up. Silas's name was mentioned again, and Kate heard her own name caught in the clamor of the crowd's cries. One woman stepped forward from the front row to challenge the councilman, and the wardens did not move to stop her. She was wearing a neat red dress, one that Kate had seen just a few days before, during her time in the City Below, and she spoke with the authority of a leader.

"My name is Laina," she said. "I represent a community that lives deep beneath these streets. Silas Dane sent messengers to my caverns, seeking help for this city. His words brought my people here. We rose up while many of your own people ran—and you expect the city to return to the place of privilege, greed, and lies that it was before?"

"We do, of course, appreciate the underdwellers' assistance, but—"

"My people spilled enemy blood alongside your own men and women," said Laina. "We came here in trust. The City Below has its own concerns. Our tunnels are being flooded, and our people have been forced to hide from the wardens, who should serve *every* citizen of Albion, not just those with the coins to pay for it. You have proved that Fume cannot stand alone. None of us can stand alone. We are stronger together. Silas Dane saw that. You branded him a traitor, yet I hear his name being called out as a hero."

"Silas Dane has been acting upon the word of the High Council in this matter," said the councilman.

"I find that very hard to believe," said Laina. "And where is Kate Winters? The girl you also named a traitor? I have heard her name spoken here tonight. I want to hear from people who did not hide behind the blades of their protectors. You are wasting your breath offering lies that no one believes. Step aside, and let those who actually know something speak."

21
A
NEW PATH

The crowd called for Silas. The councilman protested, but his words were drowned out by the shouts. The last time Kate had stood in that square with a gathering so loud, many of them had been urging Da'ru Marr to spill her uncle Artemis's blood, but this was a very different crowd.

Silas waited in his seat. He would not be drawn out so easily. He left time for the High Council to consider the gravity of what was happening around it. Soon the councilman was forced to retreat to his seat like a mouse to its hole, and Laina waited patiently beside the podium for Silas and Kate to answer her call. When Silas stood up, a few people applauded, but most stared in silence as he stood upon the city square's steps, as strong and immovable as any of Fume's statues, and let Kate walk down the steps in front of him.

Every warden present stood to attention as Kate and Silas approached. Silas's last memories of that place were of battling wardens who had attacked him at Da'ru Marr's command. Their welcome this time could not have been more different, but he did not take his place upon the podium; he stood beside it instead. He was a soldier, not a politician. He did not need to play the High Council's game. All he had to do was change the rules.

"The blood has not yet dried upon our blades," he said, letting his voice resound from the distant walls of the square. "And already the High Council is lying to us. Tonight Albion was shown a glimpse of a secret it has not seen for centuries. The veil has been hidden from you for too long. These men have used knowledge of it as bait to taunt the Continental leaders into more violent and daring attacks, culminating in the battle we have witnessed today. They will lie to you. They will encourage you to follow the same path that has always served them well in the past, but they will not serve you as leaders should. Fume was never meant for us. We have built upon land set aside for the dead, and those foundations crumbled tonight.

"The souls you have seen are not your enemies. They are our ancestors. They are the ones who helped us save this city. They, along with the warden officers who stood against the enemies' blades, the people of the City Below who answered our call, and the bravery of every one of you who remained here, standing at their side. Even the prisoners of Feldeep, who owe this country nothing but hatred, have played their part. Edwin Gorrett is not a hero. He supplied information to the enemy because he was one of them. He is a Blackwatch agent, who managed to deceive us all. But these people . . ." Silas walked over to the group of Skilled kneeling on the floor. "They have done nothing against you. They came here to help you. They should not be imprisoned for their trouble. Each of us has suffered in our own way, and some of us have done things of which we are not proud." He cast a pointed look at Greta. "We will live to be punished by our consciences for that."

He turned to address the High Council directly. "You have murdered this country. Your actions and those of your predecessors have torn it apart. The invaders in our lands are retreating. Fume is burning, and we are still here. Albion is not finished yet, but you are."

He signaled for the wardens to release the Skilled. Their hands were untied, and they stood up, facing a crowd that did not know what to make of them. Most had never encountered any of the Skilled in their lives, but Greta and her group held their heads high, refusing to look vulnerable or weak.

"I am here to call on everyone present today to let this be a new beginning," Silas continued. "We have shown what can be done when we come together. We now know what this city needs. It needs people who are not afraid to do what is right. People like this girl." He pointed to Kate. "Kate Winters has sacrificed far more than any of us to keep Albion safe. She, and people like her, are this city's future. We can rebuild Fume, not for the rich and their opulent lives but in honor of the dead who still exist within these walls. The High Council has led us to this point in our history; now we shall carry ourselves the rest of the way. Albion will be strong again, but it needs better people than these men to lead the way."

None of the High Council spoke. The wardens were no longer under its members' control, and it had no defense against Silas's argument. The crowd was cheering Silas's words. All the councilmen could do was sit and watch everything they had schemed and bribed for be pulled apart with every word that Silas spoke.

"I propose that we create a new council," said Silas, "one whose members truly represent all the people of Albion. Our army should be filled with soldiers who want to defend our country and are trained to defend it, rather than those who are stolen from their homes and sent unprepared to their deaths. This is our chance. Today we can learn from our past and build a new future. I will no longer place my hand and my sword at the will of these men."

He took out his sword, laid it on the ground, and took a step back. "My weapon is yours," he said. "This country is on its knees, but we can restore it again, together. I will fight for you and for Albion. Albion needs you to stand with me."

Someone in the crowd began to applaud, and Kate spotted Edgar standing up in his seat, clapping enthusiastically. Tom stood up beside him, and soon almost everyone in the city square was standing, cheering, celebrating Fume's survival, and sharing the hope that life could be different. The sound carried to the ears of every person and spirit in the city's streets. It rang from the towers and echoed beneath the surface of the Sunken Lake, but no one was there to see the waters of the lake shrink back to their former level. No one witnessed the shades at its edges stepping back into the buildings surrounding it and fading into the ancient walls.

When the noise died down, everyone waited for Silas to speak again. When he did, it was to give one command. "There are fires to put out and buildings to save. Fume has protected us. Let us return the favor."

At those words, people began to leave the square, filled with renewed purpose after the exhausting events of the night. The wardens grouped the disgraced councilmen together, ready to transport them to a safe place until their future was formally decided, and Laina and Greta approached Kate and Silas as the seats around them emptied quickly.

"You may not know me, but I have heard of you," Laina said to Kate, clasping one of Kate's hands between both of her palms. "What has happened here is tragic, but if it allows my people to exist freely with the City Above, I welcome it as an opportunity." She looked directly into Kate's eyes. "I can see that you have suffered. I hope, in time, your burden is lifted from you. Both of you. I hope you will find peace."

"May the same be true for us all," said Greta, her words clipped with impatience.

"I will support your plan for a new council," Laina said to Silas. "But my people cannot remain here until our welcome to the surface is sincere. We have repairs of our own to make. We shall return when we are invited to speak as equals once again. I am sure you understand."

"Of course," said Silas. "Fume is built upon what lies beneath us."

"In more ways than the High Council could appreciate," said Laina. "Let us hope the goodwill between the Above and Below does not die when the sun rises. Many good intentions can wither in the light of day."

She returned to a small group of bloodied guards who were waiting for her, and Kate noticed that Greta's mouth was pinched, as if she were making a great effort not to share what she really thought of the woman.

"In time the tunnels will dry out," said Greta. "The streets will be clear of rubble, and this night will be a story we pass on to our grandchildren; but people will forget. They always forget the warnings of the veil, and we have forgotten how to 'see' the way our ancestors once did. *You* have remembered," she said to Kate. "You have done more in a few weeks than I could ever hope to achieve in my lifetime. I am aware there has been some . . . unpleasantness between us in the past. Distrust has lived on both sides. Perhaps, now, we can begin again."

"I'm not going back to the cavern with you," said Kate, sensing the unspoken point behind Greta's words.

"You belong with us," said Greta. "You can work with us. Perhaps we can teach each other."

"No. I'm not going back there."

"But you will at least stay in the city?"

"As long as the museum is still standing, Kate will always be welcome to stay with me," said Silas.

Greta's brow furrowed. "I have seen what you can do," she said to Kate. "A gift like that should not be wasted. It should be passed on."

"That is for me to decide, not you," said Kate. "If any of the Skilled want to speak to me, they can. But not yet. Not today."

Greta looked sour; yet, she had no choice but to accept Kate's decision. "We will speak again. I may not have your Skill, but I know a veil-touched soul when I see one. I hope it does not lead you down a dark path."

"I think we have already discovered where dark paths can lead," said Silas. "Dalliah Grey's life ended tonight. It is our responsibility to never again walk the path that she chose."

"When you are ready, Kate, the Skilled will welcome you," said Greta. "But I must ask. Do you still have the book?"

Kate felt *Wintercraft* in her pocket and moved unconsciously to keep it out of Greta's reach. "I have it." Kate could not tell if Greta was relieved or disturbed to hear that news, but her answer was enough to make the older woman step back and end their conversation.

"Then I look forward to our future," Greta said curtly. "Let us hope it will be better than our past."

The rest of the Skilled followed Greta into the melting crowd, and as soon as they were out of sight, Kate dared relax a little. "I don't know what to say to them," she admitted. "I don't trust any of them."

"And that is all you need to say," said Silas. "The Skilled will find their own way. This is your life. You do not owe them anything."

As Kate walked back to meet Edgar and Tom at the carriage, Silas stopped to talk to a small group of wardens and give orders for the High Council's detainment. No one watching would have been aware of the torment that still plagued his soul. No one except Kate.

Kate knew the true cost of what Silas had sacrificed for her. She knew the place where his soul was sealed in the cold and the dark, and she could still see a shadow of that suffering within his eyes. Silas had rallied the city when no one else could. He had protected it, even when branded a traitor, and he had given the most precious part of himself to keep its people safe. He had not told the crowd any of that. He was happy to set the wheels of change in action and have others steer it along the way.

As the carriage rattled its way toward the museum

that was Silas's home, Kate could hear the shades of Fume whispering to one another, like wind swirling between the city's ancient stones. She could feel the stirring of dormant life within the trees and the fluttering of birds chased from their roosts, searching for a place to settle upon the rooftops. Even in its darkest day, Albion was filled with life. The air trembled with it. Energy rang from the earth and moved through the smoke: the essence of the living world that no other breathing soul could see.

Kate owed Silas everything. Silas would never see the world the beautiful way she did. He would live an endless life, his soul trapped in the horrors of the black, forever fighting against terror and madness. Only she knew the full truth of what he had given up for her and for Albion, and she would never forget that sacrifice. Kate could feel faint echoes of the torment twisting behind Silas's gray eyes as he drove the horses on. She had glimpsed his true spirit that day. Now it was torn forever. She had left him alone in the dark.

The following weeks and months were set to become defining moments in the course of Albion's history. The country was standing on the brink of a new era, along with all the uncertainty, difficulties, and triumphs that entailed. It had lost an entire day to the timelessness of the veil. To the eyes of anyone beyond the shore, the whole country had fallen still for many hours as its people were overcome by shadows.

The dawn that had broken after the veil's fall was the dawn of a completely new day, but no one would recognize those missing hours for many days to come.

The ancient spirits of Fume would watch the rebuilding, the lower streets would begin to be restored, and damaged towers would be repaired. Funerals would be held for all those who had not survived, including Artemis Winters, whom Kate buried in the same grave as her great-grandfather. She did not think it would be right to bury Artemis in the family crypt beneath the Winters tower. Artemis would have wanted to be near the sky.

Kate and Edgar cleared rooms in the upper levels of the old museum to claim as their own, while Silas continued living in his own dark space deep beneath the main floors, letting his crow fly freely around the corridors and streets, watching over Fume's people. Edgar's brother returned to the Skilled to continue his early training, and Laina and Greta became regular visitors to the museum, where discussions over the creation of the new council continued for months.

Under Silas's direct command, the wardens would soon reinstate safe routes between Fume and the nearest towns and begin reconnecting Albion's settlements as they had been in the past. Work upon the city would continue for many years, but repairing the country's broken way of life would take even longer. Albion's people had grown suspicious of one another over the generations, but as the wardens' harvests stopped

and the Night Train was left to rust and fall into distant
memory, the fear of war with the Continent would die down
to a whisper and towns would begin to make contact with one
another again.

Kate would watch Edgar become a formal officer of the
new wardens in a ceremony held in the charred courtyard of
what had once been the High Council's chambers, while the
men who had made up that council would be driven from the
city—leaving their dark mark upon the history of a country on
the threshold of change.

Kate did not know what lay in her own future. She spent
her early weeks in her room within the museum restoring
Wintercraft, just as she had restored dozens of other books
during her old life in the bookshop with Artemis. The spirit's
rejuvenation of the pages had only taken it back to its original
state, but with its permission, Kate rebound the cover,
strengthened the spine, and reattached loose pages that could
not restore themselves.

Tom had told her about the note Artemis had found inside
the book. When Kate found it again, she sat down and read
it for the first time. She did not want to believe that her life's
course was set, but those words, written almost a century
earlier, had changed lives long after their writer's death.
If Ravik had never written it, Kate would not have found it
hidden in the mirror and Artemis might still have been alive.
If Dalliah had not encouraged Da'ru Marr to experiment

upon Silas, he might never have gone looking for Kate. And if the book itself had never been written, Albion's history would certainly have followed a very different course.

It was impossible to know if the events Kate had seen were predetermined and prophesized by seers looking into the veil or if people's belief in what they had "seen" drove them to create situations that otherwise might never have happened on their own. She wanted to believe in free will. She needed to know that destiny could be changed, that she was not simply acting out a life whose course had already been witnessed by people who were now long dead.

Her father's family had been consumed by their search for knowledge at any price. Her mother's family had trusted the veil to show them the way, putting their lives in the hands of forces no one could truly understand. Kate did not sit easily upon either of their paths. She had her own life to live and her own history to make.

She secured Ravik's note into the back of *Wintercraft*, along with her own neatly written pages detailing how the book had acquired the Winters spirit that remained locked within it. She read the warning inside the cover and then closed the book gently, feeling the soul of her ancestor pass softly through the ink and paper within. Kate had her own story to add to the knowledge inside, but that could wait. *Wintercraft's* journey was over, for now, but her future had only just begun.